RISEN

RISEN

K.M. ROBINSON

Crescent Sea
PUBLISHING

DEDICATION

To those that sacrifice for the ones they love.
You are the difference makers.
Never change.

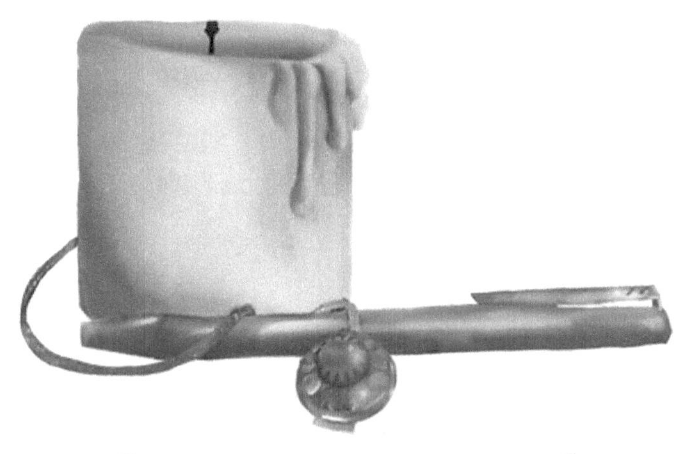

CHAPTER 1
JADE

"**W**here did you get that?" I launch myself at the Commander's hand, attempting to snatch away my mother's necklace. My Aunt Sophie has worn that necklace since my mother died when I was five. He pulls it out of my reach.

"You know where I got it." The Commander sneers at me, allowing me to take the necklace from him. I intentionally dig my nails into his palm, making him wince.

"I told you, Jade, it's not that easy to be rid of me. Now, you and I had a deal and we're not done yet."

"What do you want?" I growl, praying Roan, Lucas, or

my father would walk into the office, even though I know they are still in the meeting.

"I want you to hold up your end of the deal. Someone needs to pay for that rebellion, and it's going to be you."

I have a feeling it's also about the fact that I survived and this is payback.

"In case you've forgotten," I challenge my husband's father, "*you're* the one who killed Daniella in your office after you poisoned *your own son* in an attempt to poison *me*. You're not the one with leverage here."

"Oh, but, Jade, I am. As you can see by the necklace in your hand, I have Sophie. You say or do anything other than *exactly* what I tell you to say, and Sophie dies… and then I'll take your father out." He grins at me.

When I was five years old, my father, along with Lucas's father and several other political leaders, led a rebellion against the Commander and the Command. The goal was to reestablish a democracy in the country instead of the dictatorship we suffer under now. When it failed, the Commander found out my father was behind it. He couldn't do anything against my father publicly, but my life was fair game.

I was committed to marrying the Commander's son, Roan. His job was to gain my trust and kill me. Somewhere along the line, Roan decided he couldn't go through with it. With Lucas' help, we all managed to stay alive well past the point of intended internment.

Unlike my father, Lucas' father wasn't caught after the rebellion ended and he charged Lucas with protecting me when we were children. I never knew him, but he was always looking out for me. When I nearly died, he inserted himself into my life once again to take care of me. He even went as far as to pretend to be friends with Roan so he could watch out for me from the inside. Now that the truth is out, they are working on becoming friends for real.

My father and Lucas work together in my hometown. Their new offices are being revealed today. I'm positive Lucas has weapons hidden around the room, but I try to keep my eyes from darting back and forth to look for them as the Commander stands before me.

"And what if I go public with this?" I ask.

"You might be able to protect your father, but you'll never get to Sophie in time." He shrugs carelessly. "But you should be aware that I also have people strategically placed to watch your father too."

"What do you want?" I ask again.

"I told you—you're going to die. I don't care how, really, as long as you're dead. You've destroyed my plans long enough, and I want my son to be rid of you. I never should have trusted him to be a part of this. But I got him *into* this mess, and now I'm going to get him *out* of it. You won't bewitch him any longer, Jade."

"He came to the conclusion that you were a *monster* all

on his own, *Robert.*" It was the first time I had referred to him as anything other than his title. He no longer holds power over me...although at this point, he apparently *does.*

"Make a choice, Jade. You or Sophie."

The commander reaches out, taking the necklace back from my limp hand. He dangles it, swinging it back and forth like the pendulum on one of the grandfather clocks in Mr. Eroh's shop where I work.

"Tick tock, my dear," he sings at me.

I watch as it sways back and forth, weighing my options.

I want to run to Roan and tell him what his father is doing. I have three men in this building who would put a stop to the Commander this instant, if only I could reach them.

"Don't even think about it, Jade," the Commander says, as if reading my mind. "You have precisely one minute to answer me. One of my people is waiting for your answer. If they don't hear from me in the next few moments, they execute Sophie on the spot."

"So what exactly is your master plan *this* time?" I bite.

"Same as before." He smiles. "We make believe we like each other for the public. You don't tell Roan or Lucas or your father. You leave your people out of this. You back me on absolutely everything I say, *publicly,* and sing my praises. In a little while, you'll be in an accident. Not even your father will be able to pin it on me. And this time, Roan doesn't get hurt."

"He'll know it was you if I die. You won't fool him."

"Maybe not, but he'll never give me up. And he'll move on, you'll see. Well, *no*, actually, I don't suppose you will." He laughs. "You've caused me more trouble than your father has, Jade, and that's surprising. I should have just killed you when you were a child and spared myself all this grief."

"Clearly you should have," I agree sarcastically.

"Last chance, Jade. Agree to stand by me and die when the time is right in exactly one month from now, or say goodbye to Sophie right here and now."

Laughter erupts outside the door, down the hall. The men were coming back.

"Now or never," he says quietly.

I can't let Sophie die. I have a month until my execution date, apparently, which gives me time to figure things out.

"Tick tock."

The laughter gets closer and the Commander moves to slip out the door. He shrugs.

"Fine by me," my father-in-law says at my silence.

"Wait!" I call. He turns and I give him a short nod.

The Commander smiles as he tosses the necklace to me.

"Now be a good girl and keep your mouth shut…I'll

know if you don't—I have people everywhere" he adds and darts out the door, giving him just enough time to slip away before the men turn the corner and approach.

"Are you okay, Jade?" Roan frowns as he follows Lucas into the room.

I have one month to live... yeah, I'm great.

I give him a small smile, trying to recover from my conversation with his father.

"Is your meeting done?" I ask.

"Yes, are you ready to go home?"

Yes, I have to get out of here and figure out what to do.

"Sure," I nod.

"Lucas, you want to come over? We can hang out and have dinner," Roan suggests.

He forgave Lucas awfully fast for having learned their entire friendship was a farce. But who am I to judge?

"Yeah, sure," he shrugs. Reaching around me, he grabs his jacket and tosses it over his arm. It's far too warm for jackets, but I have a feeling it's for appearance's sake.

We stop in my father's office. He smiles when I step inside.

"Headed home?" he wraps an arm around my shoulder.

"Yeah, Lucas is coming over for dinner, want to come?"

"I wish I could," he says sadly. "Unfortunately, now

that the offices are up and running, they've got me swamped. Maybe tomorrow we could have lunch?"

Now that I was finally free to see my father publicly, we've been spending a lot of time together when I'm in town to work. Whenever he can sneak away for lunch, we meet at the bakery. If he can catch a few spare minutes, he'll pop into Mr. Eroh's store to say hello. Now that he's settled into his new workspace, I plan on visiting him at work more often too.

"Sure, that would be great."

"See you tomorrow." He kisses the top of my head and waves to Roan and Lucas as we all retreat into the hallway.

My ultimate goal is to get my father and Roan to spend more time together. Their relationship is still pretty rocky after the whole *Roan-is-trying-to-kill-me* incident.

We chat on the way back to the house. I let the boys go out to the garden while I poke around the kitchen looking for something to feed them a bit later. I've been trying to give them a little extra space in hopes that it will make the coconspirators-to-*actual*-friends transition faster.

As soon as they are out of sight, I pull the necklace out of my pocket where I hid it when they walked in. It sparkles in the same way it used to when my Aunt Sophie wore it when I was little...before she started keeping her distance. Once the marriage mandate was made public, Sophie kept far away so she wouldn't be connected to us when the time came for me to be killed. The plan was for her to work behind the scenes to help me, but it wouldn't work if people knew about her being a part of my life.

I examine every inch of the necklace, hoping Sophie left some kind of clue. Finding nothing, I open the locket. A piece of paper floats out and I catch it in mid-air.

Tonight. 11pm.

My eyes tear as I realize it's not a note from Sophie, but from the Commander. As if he didn't have enough of a say earlier. Now I have to sneak out of my own home to go and meet him.

For two months I had been free of the man and now I am right back under his control.

I wish I could tuck my hair clip back into my long tresses, but that bit of safety was revealed during my last meeting with the Commander, when he used it to accidentally kill his secretary, Daniella. The poison inside had killed her almost instantly, providing the perfect scapegoat for the Commander to avoid being blamed for attempting to kill me, nearly killing his son, and trying to get revenge on my father. Now I have no safety net as I go to meet the monstrous leader of our tiny country.

I destroy the note, ripping it into tiny pieces. Disposing of it, I wish I were banishing the Commander instead of just his note.

Dinner goes by quickly. It's nice spending time with Roan and Lucas. They've really become my best friends over these past few months. I've come to rely on their friendship.

Lucas says goodnight and heads home as darkness draws in.

"So, are you really doing okay? I know today was hard for you." Roan asks, guiding me to the couch.

I lean against his shoulder, resting my head on him.

"I hated seeing the library gone," I admit, "but the offices are nice."

"You did a great job on your father's office," he compliments me.

I smile as I stare across the room. He can feel it against his shoulder, and he grins too, his cheek moving my hair as he does.

"This is nice," he finally says.

I can't say I disagree. Being with Roan is *more* than nice.

We sit for a few more minutes before I announce I'm going to bed. He watches me walk away before I hear him get up to go to his own room. Even though we've decided to start a real relationship, we've kept our boundaries. We may be married *technically*, but we're taking things slow and getting to know each other.

Once I'm sure he's in for the night, I prop open my window and climb out. It eerily reminds me of the day I snuck out two months ago to meet the Commander... *also to make a deal for my death.* This was becoming a habit.

It's strange walking through the town at night on my own. It's never been safe for me to be alone, but even with my newfound freedom, I had yet to venture outside by myself at night.

The stars shimmer as I walk. Only a few clouds skim past the moon, hardly blocking my only source of light. It's starting to get cooler in the evenings now and I shiver as I walk. I wish I had thought to dress warmer.

The guards let me in when I reach the gate of the Commander's home. I don't even have to ask where to go; I know where he'll be waiting.

Since his first plan failed disastrously, he'll be keeping things close to the vest this time. I doubt even his wife, Alice, will know. The soft glow from the pool house tells me I'm right.

Inside, the dim light reflects off of the water, fluid white lines dancing across the walls. The last time I was here was when Roan kissed me for the first time. How I wish we were back in that drying box, air flying all around us, with Roan's arms wrapped around me, pulling me closer as our lips pulsed together.

"Surprised to see me?" I ask as I stand by the door. I leave it open with my hand between it and the doorframe in case I need to escape.

"You're a smart girl, Jade. I figured you'd find my note." He takes a step toward me and I tense. "Like I said, Jade, you have a month. Now sit down."

When I refuse, he continues.

"The good news is, I have a plan, Jade. Better than the last one. This time, I don't even have to lift a finger."

"And how is that?" I ask.

"Because, Jade, when I'm done, the entire country is going to hate you. You see, my dear, I'm turning *you* into the villain this time. No more hero status for you. You're going down, but not in a blaze of glory; *you're* going down in *flames*."

"A villain?" I smirk. He can't turn the people against me.

"They'll hate you when I'm done." He seems so proud of himself. "Like I said, you're going to agree with everything I tell you to do, so when I start letting you make public choices that the people don't like… well, they'll be angry with you—angry enough to kill."

And suddenly I understand. He *does* have the power to do that. I have to say and do everything he tells me to, and if he makes me hurt the people, they'll eventually turn on me. If he's giving me a month for a time limit, whatever I'm going to do publicly must be big…and truly terrible.

"What—?" I start but get cut off.

"You're going to destroy this country, one piece at a

time. You'll stand for everything your father hated all those years ago. You'll publicly side with me and do things even *I* wouldn't dream of doing. Now that I *trust you*— at least as far as the public is concerned—and I start giving you responsibilities and power, you're going to go a little mad, my dear. This is going to be so fun to watch." He grins. "And the people—*even Roan*—will think the power has gone to your head and you're getting carried away. They'll never even question it."

"You expect all this to happen in a month?"

"Oh, yes, Jade, I do." He smiles, flashing his teeth at me. "Because I seem to be *falling ill.* You know it's going to happen anyway because of Roan's mandate. He'll simply think I'm playing nice. And while *he* steps up, so will *you.* But, *of course,* we have *so* much faith in you that we give *you* more power than *any* Commander's wife has been given; we'll give you *real* power. And when your decisions come out shaky...well, *I'm too sick to handle it* until after the fact. And we all know Roan can't control you. Someone will step up to fix the problem, I'm sure of that."

"Meaning you'll *make sure* someone does," I comment angrily.

He touches his chest as if genuinely concerned.

"Meaning I have to keep in touch with my people. If they are unhappy, I need to know about it. I may not be able to do anything other than advise, but, my dear," he sneers gleefully at me, "I'll be careful to make sure they know they *aren't allowed to hurt you in order to stop you.* That should do the trick."

He really *does* have it all figured out. It's truly the perfect plan—much better than his first plan. Or second. And this time, his hands would be clean as far as anyone could prove.

"So, Jade, time to strike a deal," he says arrogantly.

"Fine," I whisper, unable to look at him.

"What was that, dear?" he taunts me.

"Fine," I shout, despising him with everything in me.

"Good. Then Sophie can live another day. She'll be so pleased." He drops the happy act and his usual hatred spews out. "One word—to anyone—and she dies. Push me, and your father dies. I will no longer care about public image; I'll kill him and make sure everyone knows and that is how I will lead from now on.

"Furthermore, if Roan even comes *close* to finding out, you have no idea how sorry you'll be. Now, run along, Jade. I'll be *unable* to be in the office tomorrow. I expect *you* here the day after, *with* Roan, when I tell him he's temporarily taking over. Play nice and this will all go a lot easier. Understood?"

I nod and he raises an eyebrow, waiting for me to speak.

"Fine," I agree to his sick game.

Taking a step toward me, he runs his hand down my

arm slowly, as he once did several months ago to upset my father. I wrench away from him and fling the door open. Running, I hear him laughing after me.

I signed a deal with a monster tonight.

Again.

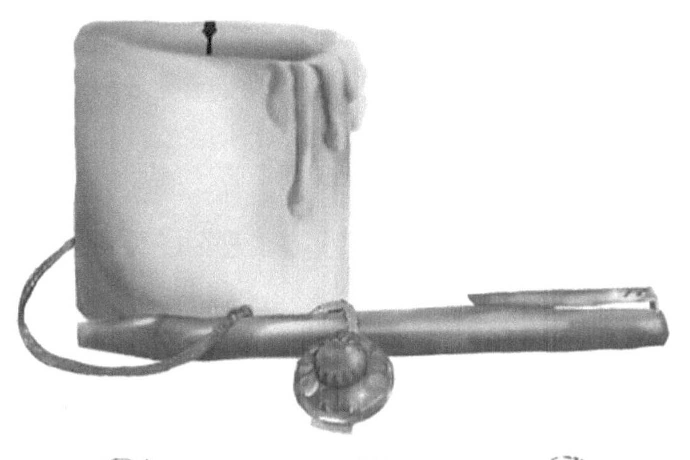

CHAPTER 2
JADE

orning is unwelcome. Usually, I prefer to rise with the sun, but today I just want to bury myself under the blankets and never take my head from my pillow.

Only the smell of food from the kitchen where Roan is cooking rouses me. I feel so sick I can't even think of food, but I need to keep things normal for Roan's sake.

"Morning, sleepyhead," he greets me with a chuckle.

I slept for an hour during the night and my head is pounding. If I could have thrown a pillow at his head, I might have.

"You okay?" he asks, noting my less than pleasant demeanor.

"Oh." I shake my head, hoping to clear away the fog. "I have a bit of a headache, that's all. I didn't sleep so well last night."

"Can I do anything for you?" he asks, carefully setting a glass of juice in front of me. He's gentle enough that it doesn't make a sound as it touches the island.

It amazes me how much effort he puts into taking care of me now.

"No, I'll be fine. I'm sure once I eat, I'll feel better," I reply.

My headache will probably go away anyway. The food, however, will *not* help with the knots in my stomach.

"Are you going to be okay to go in to work today?" He leans on the island and looks me straight on.

"Yeah, I'll be fine. If I'm not, I'll sit in the back room for a while. Mr. Eroh won't mind."

In the two months since the fire, Mr. Eroh's shop had been rebuilt, thanks to the efforts led by my father and Lucas. Even with his injuries, Lucas made sure to help however he could. The store was roughly the same size but structured a little differently. He had even set aside a corner for a small library since the town lost theirs to the Command.

Secretly, my father, Lucas and Roan had added

hiding places throughout the building that no one but our small group knew about. We could hide objects and even people if necessary. They actually created a secret escape in case of emergencies—like the fire the Commander had set in an attempt to kill Mr. Eroh and me.

"Do you want me to walk you?" Roan asks as we eat.

"No, I should be fine." When I see the disappointed look on his face, I add, "Thank you, though. I just don't want to make you late for work. Maybe we could go to the art house tonight? It's been awhile since we've gone."

The art house is one of our escapes. Growing up, Roan would sneak away to the art house run by a man I still haven't met, and create stunning works of art without his family knowing. In our small country, barely the size of a few towns put together, art was considered frivolous. If it wasn't practical, it wasn't done. If it wasn't necessary, it was a waste of time. But Roan and I love the freedom that tiny building gives us.

It houses a gallery to display the art created by the people who go there secretly and a room to create in. The gallery is pristine, surrounded by glorious works of art in the form of paintings, drawings and sculptures. The workroom is dark, dusty, and small. It's dirty and old but so secure that it feels almost cozy. I love uncovering the furniture and watching the dust sparkle in the light that peeks through the boarded up windows.

"Yeah, that would be nice." Roan smiles, returning to his usual morning routine.

If I only have one month left, I have to make the most of it. Especially since I'll need to start pulling away from him soon. I have to make this as easy on him—on *all* of them—as possible. That means not being overly attached to me. I'll give myself a few days to say goodbye in my own silent way, and then I'll start putting some distance between us.

Tonight, though, I have the art house.

"Can you take care of that please, Jade?" Mr. Eroh asks as he slips into the back storage room.

"Hi Annie, is that everything today?" I ask as the baker hands me a few silver trays.

"Yes, I'm adding a new section of mini pies to the bakery and I wanted something fancy to put them on." She smiles at me.

"These will be perfect." I smile back.

I like Annie. She's always looked out for me. Whenever I go to the bakery, she just sets food and tea in front of me. I never have to order. She always picks out the perfect thing.

She reaches up and tucks her locks into the handkerchief tied around her hair. Her pigtails bounce as she brushes against them.

"I made a new kind of scone this morning—almond with white chocolate chips. Want to try one for lunch today?" She knows she's snagged me.

"Now, see, that's just not fair…I wasn't feeling well this morning—*headache*—and now I have no choice but to be forced to go into public to eat." I grin.

"Scones always make you feel better. Besides, misery loves company," she says cheerily.

"Misery might, but headaches don't." I wink at her. "Good thing it's mostly gone."

"See you at lunch, Jade." She waves over her shoulder as she leaves with her new trays.

"New scones, huh?" Mr. Eroh comments. "You know she made those specifically for *you*, right?"

"I know. Annie's a nice lady," I reply.

The entire town has been watching out for me since the day I married Roan. Well, actually since I was five and the Commander announced our commitment. Now that my father is clearly back in the picture, the town seems a bit more relaxed, thinking we've survived it.

They'll relax even more when they see him at lunch

with me today. I'm suddenly extra grateful the headache is mostly gone.

"You seem off today, Jade. Is everything all right?" Mr. Eroh asks, taking a seat next to me behind the counter.

"I'm fine. Just a headache, that's all."

He stares at me for a long time, fighting to see the truth.

"Really, I'm fine. I just didn't sleep well last night and it gave me a migraine."

"Why didn't you sleep well? Are you still worried about Roan? You could move back in with your father, no one would blame you," he suggests.

"No, I'm not worried about Roan. Not even my *father* is worried about Roan anymore."

"So then what is it?" he probes.

He's too smart for his own good.

"I just couldn't fall asleep. Really. It's nothing to worry about."

It's everything *to worry about.*

He sighs at me and turns away to reassemble a broken clock. I watch him as he works. Eventually, he passes it over to me and tells me to finish reassembling it. I've been taught well and it only takes me a few minutes to finish fixing it.

"Wonderful, now take that over to the candle shop before you come back from lunch. Erica is expecting it today."

Erica. Which means the clock is probably a message.

"Anything I should know about it before I take it over?" I ask casually, assuming the Commander is still keeping tabs on us. After all, he admitted he had people following my father.

"Just be careful of the hands on the face. If you touch them, they are likely to snap off. It's an old clock," he replies before moving on to another project.

In other words, don't move the hands because their current position sends her a specific message. Great.

We may have won against the Commander once, but those of us in the game haven't let their guard down, which means the secret messages continue.

"Maybe I'll head over now and drop it off before lunch, if that's okay with you," I suggest, reaching for the clock.

Mr. Eroh nods and mumbles something, waving me off without turning to look at me. I smile and pick up the secret message.

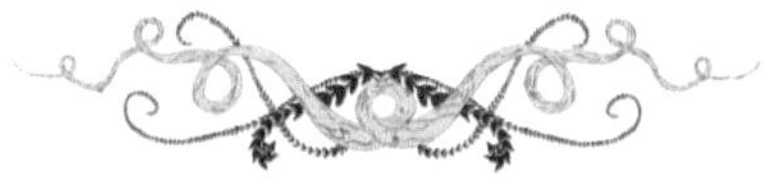

I haven't been in the candle shop for months—mostly because I'm allergic to scented things, but also because I had no need to pass along messages to my father or aunt anymore. I had only ever gone in when I was forced to for communication's sake.

Erica's shop is full of the most lovely candles I had ever seen. She makes them all by hand. Her mother taught her when she was young, and she grew up to take over the shop and expand it. Her mother had only done it as a vendor, moving from place to place, selling at markets. Erica was the one who turned it into an actual store.

Erica was a little older than me. I admired her growing up—mostly the freedom she had compared to my own life, but also because she was so accomplished at such a young age.

"I have a clock for you from Mr. Eroh's shop. He said you were expecting it," I announce as I walk into the empty store.

The brunette woman looks up from where she sits behind the counter. Some lovely scent fills the room and tickles my nose. I fight back a sneeze. *I hate being allergic to everything.*

"Thank you," she says kindly. Erica closes her book and waits for me to set the clock on the counter. She takes a moment to watch me, as if trying to place me even though she knows exactly who I am.

"It's been awhile since I've seen you. Let me think, last

time you were in, you bought candles for…your husband. Newlyweds, if I recall."

There is safety in distance.

"Yes, that's right." I smile. "I'm a few purchases away from my free candle if *I* recall."

"Perhaps you should take advantage of that today." She nods toward her collection. "It's been awhile since I've seen *anyone*, and I'd like to make a few sales today if I can. I'll even throw in some extra matches for you, if you like."

I wonder if she's talking about Sophie?

I browse her collection, settling on some cream colored unscented candles. I hand her my order and she rings them up.

Annie is kind enough to withhold my scone until my father arrives. I don't know if I could have restrained myself long enough for my father to appear if she hadn't. The moment he takes his seat, Annie is by our sides, setting down our lunch. She and my father exchange a grin and nod before Annie wanders away, letting us talk.

"Is this new?" James Jareau asks, looking at the plate in front of me.

"Yeah, Annie tried a new recipe. It's almond with white chocolate." I grin at him.

"Sounds amazing." He reaches for his and we try it at the same time. Heavenly is the only way I can describe it.

We both sneak a second bite before starting on our sandwiches.

"Jade, we need to talk," my father says.

"I know." And I *do* know…except I can't talk to him anymore without telling him everything and getting Sophie killed. "Why don't you come to dinner soon. I really want you to spend some time with Roan. You've been so busy since… everything… and you spend more time with *Lucas* than you do with the man I'm married to."

My father shoots me a look, letting me know he's still not thrilled that I'm married to Roan. He may trust Roan now that he knows Roan is devoted to me, but he still doesn't like me being married so young. I can't say I blame him. I wish Roan and I could have gotten to know each other pre-wedding-dress.

He drops the conversation, agreeing to come to dinner the following night. We enjoy the rest of our time having lunch together. I'm going to miss this when I have to start pulling away soon.

CHAPTER 3
ROAN

"What do you mean he's not coming in?"

"I'm sorry, sir, he said he wouldn't be in today. I don't think he was feeling well," Janine says, peering in from the hallway. She looks frightened to death of my reaction.

I try not to spook her, remaining at my seat behind my desk. My frown sends her leaning out the door.

"Janine, it's all right, it isn't your fault." I beckon her back in.

"Of course. I'm sorry, sir." She's practically jumping out of her skin. I don't think I've ever seen anyone so frightened, and that includes the time I dragged Jade away from work one day and she thought I was going to kill her.

"Perhaps you could do something for me, Janine." I try to smile.

Her eyes dart to the door.

"I need a message delivered. Could you see to it that this is taken to my wife? You can send any of the messengers." I smile again, hoping to reassure her.

"Yes, sir." She waits as I scribble out a note and seal it in an envelope. I hand it to her with Jade's name on the outside.

"Thank you, Janine. If you get all of the filing done, why don't you take the rest of the afternoon off? My father's not in, so he won't need your assistance and I'm just wrapping up some paperwork before I head to the site for that project I'm working on, so I won't be around either."

Relief floods her face as she races out of the room. She tosses a quick word of thanks over her shoulder as she runs from the office. I can't blame her; her predecessor *had* died only a few feet away in my father's office. Only the new carpeting covered the blood from the injury that people assumed was Daniella's.

Everyone was extra cautious about the people who worked for us now—if our loyal and trusted secretary could betray us, who else might? My father and I had no concerns about the girl, though—we knew the truth about Daniella's death and had no reason to question Janine. Even so, she was terrified we'd turn on her, even though *her* father was a highly placed politician who worked for my father. No, she had nothing to fear, but given no choice in her new job, she couldn't hide her nervousness.

When the door closes behind her, I relax back into my chair. Jade had forced me to do a little updating. '*A tribute to Daniella,*' she had called it, and I admit, the furniture she helped me pick is far more comfortable than what I had been using up to now.

An hour later Janine knocks lightly on the door and tells me she has finished her work. As soon as I release her she darts for the door. It will take some work calming that girl down. Maybe Jade can help with that.

My note to my wife quickly explained that my father wasn't at work today and that I would be late because I had to go see him. Once Janine leaves, I lock up and head to the site of my new project. I am trying to keep it as secret as possible, even Jade only knows a few details and I refuse to share anything with my father.

The site is large, large enough for building my gift to Jade. I greet the construction crew and we discuss our options for a few moments before I leave. I am pleased with the progress they are making.

Instead of taking my normal route home, I veer off and make my way to my childhood home. Maybelle greets me warmly when I walk inside.

"Roan! It's so lovely to see you! Did I know you were coming over?" she releases her arms from around my shoulders. She is starting to become less formal about hugging me thanks to Jade's influence. Guiding me into the house, Maybelle waits for an answer.

"No, Maybelle, I wasn't scheduled to come over. I heard Dad wasn't feeling well so I wanted to check on him."

It occurs to me that the last time I had come to check on my father's well being was the day he lied to me—to *all* of us—about being injured in an explosion that never really happened. He used it to turn me against Jade, nearly convincing me to kill her. I scowl at the thought of being deceived like that.

"Well, isn't that sweet? He's in his study." Together we make our way down the hall and she gently knocks on the door. "Commander, look who's here to see you."

Pushing the door open, she keeps out of the way,

giving me a small nod, she retreats back the way we came.

"Ahh, I thought you'd come see me." My father sits up from the couch he is laying on. Clearly he isn't sick.

"What is this?" I reply as unhappily as I can.

"This is your plan, remember, *son.*" He drops the happy act. "*You* wanted this, so here it is. You're in charge. Go run your country."

He waves his hand at me as if dismissing a small child.

"Why now? We weren't supposed to start for a while yet." I question skeptically.

"I have no fight left in me, Roan. I'm ready to retire and let you take over. *So what* if we start early? You're still getting what you want."

I can't tell what his game is.

"I'll start taking some days off here and there and then soon enough I'll be gone altogether and you and your precious wife can rule." He waves his hand around as he speaks. I can tell it's taking all his concentration not to scream at me like he did when Jade used to mess up one of his plans and I had to drag him away and calm him down.

"Roan?" a voice asks before I can continue.

"Hi, Mom.," I say, turning around to face her. I can't quite bring myself to force a smile.

She frowns when she sees my expression and runs her hands down her hips, smoothing her blouse.

"I didn't know you were coming over," she comments, not making eye contact.

"I hadn't planned on it until I found out Dad moved up our timeline."

Her eyes dart toward my father. She only knows a bit about what happened in my father's office that day we struck a deal. I left it up to my father to tell her, but I know he only gave her part of the story. I hadn't left Jade's side since that day aside from work, and I didn't want to waste my time coming over to my parent's house when I could be with her. I haven't set my mother straight yet.

"Are you staying? We could have dinner—"

"No," I cut her off, "I have to get back to my wife. I just wanted to speak to Dad." She cringes when I used the term *wife*. She still doesn't trust Jade and she's still afraid of James. One day, I hope to convince her otherwise.

"Maybe another time," she says, defeat in her voice.

"Yeah," I reply softly, "another time, Mom."

She gives me a tiny smile and leaves. I turn back to my father, his eyes already flashing.

"You should treat her better," he says spitefully.

"*You* shouldn't have tried to kill *my* wife," I spit back.

We stare at each other for several tense moments. He finally looks away—a small victory.

"I won't be in tomorrow either. Bring Jade and handle things. Since you two will be ruling together anyway, you might as well get her started on being Queen or Empress or whatever title you decide to give her." Rage seethes through every word out of my father's mouth.

"She'll be the Commander's wife, just like every other Commander's wife," I correct him.

"Except she'll have power." He glares at me. "Or else she'll be pulling the strings. The entire country knows she owns you, so why not give her some power and let her be her own entity and prove you can still be in charge of your own decisions? They'll respect you *both* that way, instead of despising *you* for not having the guts to be in charge yourself and *her* for being manipulative behind the scenes."

"Why do you care?" I ask, unable to keep my anger in check.

"You are my son, I raised you to lead this country. If you fail, that looks bad for both of us. Appearances matter, Roan, despite what you might think."

For once I believe him. Image is everything to that man.

"Fine." I stand up from where I'm perched on the edge of his study desk and stride toward the door.

"Say goodbye to your mother," he instructs me sharply as I leave.

"What happened?" Jade greets me as I walk in the door.

She's standing against the doorframe, her hip propped against it, arms folded over her chest. I nearly stop to watch her for a moment, but I know she won't be happy if I waste time.

"He moved up the timeline." Something flickers across her expression but I can't tell what.

"So what does this mean?" she prompts.

"It means we're starting to take over. He said you should come to work with me tomorrow." I expect her to flinch when I mention my father's wishes but she doesn't. "He says we both need to have power or else people might think you're manipulating things behind the scenes since you have more power than any other Commander's wife has ever had before."

"Is that right?" she asks sarcastically.

"I'm sorry, Jade," I reach for her hands and she lets me bring them up to my chest.

"No, he's right. We want to make sure the people trust us both and the best way to do that is for them to see us both," she relents.

I'm so relieved that I almost miss her next words.

"Are we still going to the art house tonight?" Jade asks somewhere in the back of my thoughts.

I'm still busy trying to work out how to make this transition into leadership easier on us both.

"Roan?" she asks again, making me realize I've been staring at her.

"Sorry, what?" I shake my head, trying to focus.

"The art house? Are we going?"

I smile. I love every minute with Jade, but being in the art house with her sparks something in me.

"Yeah, let's go."

She leans over and picks up a basket she already has packed with food for us. She's always prepared for everything.

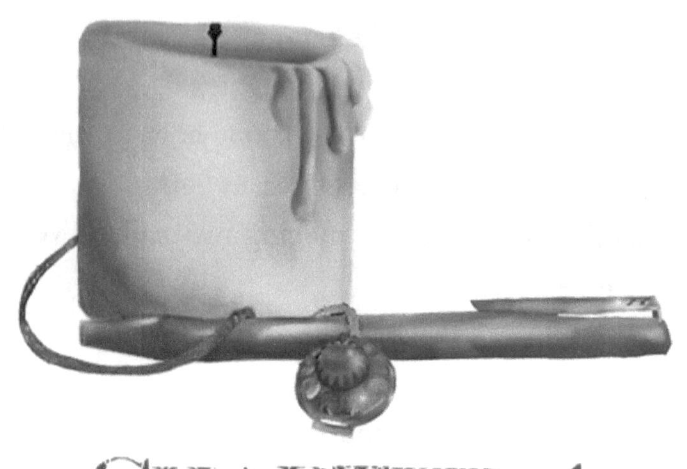

CHAPTER 4
JADE

His hand feels warm against mine. As someone who generally has rather cold fingers, he warms my hands fairly quickly. His grip is light, but firm at the same time—protective, possessive and gentle.

The walk is relaxing as bird songs guide our steps. The evening is cool and the breeze makes me shiver. Roan lets go of my hand, wrapping his arm around my shoulders, pulling me close. He snatches up my hand with his far one, balancing the basket on his arm. My head finds its way to his shoulder and I let him lead me the rest of the way to the art house.

The inside is just as we left it, sparkling golden with dust as the setting sun makes it leap to life.

"Create or eat first?" he asks.

Tipping my head to the side, I consider our options. "Create."

He grins and I know he's been itching to paint something. He sets the basket on the edge of the couch by my feet and steps away to get our supplies as I make myself comfortable against a pillow.

I can tell he's anxious to start so I don't ruin the atmosphere with words. I smile as he hands me a pad of paper and some pens. Taking a seat in the middle of the room, he begins to work, barely looking at me. I turn my attention to my blank paper and find myself lost in thought.

Sophie will die if I make a mistake—*any* mistake. My father could die too. And Lucas. I'm grateful I don't have to worry about Roan—the Commander wouldn't hurt his son... physically, anyway.

"You okay?" Roan's voice is jarring.

"What?" I panic.

"You're not drawing, are you okay?"

"Oh." I realize the sun is nearly out of sight and I've been sitting motionless for a long time. "I... I just didn't know what to draw."

I pray my smile is convincing.

When he looks back to his own creation, I know I'm

all right. I force my hand to move across the page, but my mind drifts again. With only one month to live, there are things I know I need to accomplish.

I look up when I hear footsteps walking toward me. The moon has somehow found its way into the sky and its pale white light glitters against the dust Roan is kicking up as he nears me.

He has a fierceness about him as he approaches. His eyes are focused and I track his every move. With one swift movement, he moves the basket to the ground and leans over me. Bracing his hand against the back of the couch, he takes the sketchpad and sets it on a small table behind me.

His lips are soft as they touch mine, no longer tentative and shy like our first few weeks of freedom. His kisses are possessive and reassuring because he knows I am his and he is mine.

I wrap my arms around his neck, bringing him closer until he is kneeling over me. Our hands find their way to each other's hair and we smile against each other's lips.

"You're beautiful," he whispers. "Moonlight suits you, Jade."

His words flood my ears and I wish, for this moment, we could be safe, away from his father and my impending death.

"I'd say the same to you, but I really can't see you...

you're in the shadows." I grin, reminding him his back is to the light.

Reluctantly he slides back and rests against the opposite end of the couch. Our legs intertwine, his feet holding my hips, and mine holding his. Roan stretches for the basket and hands me a sandwich I had packed earlier for our trip.

We eat in silence, watching each other. It's funny how much we like to be silent together. I've never felt so comfortable as to be able to sit with a person and stare at them for hours without being awkward. And yet, he stares right back at me, watching my every move, as I watch him.

When we finish, he packs up everything to take home so we don't leave anything behind.

"What did you paint?" I ask, breaking the silence.

"Go look," he teases.

I rise and walk over to his easel.

"Roan," I blush.

"I know I may not be the most observant of details, but did you really think I could forget that?" He rests his hand on my hip as he stands next to me observing his work.

Roan and I are surrounded by flowers and glittering lights in the painting. He's in his suit and I'm wearing my wedding dress as he spins us the length of the canvas. My dress has elements from the dress I wore to my forced wedding and elements from when I reconstructed it to prove a point at the Command party months ago. It flies out as he spins me, the dress nearly coming to life as it moves.

"It's how it *should* have been," he whispers into my ear, causing me to shiver from his proximity.

I turn to him and before I can speak, he kisses me.

"One day, Jade, I'll give *that* to you," he says, meaning the moment he painted for us—together, happy, perfect.

I believe him.

If only he knew I only had a month left…and even less time before I had to push him away. But for now, that image might be the only thing that gets me through this. I force my tears back.

This man was always meant to break my heart.

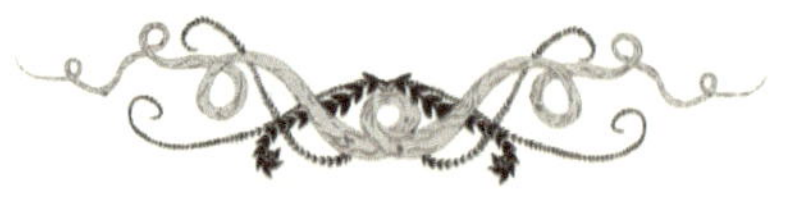

I sent word to Mr. Eroh before we left town that I wouldn't be into work the next day. When we reach our house, Roan holds the door for me, locking it behind us. Carrying the basket to the kitchen, I unpack it as he joins me.

"Are you okay with all this, Jade? I know it's

happening faster than we thought. It worries me a little that Dad's suddenly changing things."

"I'm sure it's just that he finally accepted everything and he's ready to move on. Besides, it's not like he can do anything. If he does, we'll tell everyone what really happened." I say, hopeful that I convinced him not to worry.

I can tell he's still worried, but he drops it. Stepping behind me, he pins me against the counter. I turn to face him and he lifts me onto the flat surface. He steps between my legs and I wrap my feet around his back as he settles his hands onto my hips.

"I just want to take care of you, Jade," he says with a lazy smile.

"I know." I lift one hand off the counter and place it on his wrist, running my fingers along the back of his hand. It sends a shiver down his spine and I try to suppress my giggle. Now that I don't have to hate him, I can't get over how handsome he really is with his blond hair and stunning green eyes. They sparkle as they pierce my soul.

"Kiss me," he whispers and I lean forward, closing the distance between us. It's slow and intoxicating and over far too quickly.

"We should sleep," he finally says, pulling away. "I have a feeling tomorrow is going to be a long day for us."

I sigh and scoot off the counter. His hands catch me

and slow my descent. Roan looks at me dreamily and walks me to my room, a grin slipping onto one side of his lips. Just like most nights, he raises one arm high above me on the doorframe and bends his head to give me one last kiss goodnight. Neither of us would leave if I didn't make the first move, so, like almost every night, I step backward into my room and slowly close the door as he hesitantly walks down the hallway.

"Goodnight, Jade," he says softly.

"Good night, Roan," I reply, barely above a whisper.

I'm going to miss him.

Roan's laughter interrupts my thoughts.

"Comfortable, Jade?" he continues to smirk.

The new furniture we picked out for his office is so much better than the old stuff. I could practically fall asleep on the couch, and I might have, if he hadn't spoken to me.

"As a matter of fact, I am," I say sarcastically, adding a grin to soften it.

"Want some company?" he asks jokingly, though I can see the longing in his eyes.

"Don't you have work to do, husband?" I ask with a smirk.

"It's really not fair that you get to come and relax while I have to work." He playfully mopes at his desk.

"I'd work too if you gave me anything to do," I retort.

"I could think of some things you could be in charge of." He smirks as I throw a pillow at him. He ducks and I miss.

"Sir," Janine knocks on the door. "There's someone here to see you."

The frightened thing stands in the doorway, barely peeking in.

"Thank you, Janine, who is it?" Roan asks as kindly as possible.

If a bunny rabbit sneezed thirty yards away, I'm fairly certain Janine would fall to pieces.

"Mr. Montgomery, sir."

Thank goodness.

"Send him in, please."

Lucas steps around from behind her, closing the door. She seems more relaxed around Lucas than either of us.

"Why are you here?" Lucas drops his smile and turns to me the moment the door is closed.

"Because the Commander proclaimed it so," I say haughtily, waving my hand in the air.

"Why is he changing the plan?" he turns on Roan.

Even though I'm supposedly out of danger, Lucas

has yet to drop the protector title. I have always been his first priority, and will apparently continue to be, until such a time as I find him a girlfriend or I die.

I make a mental note to find Lucas a girlfriend before I die in a month.

"We're hoping he's finally accepted his fate." I say before Roan has a chance to speak.

"When have you ever known the Commander to accept his fate?" Lucas challenges. I silently beg him to let it go.

"What choice does he have?" I point out that we still hold the cards…as far as either of them knows.

For a moment, my heart screams at me to tell them the Commander has Sophie. For an instant, I almost do. But then my head—my practical, logical, over-involved head—gets in the way and I am rendered defenseless. I will die and there is no way around it. But I'll make certain someone knows about Sophie before I die—Dad most likely.

If only I could figure out who the Commander has working for him but I can't risk my father and friends' lives.

"She's right, Lucas. Dad can't change his mind because it's four against one. We have the upper hand here. He can't hurt her anymore."

Lucas doesn't look convinced.

He's too smart for his own good. Or maybe, he's just too distrusting.

"Look, it doesn't matter. It happened. He started the plan early, so now we have to make the most of it," I say, slightly exasperated.

The boys look a little nervous that I'm suddenly so short with them. I shouldn't be, but I know it's the only way to move it along.

Roan explains that his father wants me to have some power to balance us out so that people don't think I'm manipulating him behind the scenes. It seems logical enough, but it makes the most sense to *me* because I already know the end game.

We spend time discussing our options for how I can be seen publicly working for the good of the country. By the end of the day, we've formed a plan.

"Can I help with that, baby girl?"

"You can set the table if you like." I nod to the dishes sitting on the counter next to my father's hand.

"That I can do." He nods back with a grin. "Just like old times."

He picks up the plates and turns to walk into the dining area as I add extra cheese to the pasta creation I whipped up when I arrived home. Roan finishes putting the salad together, taking a few steps toward me with the bowl.

"I think he's happy he can come over so often," Roan says in a hushed voice.

"I think he's finally starting to warm up to you," I whisper conspiratorially.

"About time," Roan smirks. "Now we just need to get my mom to play nice."

"Ha!" I accidentally say out loud. "That'll be the day."

He looks at me sympathetically. "I know. I'm sorry, babe. I promise I'll try to work on that."

Thankfully this time I keep my mouth shut instead of telling him there's not enough time to bother. Instead, I lean over and peck his lips with mine.

"All set." My father walks back into the kitchen. If he saw anything, he ignores it. "Can I carry that in for you, Jade?"

"Thanks, Dad." I hand off the chicken and pasta, grabbing the pitcher of lemonade to carry out behind him.

We settle in at the table, the atmosphere far more inviting than when the Commander and his wife join us for a meal. Roan's foot rests next to mine, every once in a while tapping against me as a gentle reminder that he exists in my life. The first time Roan did that in my father's presence, I think it was to get back at me for the time I made him jump in front of his parents. When I didn't react, it became a game for the next few meals to throw me off. It never worked and now he just hovers near me to be near me... I think, anyway.

"Jade, this is really good," Roan comments between bites.

"Her mother used to make it like this," my father says softly. "A few years ago when Jade started taking over cooking for us, she asked what Elizabeth used to make for us, and I must say, Jade really matched this one perfectly."

I look down at my plate, trying to suppress my grin. I don't know how accurate that statement is, but it makes me happy every time he tells me my cooking reminds him of my mother's.

When I look up, I find Roan watching me. I can tell he wants to ask questions. He patiently waits every time I redirect the conversation. I had managed to tell him some of the stories my father had told me, but I had never been able to talk about losing her.

"Roan?"

My father's voice convinces Roan to turn away from me.

"You look like you have a question." The kindness in his voice is meant to give Roan permission to ask about my mother, but I hope he won't pry. I couldn't bear the idea of talking about her death now.

"How did you meet your wife, sir?" Roan asks instead.

"Elizabeth was a physician. Both her father and uncle were well respected during the war when they were very young. They taught Elizabeth from a young age and she fell into the life, so to speak."

"I see." Roan comments, nodding his head.

"Once your grandfather formed the Command, he kept them on as part of the lead medical team and eventually Elizabeth worked as a nurse. She could have run her own team if she had wanted to, but she specifically held back because she knew what a time commitment that would be and she wanted a family one day." He glances at me. "You were always her greatest goal in life."

Out of the corner of my eye, I see Roan's breath catch. I assume he is thinking back to the day in the cemetery when I introduced him to the letters my mother wrote me before she had died. I feel a little bad at using those against him, but not enough that I wouldn't do it again to save my life—too bad the letters can't save me now.

"I think she's everyone's greatest goal at this point," Roan recovers, making my father's smile widen.

"They were a little more lenient back in those days on marrying young, so Elizabeth and I had more time. We were from different towns, but I had been selected to join the Command. One of the men who worked for your grandfather was giving us a tour of the Command building when Elizabeth walked in. She had been assisting the Command on that occasion, filling in for a service day event they were hosting.

"I admit, I missed part of the lecture when I saw her. I might have strayed from the group a little until they caught me and called me back. I made it my mission to look for her after that, but I didn't see her in the Command building again during my training in those following weeks.

"Her father, however, noticed me. He never admitted it, but I think he worked a little magic."

Roan smirks, propping an elbow on the table.

"Of course, Grandpa got to know you first," I add.

"He did. I didn't know who he was at the time—I didn't even know Elizabeth was a Donnelly—but somehow he figured it out. Once he trusted me, I found myself invited for dinner one night with a handful of other young politicians. It was there that I formally met my wife-to-be."

"I love that story," I comment before turning to Roan. "There's more to it, of course."

I bat my eyelashes flirtatiously for a moment before realizing my father is watching. I quickly look away as Roan snorts over my bright red face, making my heart— or some other organ—jump into my throat.

"I wish you two could have had a story like that," my

father suddenly says ruefully. "I wish I could have given you that."

"I like our story, Dad. It might have started a little… painfully…but I like where it ended."

I suddenly regret speaking as I realize I'm about to break Roan's heart thanks to his father's command. I'm about to break my father's too, come to think of it. Even with everything happening, I don't regret my time with Roan Diamond.

"If we hadn't been through everything we had to go through, Jade and I probably wouldn't be together, so for as horrible as it was, I would go through it again to get to Jade." Roan reaches over to take my hand. He looks questioningly at my father.

"I hope that one day you and Jade share the same love Elizabeth and I shared," he replies.

"Thanks, Dad." I smile at him.

"Let's just keep Sophie out of it," he replies, waiting for my reaction.

If I had liquid in my mouth, I would have spit it all over the table. Sophie had done a number on my parents in the early stages of their relationship. They forgave her because she was so young, but it made for great stories. I always laughed as a child when my father quietly told me of her antics. I imagine it's what made her so good at helping to save me.

"Should I ask?" Roan questions, looking back and forth between us.

We both shudder as we try to keep the laughter in. Roan's curious smile grows as his eyes dart between us faster.

"No," I squeak.

"Not tonight, son," my father adds, picking up his fork. He pauses for a moment, food in mid-air, to regain his composure before he takes a bite to avoid choking.

Roan lets out a sigh, curiosity mixed with exasperation, but he lets it go. I know I'll hear about it later.

"So, Roan, how is life at the office?" my father redirects. "I hear you have a new project you're working on."

Roan spends the rest of the meal craftily working around answering the question about his new project. So far I haven't pushed his secret, but I'll find out soon enough.

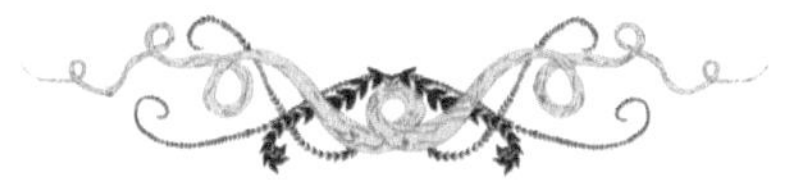

"Your father seems more comfortable around me," Roan comments as he washes the dishes.

I pick up a new towel to dry the plate he hands me,

tossing the wet one aside. The plate is warm to the touch, having just been pulled from the hot water.

"He's definitely relaxed. I mean, he accepted you once you, umm… drank that poison for me." I glance at him. "But I think he's starting to respect you for more than that."

"Yeah, that's what I was thinking." He takes a step toward me and bumps me with his hip, still rinsing a dish with the sink hose. "Now that I'm not torturing you and he knows I'm keeping some space between us in the house."

"Yes," I laugh, "I'm sure he appreciates that."

"Speaking of our arrangement in this house…" He eyes me shrewdly, inching closer. "I do believe I owe you something."

Unsure of his intent, I follow his eyes as he glances down at the hose in his hand. It's poised in his hand, ready for an attack.

"Don't you dare, Roan Diamond!" I shriek as I jump back, nearly dropping the plate. "Roan, I'm serious, don't."

"But why?" he asks innocently, raising the nozzle. "You did it once to me not too long ago."

"Because I was trying to flirt with you!" I yelp, looking for an escape that didn't involve throwing the plate at him.

"What if I'm trying to flirt with you now?" He grins.

"Roan," I plead.

He laughs, returning the hose to its place along the edge of the sink.

"I would never do that to you, Jade." He steps toward me, reaching for my waist. "I'll throw you in a pond fully dressed, but I'll never spray you with the kitchen hose if you begged me not to."

I tentatively let him slip his arms around me.

"Besides, it's far more cute when you do it." Roan nuzzles into me, our foreheads and noses touching, making me relax. "You were pretty convincing."

"Hmm?" I question, distracted by the scent of his shampoo so close to my face.

"You were pretty convincing when you were flirting with me back then," he clarifies, chuckling quietly as he speaks.

"*Just* back then?"

"*Then*…and now." Roan bites his lip.

"Roan…what were you *really* thinking that day when I pulled the sink hose on you? You looked so angry when you left, I thought I had done something wrong."

"I was upset." He pulls back. "You looked so vulnerable pinned on the floor like that. There was just a lot going on."

"Oh." I would have to settle for that as an answer.

"Come on, we should finish the dishes." He guides me back to the sink.

"Roan, do you ever wonder what would have happened if your father had succeeded?"

He glances at me, holding my gaze for a moment.

"I wouldn't have let that happen." His voice holds something dark in it.

"But what if we couldn't have stopped him?"

Was I actually considering telling him?

I can't, there are too many lives at stake.

"What if he had found a way around everything?"

"I wouldn't have let him win, Jade. I would have done whatever I had to do to keep you safe. Your father and Lucas would have too. You saw the lengths that they went to… Even Mr. Eroh was protecting you."

"But what about the country?" I change the subject. "What would have happened to all the people had your father remained in power?"

"I don't know, but I imagine we would have made sure they were all safe too. Why are you asking this Jade?"

"I was just thinking about it, that's all," I cover. "Especially now that I have to start stepping up into a leadership role."

"Are you nervous about that?"

"Yes," I answer truthfully, but not for the reasons he thinks.

"You'll do fine. We're all here to help you."

"I know."

"Maybe your first task could be calming Janine down."
Roan jokes.

"I hardly think that's part of your father's plan." My
laughter goes cold when I realize what I've said. Roan
doesn't catch it.

"He doesn't get a say in this, so you can do whatever
you want to do."

Roan launches into details on my upcoming jobs, not
realizing just how wrong that statement is.

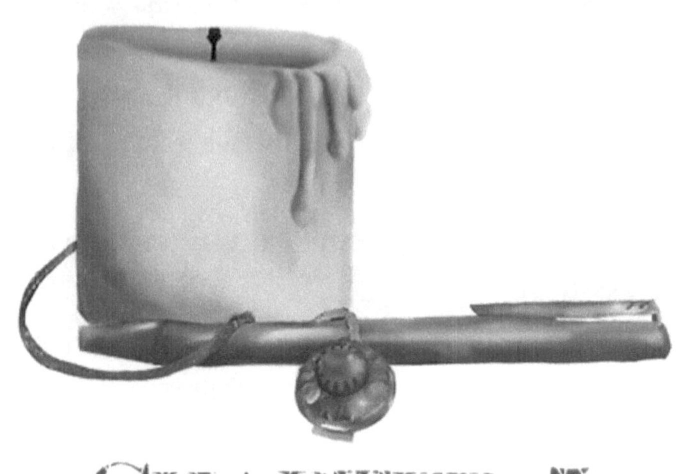

CHAPTER 5
JADE

"**A**re you okay over there?" Roan asks from his desk.

"I'm fine." I sort through papers on the coffee table as I lean over from the couch.

"We should probably get you a desk if you're going to be spending more time here," he mumbles, leafing through his own paperwork. "Unless you want to take over Dad's office."

My head darts up and I find him smirking. I roll my eyes as I look back down.

If I had longer than a month, it wouldn't be too hard

to transform one of the meeting rooms into an office for me, but for now, this would do.

"How is the organizing going?" he asks after a moment.

"Good, I think I have most of it planned out. Lucas made a good call when he suggested the bake sale."

"Not so thrilled he thought of it because of the first time he met you at the school, *but sure*," Roan grumbles.

"I thought you were over that," I challenge.

"I am. Mostly." He shakes his head. "Back to the bake sale. Do you think we can pull it off so quickly?"

"I think so. I wish I had more time to plan it, but I'm sure everyone will chip in."

"The school is really going to appreciate it. They've needed an upgrade on that playground equipment since *I* was a kid there."

"We're not very good about updating things around here, unfortunately," I admit.

"That's about to change though. You and I are going to redefine the way this country works. Are you going to see Annie this afternoon?"

"Yes, I think I'll go after lunch. I wanted to stop in and see Mr. Eroh anyway. He will probably have some good ideas for some things I can do to help the country."

"Do you want me to come with you?" Roan asks, eyes flitting over to his pile of papers.

"You have too much to do as it is, Roan. You're doing

your job *and* your father's job. I imagine in the not-too-distant-future you're going to have to spend a lot of extra time helping me out too. Get your work done while you can. I can walk to my side of town by myself."

"You sure?" He looks torn between being grateful he doesn't have to add anything else to his plate and sad that I'm going without him. He's going to have to get used to that, especially if the Commander is only giving me a month.

"I'll be fine." I smile, trying to reassure him. Everything in me screams to let him come along. I'm running out of time, though I know better than to give in. "But if you're convinced you can't do this alone, Janine is always here. I'm sure she could step up and—"

"Yes, I'm sure that would work out in my favor." Roan shakes his head at me. "I'll be fine, *wife*."

"I'm so glad to hear it, *husband*," I retort. "Actually, I have to talk to Janine. I need her to do a little research for me."

Roan watches as I stand, laying half the pile of papers on the coffee table as I move. Making my way to the door, I notice him tracking my moves and consider taking the opportunity to give him a reason to watch. I cut off thoughts of being coy, knowing it would only make things harder on myself later. I reach the exit and slip out into the spacious lobby.

The girl looks up when she hears my shoes hit the

marble floor. She practically quivers behind the folder she is holding at her desk.

"Hi, Janine," I say as sweetly as possible. "I have a mission for you, if you have time, of course."

She nods, trying to force a smile.

I sidle up next to her and lean over the desk. Setting a few papers down to her left, I wait for her to place her folder on the table and turn to what I'm about to show her. Tucking a strand of hair behind my ear, I smile as she turns to the papers in my hand, avoiding eye contact.

"You heard we're doing the bake sale this weekend, right, Janine?" I wait for her to nod. When she does, I attempt to gush over the project, hoping it will inspire her to get involved out of more than just fear. "Well, I'm really excited about it. We're going to get as many people involved as possible, but I also want to make sure that we're totally prepared with information.

"Would you be able to do a little research on costs for some of the equipment we're going to have fixed up? I want to be able to give everyone a specific goal for how much we're trying to raise. I'm hoping to be as practical as possible, but also make sure we do a really good job on the upgrades. Would you mind doing a little investigating for me? I'd do it myself, but I'm going out to round up volunteers and collect donations today."

"I can do that," Janine says quietly, tucking her hair behind her ear like I had just done.

"Fantastic, I really appreciate it!" I riffle through the papers, explaining what we're looking for and hoping to accomplish. She seems a little less wary by the end of the conversation.

"Hey, babe," Roan says, entering the lobby. "You know it's lunchtime, right?"

I look up as Roan approaches, realizing I had stayed out of the office much longer than I had thought.

"Oh." Losing track of time at this stage of the game was probably not my best move. A missing hour in the grand scheme of things is nothing; missing an hour when you have less than seven hundred of them left is a definite problem.

"You should probably head out if you're going."

"Right," I recover, smoothing my hair back. "I need to get a move on if I'm going to make it everywhere today."

"I'll walk you out." Roan motions me to step in front of him. He darts around me and holds the door for me.

Light smacks me in the face, as tangible as the gust of fresh air that shifts my hair back. I breathe in, stepping out into this new world. It's hard to realize how suffocating the indoors actually is until you walk out of a building and into the sunlight.

I squint against the brightness of the day, a drastic difference from the lighting inside the offices. It feels good to be outside and I suddenly want to go visit the pond.

"It's hard to be locked up all day when there's all this out here, isn't it?" Roan reads my mind.

"Roan," I say suddenly. "Just promise me that in the future, you won't always keep yourself locked up doing work. Promise me that you'll make the effort to keep living and not be chained to your work for the rest of your life."

He looks at me curiously.

"I don't want you to only ever focus on work. I want you to have a life too. See people, do things, take walks, keep going to the art house. I don't want you to fixate solely on your work. I know you, Roan, and I know that one day you're going to get so involved in taking care of other people that you don't take care of yourself."

Roan laughs.

"Jade, I'll be far too busy taking care of you to only ever focus on my work."

"My father only focused on others when I was little, remember? I don't want you to be so blinded by caring for others—even when it's the right thing to do—that you forget to look after you. Promise me, no matter what, that you will make the time to get outside and do something fun at least once a week."

He shrugs, a lopsided grin peeking out from under his blonde bangs, as he steps toward me.

"Anything you say, Jade." He places his hand on my wrist at my side.

"I'm serious, Roan, promise. No matter what happens, promise you'll do this for me." I try to keep him from seeing me get worked up, but the knot in my stomach jumps around like my life depends on it.

"I promise." He leans in and kisses me quickly.

"I'm holding you to that," I insist, knowing I'm probably pushing my luck and he will start asking questions. "Just remember this conversation, Roan."

He opens his mouth to ask something, but I silence him by darting forward and kissing him. He seems to accept it as an answer—or I convinced him to forget he had a question—because when we pull back, he allows me to go on my way without further question.

"See you tonight," Roan shouts when I make my way to the edge of the walk. I turn and find him waving.

The town surrounding the Command is strangely different than my town—or rather, my former town. I live on this side now. The houses all look the same, the people speak and act the same, but it feels different. Maybe it's the way I grew up, or maybe it's the fact that I know these people are more likely to side with Commander Diamond at the end of the day, but I haven't been able to shake the feeling that I don't belong.

A few neighbors wave as they see me walk down the streets. I lift my hand and throw around greetings. I'll need these people on my side so they aren't quite as ready to fall for the Commander's plan as he'd like to think they will be.

Everything quiets as I walk toward the invisible line dividing Roan's town and mine. The houses are more spaced out, the dirt road a little wider than necessary as it marks the divide between his and mine.

My shoulders sink as I step off the main road onto the division that leads passed Erica's candle shop. Every muscle loosens as I enter my hometown, reminding me that for as at home as I feel with Roan, I don't exactly feel safe.

I pass by the candle shop, making my way to the bakery, where I'll have the best chance at talking to the most people at once. The scent hits me before I reach the door. It swings open as Mr. Zuckerman walks out, the noise following behind him.

"Well, Ms. Jareau-Diamond," he says, emphasizing my connection to my father. "So nice to see you."

"Lovely to see you as well, Mr. Zuckerman. Does Annie have any new treats today?"

"I tend to stick to my staples, but she usually has something new and wonderful for you adventurous types." He nods politely. "Enjoy."

"Thank you. Have a good day, sir." I step past him as he holds the door for me.

"Jade!" Several little girls shriek my name, jumping up

from their chairs where three mothers are trying to convince them not to bombard me.

"Hi!" I greet them as they throw themselves around my legs. "How are you girls today?"

They all vie for my attention until Annie interrupts.

"Hi, Jade, you hungry? Do you want something?"

"Yes, please." I walk over to join her as she sets a plate in front of Mrs. Thompson and her friend.

"I heard you've got an announcement you'd like to make?" Annie's eyes sparkle as she bumps me with her elbow as she leans over.

She's talked to Lucas. *Of course* he would have paved the way for me.

"Everyone, listen up," Annie shouts, silencing the room except for one small child who wasn't old enough to have respect for the lady in charge. "Jade has an announcement."

Everyone shifts to look at me as I quickly explain the fundraiser. They smile and nod as I speak, becoming even more engaged when I tell them my next goal is to fix up the pond and get all the dangers out from under the dock. By the time Annie pushes me into a seat and sets a sandwich in front of me, I have plenty of volunteers.

"Easier than you thought, wasn't it?" Annie mumbles as she sets the plate down.

"Lucas?" I question, already knowing the answer.

The bell rings in the background, covered over with the sounds of utensils hitting plates and conversations. A cool breeze sweeps around my feet as the door swings shut somewhere behind me.

"Ask him yourself," Annie replies, walking away.

I turn to find Lucas walking toward me—the definition of swagger. He pulls out the chair across the table and sits, propping his feet out slightly into the walkway as he crosses his ankles.

"Hello, Mrs. Diamond," he smirks.

"Really?" I roll my eyes. "To what do I owe this pleasure, *Mr. Montgomery?*"

"I thought you could use a little company," he drawls, folding his fingers together on the table. He eyes me. "Is that unacceptable?"

"Perhaps," I challenge. "But why are you *really* here?"

"Oh, Jade. Didn't I ever tell you I have an obligation to watch over you?" Lucas leans forward conspiratorially.

"Didn't that obligation end a few months ago?" I tease.

"I sincerely doubt that obligation will *ever* end, Jade." Lucas leans back in his chair. "Besides, have you seen yourself? Runaway bikes, crazed enemies, toxic hair gadgets, and a backyard out to kill... You're kind of a walking time bomb. You really think the second I walk away, that your world isn't going to explode? Face it, Jade, I'm the only thing holding your life together."

We face off, staring at each other across the table, daring the other to blink first.

"Toxic hair gadget?" I finally say, realizing he had slipped that strange phrasing into the conversation.

"Well, what else do you call it?" He grins, deeming my break of silence a victory on his behalf.

"Not a 'gadget,'" I criticize.

"Mr. Eroh might beg to differ," he protests.

"Mr. Eroh is a highly intelligent man who knows the term 'hair comb,'" I defy him.

"Are you saying that I'm not intelligent?" He feigns shock.

"Is that something that needs to be said?" I ask innocently.

Lucas' face contorts just enough that I have to hold in my laughter. Someone at the next table glances our way and we both fight to contain ourselves and not draw extra attention.

"Bold, Jade," he finally concludes. "Just remember what I mean to you."

Six different snappy replies race to my lips, but before I can throw another insult at him, Lucas reaches his hand out into the walkway.

"Ah, Erica," he says, waving toward the table. "Join us, won't you? We need you to settle something for us."

Lucas turns in his chair and grabs an empty seat from the table behind him. He drags it noisily into the aisle as

Annie eyes him. Only Lucas or I would be able to get away with blocking her walkway, but she doesn't lecture us.

Erica glances around uncomfortably, still trying to maintain distance from me. She quietly takes a seat where Lucas has angled it to face himself.

"Hello, Lucas." She gives him a forced smile before turning to nod to me. "Hello."

"Jade, you know Erica, right?" Lucas says, keeping up the charade. "She owns the candle shop."

"Yes, I've stopped in a few times on my way home from work."

"Erica and I went to school together." Lucas continues to explain as if the introduction mattered. "Jade here is Roan Diamond's wife and the Commander's daughter-in-law. Her father and I work together."

Erica nods again, acknowledging me.

"We need you to settle something, Erica." Lucas leans forward and grins at her, as I suddenly realize just how good he is at hiding his charms when he needs to.

The man is practically irresistible and he has gone all these years without droves of women following him around. I have been aware of this since the day I formally met him, but it still shocks me how good he is at hiding his allure. I watch Erica's eyes widen just enough to be noticed.

"You see, Jade here thinks I'm not very smart—"

"I didn't say that!" I interject.

"She did," he continued, leaning back to drape an elbow over the back of the chair. Annie shoots me a look, trying to figure out what he was doing from across the room. "Frankly, Erica, she's not being very nice. But what do *you* think? Am I good at what I do?"

He looked out at her from under his dark lashes, flirting to get his way. No wonder he had risen in the ranks so quickly. With charm like that, he could talk his way in and out of any situation he wanted and people would readily believe him.

"I'm sure you're good at what you do, Lucas." Erica looks down, slightly flustered. "But then again, I remember you back in school that day you walked into a door, so…"

She redeems herself and calls him out.

I slam my hand against the table, making several people jump as I burst into laughter.

"You walked into a door?" I gasp. "How on earth did you manage that?"

"I imagine you would have loved to have seen that, Jade," Erica laughs, a crack in her hard-fought façade. "Slammed right into it. The entire class heard him collide with the door."

"Which might explain some of his choices now," I venture. "Right, Lucas? Seriously, how did you manage that?"

He took a breath, calming his frustration at not being seen as perfect.

"I caught sight of a pretty girl." He looks pointedly at me, trying to silence me.

"Was she worth it?" Erica asks between chuckles.

"Most days," Lucas answers after a moment of silence. His gaze sweeps back to Erica. "You're really going to side with *her* over me?"

"Always," she replies with a straight face.

"I knew I liked you." I push the plate of tiny cookies Annie had left for me toward Erica. She picks one up and we both crunch on one as we wait for Lucas' reaction.

"Oh, I see how it is. Some kind of girl thing. Well, fine. I'll take my lunch to go. I have to go see your father anyway."

He winks at us before sauntering over to the counter to have Annie bag his lunch for him. Maybe leaving me with Erica had been his plan all along.

Lucas glances over his shoulder to check on us, leaning one elbow on the counter as he waits. I turn away, pretending not to notice.

"So tell me more about *Lucas: The Younger Years.*" I can't help but turn and catch his gaze out of the corner of my eye. I smile mischievously.

He pales slightly, but resigns himself to suffer through the torture I'm about to put him through for the good of whatever little mission he has set up here. Lucas takes his food and thanks Annie before bolting for the door.

Erica shifts over to Lucas' seat, moving the extra chair back to its original place behind her. She smiles politely but I can tell she's eager to talk. Keeping her voice even, she regales me with tales from her past, many of which I plan to use against Lucas later.

"That was so kind of you, thank you, Jade." Mr. Eroh says, unwrapping the sandwich I brought from the bakery.

"I think the fundraiser is going to go well," I smile, picking up a small trinket on the counter. It's cool in my hand as I flip it over.

"That's good. I'm sure the school will appreciate the update of the playground equipment. Last time I was over there, it looked to be in pretty rough shape."

"It is, unfortunately, but once we pull some money together and everyone pitches in to help, it will be much safer."

I twirl the metallic trinket in my hand. I half expect it to transform into something more sinister, but it doesn't change form as I move it. Perhaps not everything in the shop has a dual purpose.

"It's nice when everyone helps, isn't it?" Mr. Eroh says absent-mindedly. "Rebuilding is hard. Take this shop for example..."

He gestures with one hand, securing the sandwich with the other. His eyes roam over the new shelves, covered in more items than either of us know what to do with. My tiny library sits in the corner, patiently waiting for someone to visit.

"It wasn't easy rebuilding this after the fire. Your father, husband, and Lucas spent so much time on this. Everyone did, really. So much work and effort went into creating these walls. This structure is sturdy. It's protective. Despite all the extra work and effort, do you think it was worth it, Jade?"

I look up suddenly at his question.

"Yes," I answer. "Of course."

"Good answer," he smiles with a nod. "It's not easy to rebuild a building, Jade, as you well know. But it's also not easy to rebuild a life...or even *build* one for that matter."

His eyes sparkle as he looks at me, taking a bite of his sandwich. The piece of metal weighs heavy in my hand.

"Just because something isn't easy, doesn't mean that we shouldn't do it." He waits for me to catch on to his point. "People—and buildings—go through a lot. We all have our *fires* so to speak, just like the shop here. But when we build it back, it can be stronger and better than before.

"What I'm saying, Jade, is that building your life back might be hard, but that doesn't mean you should stop fighting for what you really want. This is your life, and you need to live it. Don't give up on him, even when times get hard."

"Him?" I ask.

"Roan," Mr. Eroh winks at me. "Don't give up on him. He's gone through the fire with you. Now you can build your lives together."

A dull ache grows in my chest, as heavy as the trinket in my hand. I set it down a little too loudly on the counter. I hurriedly try to recover.

"We're working on it," I inform him.

"Still getting along all right?" he asks.

"Yes, we're fine," I force a smile, knowing it's only going to last a few more days.

"Still taking things slow, I hope?" he pries.

"Yes," I narrow my eyes and shake my head in mock annoyance.

"Good. Now," he nods to the trinket on the counter, "open that."

I give him a skeptical look, already having tried to open it. My boss squints an eye and ducks his head, indicating that I should look underneath. When I find nothing, he quickly explains how to open it.

The lid pops up and a soft tune fills the air, just loud enough for the two of us to hear the melodic little plunks. Of course he had more secrets.

"Take it home," he encourages me. "Speaking of, shouldn't you get back?"

"I suppose," I sigh, slowly standing. "I wish I could stay."

"Me too, but you're on a deadline now," he says, sending me into a panic. *Did he know?* "The Commander is only going to play nice for so long. You need to position yourselves properly while you still can."

I held in my sigh of relief…or maybe it was of regret.

"We're trying," I assure him.

"You said you're working on the lake next, right?"

"Yes," I say over my shoulder.

"Good, we need some good on this side of town too, and that dock is too dangerous to let go."

"I promise it's the next thing I'll do."

"Sometimes it's the little things that slip by and lead to our undoing, Jade." He turns his back, bending over a broken watch as he hums to himself.

What does he know?

CHAPTER 6
ROAN

"That's not a bad idea," I nod, taking in his suggestion.

Lucas shifts on the couch.

"Jade really did a good job picking this out," he smirks as he pats the cushion. "I think it's smart to do an open forum though. It shows a shift in power and a willingness to listen to the people."

"I agree," I nod. "Do you think we're moving too quickly though? I mean, my dad has only been out for two days."

"I don't think it matters, Roan. I think we need to move forward with this. We need to get Jade positioned as a leader quickly. I don't think it will hurt to bump up the open forum. We were planning on doing it anyway, so why not this weekend?"

He thrums his fingers on the couch arm as I consider his position.

"It can't all be about Jade though," I muse. "People might be wary if it's just her."

"Well, then give James more power too," Lucas suggests. "Wait, I see what I did there. It can't just be James and Jade. It has to be others too or it will seem like James is trying to take over."

"You know," he pauses, "we could have avoided this if James had just won."

"Yes, I'm aware." I resisted the urge to roll my eyes. "*Congratulations*, Lucas, *you're* being promoted too."

"What?" he looks up at me. "I don't need to be promoted—"

"Oh, but you do. Besides," I wave a hand at him, "The cocky, arrogant politician you pretend to be would be angling for a job upgrade anyway. Ride it out."

He sighs dramatically.

"Why must this all be so difficult?" Lucas asks.

"I know you like keeping a low profile, but you don't have to anymore. I'm sure James will approve, but you can talk to him about it if you want," I offer, knowing he respects James' opinion as much as he would have respected his own father's. "Besides, he's getting roped into it too."

If I had known Lucas was coming to see me, I would have had him bring me something from Annie's as well. It's a good thing I ate before he came in, or I would be very jealous.

He sees me eyeing his food and taunts me with a shrug, picking up the second half of his sandwich.

"So how are we going to play this?" he asks.

"I thought we could start with a few updates of what the Command is working on right now and then perhaps we could open it up to questions," I reply.

"You're just going to *open it up to questions?*" he gapes at me.

"Bad idea?"

"Only if you don't want to be blindsided by some insane rant from someone who has no idea what they are talking about," he chides. "I imagine you didn't get much of that while your father was still in charge, but I had at least one lecture every other week.

"James was lucky. They knew where he stood and left him alone," he shakes his head. "That, or they didn't want to be seen with him and labeled as a rebel by proxy."

My father's reign of terror strikes again.

"I can't say I'm jealous that I missed out on the lectures," I grin at him, finally having the upper hand. "Now, what do you suggest for this meeting?"

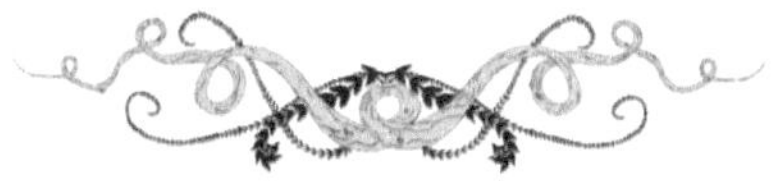

Jade's door closes with a gentle click. I stare at it for what feels like a long time before my feet move.

"Can I get you anything?" I ask through the door.

"No," she calls softly.

"Are you hungry?" I try again.

"No, I'm just tired," she calls. Her voice is softer as if she's stepped away from the door. "I'm just going to rest."

The bed quietly shifts as she sits down. I can barely make out the sound from where I stand on the outside of her door.

When I arrived home, she tucked her hair behind her ear, claimed to need a nap and had retired to her room. In all the time I have known Jade, *never once* has she taken a nap.

My first thought is to pound on the door, but if she's coming down with something, I don't want to make her feel worse. My finger tips drag along the wooden door gently.

"Are you sure I can't do anything for you?" I ask softly.

"I'm fine, Roan," she sighs from across the room. "I just need a little space."

Space? What does she need space from?

"Okay," I reply, defeated.

I'll leave her alone if that's what she wants. I'd give her anything she asked for, but the separation—even by a simple wall—makes my chest want to cave in. Somehow, this feels different.

I wander into the kitchen, feet feeling heavier than they did on the walk home. I consider making dinner in case Jade wants something when she gets up from her nap, but I doubt she's coming back out tonight. Glancing around, I try to find something to occupy my time.

The house is quiet. Any noise I make might disturb Jade as she rests, so I walk out to the back yard, looking for something to do. The steps barely creak as my weight shifts against them.

Flowers still grow all around the yard where my mother had them planted. I regret ever letting her plan the house before the wedding. I'd pull every last flower to prevent Jade from getting sick, but I know she'd yell at me. She still appreciates their beauty, even though she can't get too close.

The hammock sits in the middle of the grass and for a moment, I think about resting myself, but I'm too wired to lie down. Grabbing the watering can, I tend to the flowers. The only area free of them is the far fence wall. I move around the perimeter, giving the plants a much-needed drink.

As I reach down to set the watering can back in its

place, I notice the stones surrounding the lower flowerbeds. My mother had found enough rocks to surround the garden, encasing it in a light gray pathway.

I step over one of the stones as I replaced the watering can, spilling a drop of water on it. It was strange that I hadn't really noticed them before. I was aware that they were there, but I hadn't paid any attention to them as they curved their way around the yard over to the far fence where Jade usually drags a chair to sit, as far from the flowers as she can get.

The sun has disappeared from the sky, but it is still light out. I glance inside. I can't see or hear Jade, but I assume she is still quietly tucked away in her room. Visibility and time are on my side, though the noise would work against me.

I might be able to pull this off if I hurry.

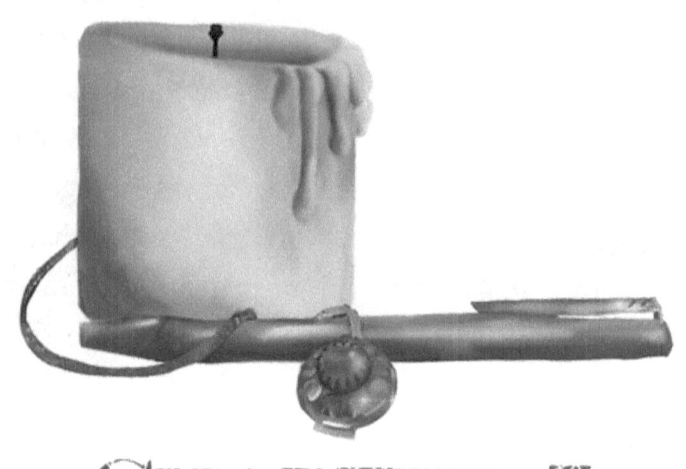

CHAPTER 7
JADE

For a moment when I open my door, all of the old feelings come rushing back, and I think, perhaps, for a moment, Roan Diamond is trying to assassinate me again—this time it's death by blood loss from a severe paper cut to the eye.

The paper dangles in front of my face, narrowly missing my eye. I throw myself backward, slamming my eyes shut, praying I avoided it. Hanging a paper at eye level probably wasn't Roan's best idea.

I eye the square dangling from one of my favorite ribbons. Roan has obviously been in my sewing kit. I remind myself to wrap my favorite ribbons up tighter so they are harder to get into in hopes that he will use the more common ribbons. I nearly snort as I remember in a few days it won't actually matter. Let the boy use the fancy ribbon—what do I care?

I take a stabilizing breath and reach for the note. My stomach rumbles, making me extra glad I had thought to eat something before hiding away in my room all night. For as hungry as I am now, I can't imagine how starved I would feel had I not eaten last night.

Curiously, the note was blank except for a tiny sketch of a flower in the bottom left corner of one side of the square. I shouldn't get involved in his games, I know. I'm *supposed* to be pushing him away. I'm *supposed* to be making this easier on all of us. Stupidly, that doesn't stop me from walking into the living room, leaving the note dangling in front of my room.

My stomach protests again, begging me to feed it. Masochistically, I stick my head into the kitchen, just in case the flower drawing was actually a riddle for *flour* and I was supposed to be in the kitchen. Roan isn't there.

The living room is empty, as is the hall. I don't bother checking in his room. The door to the backyard is cracked open slightly, telling me I need to go outside.

I approach the door, pushing it open just enough to see outside. The sun is a bright golden color, bathing the grass in a harsh yellow.

I jump out of my skin as Roan sidles up behind me. *I should have checked his room.*

He chuckles as my hand flies to my chest but I refuse to turn around. Roan reaches forward and moves my hair off my neck, but doesn't ask me to turn to him. Instead, he waits for me to open the door.

Nothing looks out of place—nothing seems unusual. The steps are still there. The hammock still sits in the middle of the yard. The fence holds its defensive position, keeping our neighbors at bay.

As I walk down the steps, my eyes immediately fall on the fresh dirt. It's brown and earthy. I can smell it.

One rock is missing. Now two. Now three.

The entire length of the yard is transformed into rings of dirt where stone had once sat. It wasn't until the end of the trail that I realized why they were missing.

"What—?" I start to ask.

"Do you feel better today?" Roan asks, throwing me off.

"What?" I repeat, this time looking for a different answer.

"Are you," he punctuates his words, wrapping his arms around my waist, "feeling better this morning?"

"Yes," I shake my head, trying to piece this strange puzzle together. "What is that?"

"You've never seen a bench before?" he asks innocently.

"Why is there a bench in our yard?" I demand softly. "And why did you tear up the garden?"

"I think the better question is how long are you going to stand around talking while your breakfast gets cold?" he guides me across the yard to the tray of food waiting on the stone bench at the far end of the yard. Pillows sit on the bench, acting as cushions. He picks up the tray and hands it to me, guiding me to sit as he takes a seat beside me. "And I didn't dig up the garden. I moved some stones around, that's all."

"But why?" I question. "And where did you get the other stone, because I *know* we did not have enough to build this thing—it's huge, Roan."

"I know you like it out here and it's not right that you have to drag chairs all the way over here all the time. I thought a stone bench would be pretty. I didn't have time to find cushions, so you'll have to forgive the pillows from the closet, but we'll get some."

"Roan—"

"I wanted to," he cuts me off.

"Because you want me to be comfortable here," I sigh, finishing his sentence. "This is lovely, thank you, Roan."

Every bit of me is on fire. I feel like I'm being burned at the stake, flesh melting off my bones, ripping my organs from my body as they turn into puddles of liquid running down my legs to the ground. *It hurts.* His kindness *hurts.*

Roan Diamond was not making dying easy.

"Eat," he nods to the food on the tray.

Fine. One more day. I can give myself one more day.

The pancakes smell amazing as I pick up the tiny container of syrup and pour it over them. Roan picks up a second fork and cuts a bite off. Before he can lift it, I dart forward and kiss him quickly.

I shouldn't. But I do.

"I got them from town," he says as I pull back.

"Hmm?" My face falls in confusion.

"The stones. When I had used all of ours, I walked around the town and collected them."

"You walked around town last night without me knowing?"

"You were sleeping and I was quiet. You're not the only sneaky one around here, Jade." He grins, lifting his fork to his lips. *Stupid fork.*

"You are so sweet." I shouldn't have said that out loud. If he wasn't watching so closely, I'd jab my fork into my lips as punishment for the betrayal.

Roan moves closer, shifting so that his knee touches mine. The warmth of a person being so close to me is still a little surreal at times, but in a good way.

The food is amazing. Roan's cooking is always good, but this is something I'll remember for a long time. I realize, of course, it's probably because of its association to the gesture, but it doesn't matter—I have a month and I'm going to savor everything.

I put my head on his shoulder. It makes eating harder than it should be, but I manage as gracefully as possible. Roan looks pleased with himself and everything in me screams to encourage him. My brain reminds me I shouldn't.

I leave my head on his shoulder but stay quiet. It's a compromise I can live with.

After a few moments, he hurries me along. We're supposed to be getting ready for work. By now, the sun is higher in the sky, blindingly peeking over the fence over our shoulders. When we stand, we cast long shadows leading back to our house.

Roan takes the tray from me, tugging me along with his other hand. I reach back, pulling the pillows into my arms, not wanting to leave them out in case the weather turns unexpectedly. He quietly leads me into the house.

"Go get ready, I'll take care of this," he murmurs, giving me a fond look before wandering off to the kitchen.

It takes a moment before I can move. Navigating to my room is anything but easy. I finally manage, making my way to the sink to brush my teeth.

Standing in front of my closet, I consider my options. Somehow, it was easier to pick outfits when I didn't know which of them would be my last. Should I pick a different outfit for every day until the big moment or should I wear my favorites as much as possible? The choices are agonizing.

In the end, the important thing is to get dressed.

Royal blue wins out. I slip into the asymmetrical dress, the front falling just above my knee while the back trailed behind me nearly to the floor. I wondered if the three-quarter sleeves will be comfortable if it gets windy later.

I slip into my shoes and step outside to find Roan sitting on the arm of the couch as I so often do to him. He grins slyly at me.

"Ready for work?" he asks.

"I am," I nod, trying to hold in my giggle.

I was able to keep him from affecting me back before he switched sides to protect me, so why can't I withstand his efforts now? Circumstances affect the powers of his charm.

He stands, offering me his hand.

I'm powerless, so I take it.

We make it three feet before he jerks to a halt. Grabbing me, he dips me toward the floor, kissing me as I cling to him to keep from falling. Roan holds me as his lips brush over mine. I'm lightheaded, though I don't know if it's from the electric kisses trailing along my neck and collarbone, or from being nearly upside down with blood rushing to my head.

"Okay," he breathes as he rights me, "*now* we can go to work."

"I didn't realize that was a morning requirement," I tease, fixing my hair.

"It *should* be," he demands, "and for the record, I didn't like not saying goodnight to you last night. Please don't make me suffer through that again…or you may end up upside down again. That's your warning."

He laughs quietly as he moves toward the door. If the Commander doesn't kill me first, the agony of pulling away from his son surely will.

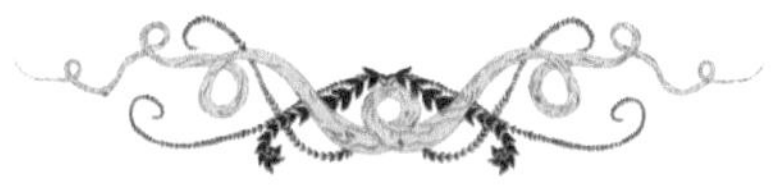

"Mom," Roan's voice catches me off guard. "What are you doing here? Is everything okay?"

"Janine let me in," Alice says as she backs away from Roan's desk. "I brought a cake."

She points to the desk where a simple white frosted cake sits on the right side nearest to the door. It's garnished with a few berries and a sprig of something green.

"It's for the bake sale," she clarifies. "I had Maybelle

make it. "Your father needed a book from his office, so I brought it over."

She glances at me nervously. I can see her fingers itching to grasp the pearls around her neck but she fights back the urge, keeping her hands at her side. Instead, she smoothes her dress over her hips and nods to me with a forced smile.

"That was nice of you, thanks, Mom. Tell Maybelle it looks lovely as always."

"It really is quite beautiful," I add.

She nods again, assuring Roan she will pass the message along. "I should get that book," she adds, backing up to step around us. She looks down as she tries to pass.

"Let me help you, Mom," Roan follows her. His tone is far less icy toward her than it has been these past few months. He mumbles to her in the hallway as they walk to the Commander's office.

I need to find ways to avoid Roan today. Sitting on his couch certainly won't help my case. Perhaps I can take the cake to the school and set it up. I don't mind moving the tables around by myself, especially if it means a little distance. I need to clear my head after this morning.

Waiting for Alice to leave is like a full-time job that never ends. I hover by the door, straining to hear while still staying out of sight of the lobby. I should probably be paying attention to the book Alice is taking to the royal swine in case it's a message for me, but I'm not sure I can handle any more messages today.

I need to figure out where the Commander is keeping Sophie. There are only so many places in the Command that he could hide her. Then again, I didn't know about all his secret rooms in *this* building until the day he drugged me and sent me out on stage to be poisoned, so what do I know?

Alice's clicking heels are my first indication that I should throw myself backward, ensuring that I'm out of sight. She walks away, proper as ever, as I dart to Roan's desk to scoop up the cake. This is my best chance.

I nearly collide with Roan as he walks into his office.

"Easy there, Jade. What are you trying to do, kill me? I thought we were over that stage of our relationship." His hands settle on my elbows as I steady the cake. My face flushes.

"I thought I would take the cake over to the school. There's not much I can do here yet, so I figured it wouldn't be a bad idea to set up early." I try to shrug casually.

"Well," he looks around, "give me a few minutes and we can walk over."

"No," I say far too quickly. I need to calm down. "You don't have to come. Stay and get your work done. I can handle this."

I pray my smile is convincing. He looks at me skeptically.

"Besides, it doesn't take two people to carry a little old cake. I'll be fine."

"Jade, what is going on? You're acting out of sorts."

"Am I?" Nope, I'm definitely failing at this. How could I have survived him so easily before and now I can barely speak around him? It's like I've lost my ability to protect myself. All of my grace and quick-thinking is gone.

He reaches to take the cake from me and I can see in his expression that he wants to have a "serious talk" with me. I duck under his arm and bounce toward the door.

"I'll be back in a bit." I angle my body to the door so that I can lean sideways and peck him on the lips. I smile before walking out, hoping he doesn't follow me.

If I hadn't made it awkward enough already, I'd be making it worse soon if the Commander's plan had any say in it.

I keep up a brisk pace as I walk to the school, not slowing until I see the playground.

"Good morning, Mrs. Diamond," the woman in the office greets me. "What can I do for you today?"

"I was hoping I could set up for the bake sale, if that's all right with you all." I hold up Maybelle's cake as if it validated my point.

"Let me check for you," she smiles politely, standing from her swivel chair. It creaks as she walks toward the principal's office to get permission for me to close down their gymnasium.

"Right this way, Mrs. Diamond." She waves for me to follow her when she returns.

She guides me down a hallway, into a large room used to teach the children to exercise properly. Light filters in through the high glass windows, the floating dust particles reminding me of a far-less-exciting art house.

"If you need any help, you can ask the janitor. He's down the hall on the right." Her shoes tap as she walks away, leaving me in silence.

A few tables sit at one end of the room. For a moment, I think about rearranging the space, but it *is* just me and I'm not too keen on the idea of rolling tables on my own.

I sigh and walk over to the tables. For the longest time I wished to be alone and now the only thing I wanted was to be surrounded by people.

Mr. Eroh had collected a few table clothes for me and sent them to the school with one of the boys a few days ago. They sit at the end of one of the long tables. Setting the cake at the far end, I pivot and walk toward the box.

It only takes a few minutes to spread out the linens on the tables. I set out tags at one end so that we could write the name of the donations on the cards and place them on the table with the appropriate food.

I still needed to bake my contribution tonight, but I'm sure Roan won't mind as long as I make a second version to keep at home. Maybe I could let him help a little tonight since I will have avoided him all day. *Baby steps.*

The ribbons on the table add a little visual interest to the display, though I'm sure they will be overlooked tomorrow as hungry eyes search for the desserts they will be taking home for later. I spend as long as I dare rearranging the twisted ribbons, hoping to delay my departure, but not wanting to be overseen and judged for fiddling with ribbons that don't actually matter—arranging them so intentionally has all of the importance of twirling one's hair.

Finally, I give up, scooping up the box the tablecloths were in and setting it under the table. One last look and I make my way back to the office to say goodbye. It is time to face Roan.

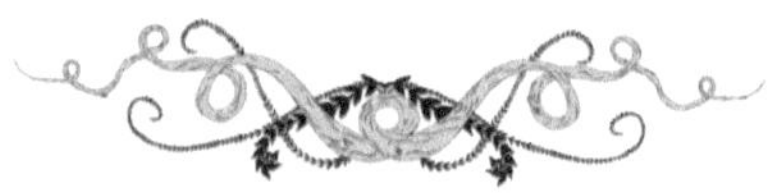

"Mrs. Diamond," Janine greets me as I walk in.

"Janine, please call me Jade," I remind her.

She rushes over to me, papers in hand.

"I have that information you were looking for." She hands me a stack of papers.

"Thank you, Janine," I say as I leaf through the pages, "this looks great."

"Mr. Diamond is waiting for you in his office," she looks expectantly at me.

My heart jumps at the thought of him waiting for me and I wish I could appreciate it more.

"Thank you, Janine."

She scurries back to her seat, looking a little less nervous than usual. Perhaps she's warming up to us.

Roan's door is open so he doesn't hear me when I slip in. He's bent over his work, leaning in toward the papers in his hands. For a moment, I consider walking behind him and working out the kinks in his neck and shoulders, but I'm supposed to be keeping my distance.

I do it anyway.

He's surprised to see me as he finally notices me when I'm halfway to him. Before he can speak, I set my papers down on the corner of his desk and tuck myself behind his chair.

His skin is warm and he cringes into me as I hit a sore muscle. Roan relaxes, closing his eyes as I work. His muscles tense as I touch them, bunching up under my fingers.

I work quietly for a few moments and Roan pretends to try to do his work while I'm standing so close. When he can't take it anymore, he reaches up to cover one of my hands with his. Freezing, I wait to see what he will do.

Roan quietly tugs at my hand, pulling me around in front of him. I let him guide me to his lap. We sit facing each other.

"Are we okay?" he asks quietly as I stare into his eyes.

"Yes," I answer truthfully. He's done nothing to provoke my actions. His father on the other hand…

I twist so I can face him more easily, putting a bit of space between us. The edge of his desk digs into my back.

He leans forward, the question of a kiss lingering between us once again. As far as he knows, I have no reason to hold back and it would be entirely out of character. I need to ease up on pushing him away so quickly.

I meet him halfway.

When we finally pull apart, he murmurs, "That's more like it, wife."

I roll my eyes, forbidding myself from giggling.

"We didn't get to talk last night, but Lucas came to see me yesterday," Roan tells me, finger stroking the inside of my arm.

"Oh?"

"He said you did a great job at Annie's." He smiles at me.

"Lucas wouldn't have any idea—he didn't come in until after."

"He says he saw the aftermath…and Annie told him."

"*That's* more like it," I smirk. In an effort to get a little revenge, I play with Roan's collar and watch him swallow as my finger brushes against his neck.

"He also suggested," Roan pauses to lower his voice again, "that we move up the open forum to this weekend."

"What?" I gasp. My hand freezes against his neck uncomfortably. I have to intentionally force myself to move it as the rest of my body is unable to be thawed.

"With Dad changing the plan, we have to adapt. We need to get you into a place of authority and change the dynamics for Lucas and your father as well. We don't want it to just seem like a power play by James."

He makes a good point. Singling my father out as manipulating me into power would be a dangerous twist to this little game and an opportunity I certainly don't want to give the Commander.

"It can't just be us though." My mind races to think of who else we could elevate.

"No, there will be a few others. Mr. Zuckerman, maybe. Lucas made a few suggestions." His finger runs over my leg just above my knee. "It will all be all right, Jade. You don't need to be so jumpy."

"When are we doing this?" I ask, trying not to look worried. I had better control over my face the day Roan came to pick me up for our wedding.

"Sunday," he responds, glancing around me to look at his desk. "Lucas suggested we don't open it up to questions on the first night, but I thought it might be good to let the people bring us their concerns. What do you think?"

I pause, thinking it through. Lucas likely thought that an open forum would invite trouble and I tend to agree. I'd much rather guide the people into having an open conversation by showing them what it should look like first.

"What if we screen a few questions first? We could have everyone write down something that they would like addressed when they join us and someone could go through them in the back and pull a handful of good questions to address.

"That way, we can answer a few questions, but things won't get confrontational, and we can agree to go through all the questions and get them answered in the upcoming forums."

Roan wraps his hands around my waist, pulling me closer. I'm relieved when the sharp pain of the desk is no longer digging into me.

"I like that." He nods before leaning his forehead against mine. "You're going to make such a good Commander's wife, Jade. You're brilliant. And practical and sensible."

Before he can go on, I interject. "And *you're* stalling to keep me here longer, husband. But one of us has work to do—"

"Surprisingly enough, you're not referring to me. And here I thought I was the only one who ever worked in this office."

I shoot him an annoyed grin before tightening my fist on his collar. One more kiss won't hurt.

His smile dares me to walk away from him. He has me right where he wants me, but I can't let him win.

I stand, shattering his plans for a perfect afternoon of kissing. Moving to the couch, I work through the papers Janine has constructed for me, planning out every last detail before the fundraiser tomorrow.

Roan sits quietly at his desk until it's time to go home, only walking out of the office a few times to handle things and talk to a handful of people. When he goes, the room gets overwhelmingly silent, even though he hasn't been making any noise in the first place.

He slips out one more time to speak with one of the representative's aids, leaving me in silence once more, which is why I nearly have a heart attack when a voice sounds at the door.

"Well, look who is hard at work," the Commander sneers.

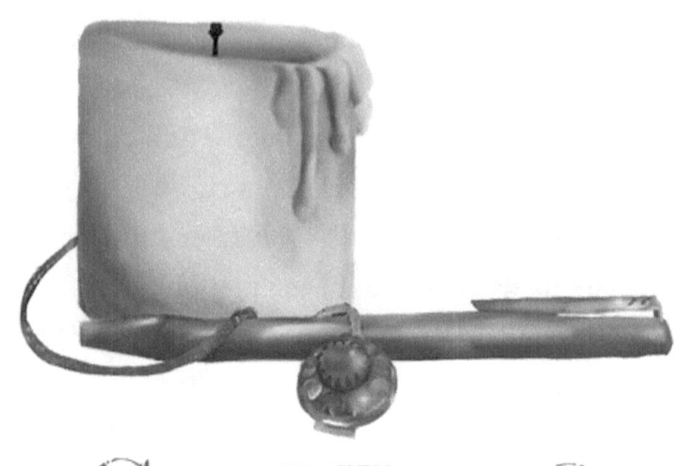

CHAPTER 8
JADE

"What are you—?" I jump.

"Shh, shh," the Commander wags his finger at me. "No one knows I'm here."

"How did you get in without them seeing?" I drop my voice to a hushed tone, complying with his command.

"I have my ways, Jade. How do you think I got around this place before?" He pauses thoughtfully. "How do you think I got *you* around here before with no one noticing? *Stupid girl.*"

"If you're trying to avoid your son, he could be back any minute," I protest.

"No, he won't. Sean will keep him occupied for a few minutes so we can talk."

Sean. I made a mental note to find him and let Roan know he worked for the Commander without telling him how I knew before I die.

"Your wife was here this morning," I inform him as he approaches.

"I'm aware."

"Why are you here?" I question.

"I haven't heard from you in a few days, *daughter*," he leers at me, "I thought I should check in and make sure you're holding up your end of the deal."

"I haven't told Roan yet, if that's what you mean." His very presence disgusts me.

"*Yet?*" his face falls just enough to let me know he's concerned. He still has the upper hand though, because I haven't figured out where Sophie is yet.

An idea hits me in the instant it takes for him to recover. Most people will be at the bake sale tomorrow. That means the town will be empty for the majority of the event—or at least more quiet than usual, even if they show up at different times. If I make an appearance and then rush off to do something official for the sale—like find more cookies or pick up extra trays—no one will think anything of it and I'll still look professional to them. If I play my cards right, I can do a little digging to see where Sophie might be held.

"Do I need to remind you what is at stake here, Jade?"

"No," I cut him off. "I'm perfectly well aware of where things stand."

I put my hands on my hips and rise up to my full height, preparing to change the game.

"I want to see her. Sophie," I inform him. "I need to see her to make sure she's all right before I go through with any of this."

"You don't get to dictate what we do—"

"Yes I do," I challenge him, bravado washing over me.

The Commander grows as irate as he was the day of my wedding and I expect to see him start foaming at the mouth again. Instead, he grins.

"We'll see." My father-in-law backs toward the door. "But only if you play nice, daughter."

He slips out without another word, leaving the room feeling like it pulled my soul out and stomped on it. The encounters I keep having in this building are not worth the pretty marble columns out in the lobby.

"Ready to go home?" Roan asks when he returns.

"Yes," I gather my things, bringing the papers with me.

On Monday, I will need extra space to work and will tell Roan I'll be working in his father's office for the day. I can get my work done, of course, but I'll also explore the room and see what the man had hidden there. By mid-week, I will know every hiding place in this country if it kills me.

I take Roan's arm and follow behind him as we step through the door of his office. Tonight I will bake pies for the bake sale with my husband, and later tonight, I will get more of this work done so that I can spy tomorrow.

"You're not going to share?" Roan asks, reaching across the table.

"No." I lash out at him with the back of a spoon. He pulls back quickly, trying to avoid my mock-wrath. "Now hand me those already."

I use the spoon to point to the bowl sitting beside him. He picks up a berry and pops it in his mouth before handing the bowl over to me. I take it from him as he turns back to pick up the second bowl.

When he hands this one to me, Roan brushes his hand against mine sending tingles up my arm. Here I thought I was comfortable with him, but apparently being on edge has reverted me to the giggly girl I pretended to be during the latter half of our wedding day when I was proving a point.

I add the berries to the pie crust a few at a time, drawing out the process as he watches me.

"How many do you think we'll sell tomorrow?" he muses.

"I'm sure we'll raise enough to fix the playground," I respond, keeping my eyes fixed on the pie. "It's our first big fundraiser. Your father never really did anything that didn't directly benefit the Command, so it's a bit novel. I imagine people will come out just to see what we do."

"Have you picked out your outfit yet?"

He knows me too well.

"Not yet, but I have a few ideas." I turn away to reach for the strips of dough that will become the top of my pie crusts.

"Perhaps a fashion show?" Roan anchors his elbow to the kitchen island, tapping his chin as if the thought had just occurred to him.

"You really want to sit through another of those?"

"Last time I ended up in your closet and it wasn't half bad," he smirks.

"Last time you got *pushed out of* my closet," I remind him, twisting a piece of dough between my fingers.

"This time you won't push me out," he goads me.

"This time you won't get anywhere near my closet in the first place," I level a veiled threat at him. "*If* I show you any of my outfits, it will be with you safely restricted to the couch."

"You're no fun," he protests, reaching for one of the left over berries.

"Never said I was," I mumble.

"Do you want to hurry up and put those pies in the oven so we can make out a little?" His question nearly makes me choke on the air I was breathing. "Well, we have to do *something* to pass the time."

"I thought you wanted a fashion show," I respond in a flat voice, realizing that was a much safer option for my heart.

"We can do both," he shrugs casually.

"You're a difficult man to please," I say, setting the twisted dough on top of the open pie.

"Not really," he grins evoking a dramatic sigh from my lips.

"Are you going to help me or not?"

Roan reaches over, mimicking my motions as he twists the dough. I lay my piece down before reaching for his as I weave a seemingly intricate design on top of the fruit.

"Will you be comfortable answering questions on Sunday?" he asks eventually.

"I'm answering questions?"

"I think it would be a good idea. You don't need to hide behind your father or me anymore, especially if we're trying to get you in the spotlight." He offers me a tentative smile.

That's exactly what I *don't* want—but precisely what I need—for Sophie's sake.

If I can find her this weekend, maybe I can avoid all this. I just have to locate her and get her out. *Simple, right? Right.*

Wishfulness takes over, reminding me that if I really *can* find my aunt, then I won't have to pull away from Roan or my father. Maybe one night won't hurt.

"I've managed dinner with your parents *how many* times now? I think I can handle a few questions in an open forum." I prop my elbows on the island as I place the last piece of dough in place. Leaning forward, I bat my eyelashes at Roan.

He responds by leaning in but before he can get too close, I spin around, pie in hand. I slide the first one into the oven, grabbing the second so quickly that Roan doesn't even have time to stand to help me.

"There," I say, walking to the sink to wash my hands. "Now we just have to wait."

"Perfect," Roan stalks toward me and I consider grabbing the hose from the sink.

He touches my waist, spinning me around. I flick the last droplets of water off of my hands, sending them toward his face. He shakes his head, tossing them off before kissing me.

"Roan," I giggle, squirming to get away. "Fashion show."

I duck under his arm and he tips his head, restlessly watching me walk away. His hand rests on the counter but his entire body leans toward me. He lets me walk a few feet before making his way to the couch, sweetly waiting for me.

Inside my closet, I glance around quickly. I had planned on wearing a bright-colored dress, but if I am going to sneak through the school and town, standing out won't be helpful. I gaze around looking for better options.

My first instinct is to pull the black lace dress out, but if I snag it on anything while I'm hurrying through my search, I could be caught. Pushing it aside, I look at my mint dress. *Too noticeable.* Lavender could be a good choice.

I pull it out of my closet and hold it up to my body, twisting to look in the mirror. It's the one I'm going to wear, but it wouldn't help my case to walk out in the one I was choosing for my first outfit.

Roan liked the mint dress before. My finger runs over the fabric. It's too light to withstand the cooler temperatures. Pushing it aside, I look for another.

Slipping into the cranberry dress, I model it in front of the mirror. It's cut lower than most of my dresses, but still high enough to be modest. The halter top shows off my shoulders and I imagine Roan's lips trailing across them. The breeze catches the back of the asymmetrical dress, sending it floating behind in my wake.

Roan's eyes grow wide when he sees me.

"Why haven't I seen this before?" he demands playfully as I sashay toward him.

"It was in the trunks my father sent over. I've been keeping it tucked away for the right occasion." I grin. "Do you like it?"

"It's perfect, Jade. Not for tomorrow, but it's perfect." He studies me as I spin slowly. "Actually, that might be good for the Command Christmas party in a few months."

Roan stands up, pulling me into his arms with a sneaky smile. It will be my first Command Christmas party...if I survive. What Roan doesn't realize is that I was planning to alter this very dress for the party.

"I was planning on adding lace sleeves," I bite back my smile, not wanting to let myself think as far ahead as the party.

Roan moves his feet, tilting me into a slow dance.

"That would be perfection. You could sweep your hair off your neck like this," he brushes my hair away from one side, pulling it in front of me on the other. "We could find you a glittery hair comb and dangle it in front of my father."

His words take on a harsh tone, but his eyes tell me he is teasing.

"You'll be the loveliest one there. Now," he pauses, "go try on another dress for me and meet me back here."

Roan spins me toward my room with a gentle push.

The door clicks behind me as I walk back over to the closet. I pull out the lavender dress and slip into it. It sits off my shoulders with a simple halter collar leading up to my neck. I pull out my matching wedges with floral accents up the front and tug them on. In front of my mirror, I sweep my hair up into a high ponytail, pulling it tight to add extra height.

"Ready for outfit number two?" I call, stepping into the hallway, fully prepared to march over to Roan and loosen his tie.

I expect to find Roan where I left him. He is not there.

"Roan?" I ask, glancing around. When he doesn't answer, I ask again, more forcefully. "Roan?"

I walk over to the back door to see if he's outside. It's dark enough that I couldn't see even if he was out there. The shuffling behind me tells me I was wrong.

"Wow," he breathes as I turn.

"Whoa," I reply. I blink a few times before I can continue. "When you get dressed up..."

He really knows how to dress up.

"I didn't think it was fair that you were the only one showing off."

"I like this version of our fashion shows much better." I grab his tie, pulling him close. "Please tell me you're wearing this tomorrow."

"I was thinking a bake sale required a more casual

look," he says, taking me in his arms. "Somehow a tux feels like it's a little much."

"Whatever gave you that idea, Mr. Diamond?" I inquire absentmindedly.

"Well, I suppose I *do* have to compete with you," he pretended to give in. The tux wouldn't be the worst choice in the world.

I laugh as he sways us along to music that doesn't exist. Just before he leans in to kiss me, I pull back, ordering him to finish the fashion show. Planting myself in his normal spot on the couch, I wait for him to show me another outfit and try to plan my route for my spy mission tomorrow.

"Can I take that for you?" Roan asks.

"Thanks," I reply, handing him one of the baskets with the pies in it. I slip the other over my arm. Inside, I've tucked a few extra things away inside.

Roan helps wrap a shawl around my shoulders. The temperature will warm up by the time the bake sale starts, but the walk over might be a little chilly.

I blink back the tired feeling in my eyes from staying

up so late with my work. Roan can't know I am changing the plans. Ducking, I adjust my shawl, hoping he doesn't see me yawn.

I keep to the walkway as we step outside, avoiding the dew-covered grass. My wedges offer me height, but never once promised to keep my feet dry. Roan leads the way until we reach the main road.

The school is quiet, even more so than when I had been here yesterday. My husband raises his hand and calls a greeting to the secretary who helped me yesterday.

"Mr. and Mrs. Diamond, good morning," she greets us. "I was just opening up. The others should be here in a few minutes."

"Thank you." Roan's smile is easy as he waits for her to finish unlocking the doors.

Inside, I lead him to the gym, as if he hadn't grown up there. He asks me to put him to work so I point him to one end of the tables.

"Can you handle sign in?" I ask, hoping it will get him to stay in one place long enough for me to escape. I don't have to worry about others noticing me walking around where I shouldn't be, but if Roan catches me, I'll have to come up with some kind of explanation.

"Sure." He pulls the clipboard out of the box and moves over to the small table by the door where people will sign in, give extra donations, or check in the food they have brought to sell. I should probably find someone to help him. Maybe I could assign Janine to give Roan a hand. Seeing us outside of the office might help her to feel more comfortable with us.

It isn't long before the initial wave of volunteers arrive. Surprisingly, they're mostly from my side of town.

"Good morning, Jade," Annie bustles in the door, carrying so many trays of food that she nearly tips over as she tries to maneuver between the doors.

I rush forward, trying to help. Roan jumps up from behind the table, reaching Annie long before I do. We both try to take containers that aren't strategically balanced in a way that would topple the others if we removed them. We finally get everything to the table and I help Annie arrange the trays.

"These two are for you," she scoops up individually wrapped scones and hands them to us. "I wasn't sure if you had breakfast or not this early, but it's going to be a long day, so I thought you should eat."

"Thank you, Annie," I say, unwrapping my vanilla scone. I inhale its scent before taking a bite.

Roan thanks her as well and finishes his in three bites. "Amazing as always, Annie."

Annie gives him an approving smile before nodding to the door. "Looks like more recruits are here."

Lucas and my father walk in mixed among other people. Their presence would make my job harder.

"I'm not staying," my father kisses the top of my head,

"I have to go help Mr. Eroh with a little project, but I wanted to make sure you didn't need anything first.

"We're fine, Daddy," I drop my arms from around his waist. "Lucas, maybe you could help Roan until Janine gets here though? He's in charge signing people in and taking donations."

"Sure," Lucas takes his folded jacket from over his arm and lays it on the back of the chair. His sarcasm takes over the moment no one is within hearing range. "I hear you can't handle this without me, buddy. Don't worry, I'm here to help."

"I liked you better when you were pretending to be nice," Roan pretends to sneer.

"You've always liked me," Lucas counters and I can see the conversation taking a bad turn.

"All right, boys, let's get to work," my father jumps in, obviously sensing the potential turn of conversation. "Jade worked very hard on this and we need to make sure it's a success."

He turns to me, adding, "Maybe I should stay."

"No," I say too quickly, "You have other things to do. We'll be fine."

"If you're sure," he says skeptically.

"I'm sure, Daddy. We'll be fine. Annie's here if we need her anyway."

"Good point," he chuckles, knowing no one can mess with Annie. "Do you need anything before I go?"

"Umm," I glance around. "Would you be able to hang the sign up outside when you go?"

"Sure," he nods, waiting for me to get it for him.

I dart over to the table and return with the sign.

"Thanks, Daddy."

"You're welcome, baby girl. I'll see you later." He winks at me as he turns to leave.

I quickly explain the sign-in sheet to the boys, showing them the different pages to be used for different things. I am hoping to use the information we collect for the next time we want to run a big fundraiser.

I turn to walk away and nearly collide with a woman.

"I'm sorry, Jade," Maybelle says, smiling gently at me. "Here."

She hands me a bag of cookies before quickly turning to Roan.

"Can we talk?" she asks him urgently.

CHAPTER 9
ROAN

ade gives me a concerned look as she passes off the bag of Maybelle's famous cookies to a volunteer to take to the table. She quickly walks around the registration table and takes my place so I can follow Maybelle out.

When we reach a secluded part of the school, Maybelle turns to me.

"Now, Roan," she begins, folding her hands together like she's about to sing an opera. "You know I've always minded my own business. I've never asked too many questions and I've never inserted myself where I don't belong."

"Maybelle, what's going on?" She's starting to worry me as she grows more flustered.

"I've always tried to look out for you, Roan, but I never overstepped, even when I wanted to."

"No, Maybelle, you've always been wonderful," I confirm. "But what is going on?"

"Roan, I need to ask you something." Her lips twitch as if she might continue speaking. Instead, she looks away, eyes trained on the floor.

"You can ask me anything, Maybelle. You know I'll tell you anything."

The muted light from the tinted window gives the hall a green, hazy glow. It's the color of algae in the pond on Jade's side of town in the early summer when it's just creeping out onto the surface of the water, stretching its cells and testing its new home.

"What is going on, Roan?" She holds absolute seriousness in her eyes—she's concerned. "I didn't ask questions when you brought Jade home. I knew your parents hated her, but I didn't ask. I didn't ask questions when you fell for her for real, nor did I ask why it made your parents so angry. I didn't ask when you and your father shouted in his study, and I didn't ask after your father's accident, nor after the time you were poisoned and that woman died in your father's office, but, Roan, something is going on here and I can't ignore it this time. The last time I ignored it, a woman died, and *you* almost died.

"I can not lose you because I didn't ask this time, Roan, so what is going on?"

Her response shocks me. Other than Dad changing the timeline, nothing was out of place, and yet suddenly the situation was so dire in her mind that she came all the way to the school to drag me out of a bake sale to ask what was going on? No, it doesn't make sense.

"I don't understand, Maybelle. Nothing is going on—and before you protest, you know I would tell you if there was and you asked."

"Your father is suddenly handing over control to you? *Yes,* I heard your parents talking about that. He's just... walking away? *Your* father?

"When has your father *ever* walked away from *anything*?" Her demeanor shifts as she places her hands on her hips. "And now suddenly he's sneaking around, going out at all hours—"

"Wait, what?" I interrupt. "What do you mean he's going out?"

"He's telling everyone he's not feeling well, but he walks around the house perfectly fine. I understand that he does that sometimes—especially when he needs to get work done—but he's also going out more than he's staying in."

"Maybelle, where is he going?"

"If I knew that, do you really think I'd have to sneak out of your house under the guise of bringing more desserts here so that we could have this conversation in the middle of this mildew paradise?" she chides me. "You tell me what's going on right now, young man, or so help me, if something bad happens to you..."

"Nothing bad will happen, Maybelle. I promise." I reach out and touch her elbows to convey how genuine I'm being with her. "I don't know why he's going out or where he is going, but I promise you, we'll all be safe."

I debate telling her the truth about my father, but I know her well enough to know that if she is aware of what has been going on, she won't be able to work for my parents anymore, and she needs this job. Being oblivious is one thing, but knowing and turning a blind eye is against Maybelle's code. She's only looked away this long because she wanted to be around to take care of me.

"I will look into it and report back," I vow. "Just keep me posted on what you know."

If my father is up to something, I want to know about it sooner rather than later.

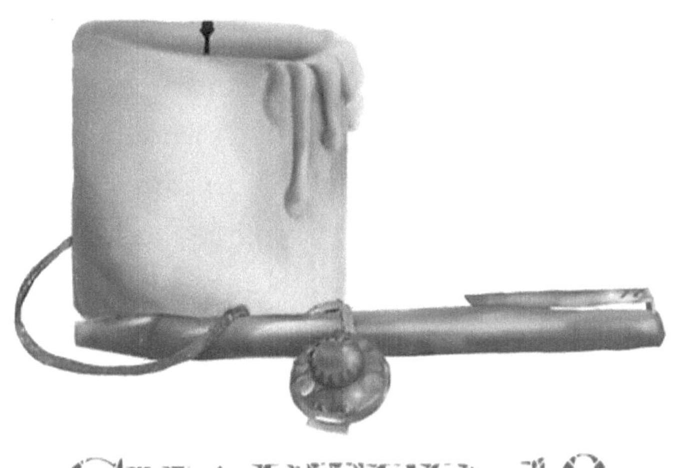

CHAPTER 10
JADE

 stand as soon as Roan walks back in. It's hard to read his face.

He shakes his head, telling us he will explain later as he rounds the table to take his post back.

I leave him and Lucas to check people in for the sale. Their invitations to tomorrow's open forum filter across the room as it starts to fill up.

Excited people lean over the tables, examining the covered treats. A few children shriek in happiness as their mothers allow them to buy a snack.

I make the rounds, ensuring that I talk to each volunteer behind a table. They will be my alibi.

I spend my time rushing between tables, fetching extra bags or small trays for people buying more than they can carry. I start to feel the muscles in my legs pinch from moving around so much, but it's a necessary part of my plan. If I move enough that I'm never in one place for more than a minute or two, it will be much harder for people to tell when I conveniently go missing.

My opening is bound to show up sometime soon. I just have to endure until then.

"Are you in charge?" a man I don't recognize asks, bustling up to me.

"Yes," I say, trying not to sound timid as he draws closer.

"They sold my cake," he announces.

"Oh," I give the most generic response I can until I can figure out how he wants me to react. If they sold a cake he baked, that was awesome. If he meant something else, I could be in trouble.

"I was trying to buy it and they sold it." His words were clipped as he struggled to control his volume. "I told them I was buying it, but they gave it away anyway."

"Oh, I'm so sorry," I try to manage his barely-contained anger. "Perhaps we can find you another one."

"I don't *want* another one, I want *that* one. *She* has it," he points at a woman across the room, "and *she* gave it to her."

He turns to point at one of the workers behind the table who immediately blanches upon being called out.

"I'm very sorry, sir, she must not have realized at the time—"

"I *told* her before she gave it away—" he shouted, making the entire room pause as Lucas rushed over.

The man steps closer to me, shoving a small plate of cookies at me. Each step I take away from him is matched by a step toward me as he becomes increasingly irate.

Out of the corner of my eye, I see Roan dart to his feet behind the table next to Janine who had apparently slipped in at some point. He only rocks back onto his heels when Lucas makes a beeline for me.

"Step back, Timothy," Lucas warns as he approaches us. He moves faster than he had the day we were locked in the Commander's office.

"No," Timothy challenges.

"Do you know who this is, Timothy?" Lucas lowered his voice to a whisper loud enough for the three of us to hear. "This is the wife of the future Commander. You will not speak to her this way."

For a moment, I consider explaining the situation to Lucas, but I have a feeling that will turn the already-tense situation into a volatile one. Moving toward the table to find a replacement might be equally as bad of a decision so I stay put, waiting for Lucas to tell me what to do.

"You have no business here, Montgomery," the man refuses to back down.

"*Everyone* now has business here, Timothy. You made it their business when you shouted and disturbed everyone.

"Now, you can either find something else to purchase or you may leave. The choice is yours, but you will not stay here and cause a scene.

"There are perfectly good baked goods over there," Lucas points to the nearest table. "I happen to know your wife loves Annie's scones—I see her in the café once a week picking them up—and I can see Annie has a few left over there, so go help the school out, buy one for your wife and go home."

Timothy finally backs down, following Lucas' orders to go see Annie. She stretches up, unwilling to take any flack from him. She plasters a tight smile on her face and waits for him to approach.

"You okay?" Lucas asks, eyes still trained on Timothy in case he needs to intercede again.

"Over a cake? Really? What is this country coming to?"

"I don't know," he grins. "Maybe we should invite him to the open forum tomorrow and he can confront you again."

I give him a *don't-you-dare* glare, making him smirk.

"You want to tell me who he is?" I ask after another

minute of watching the man. He saunters away from the table, scowling at anyone who dares to get in his way.

"Let's just say that Timothy has a bit of a reputation. He used to be a thorn in Dad's side back in the day and now he's one in mine. Every time he takes issue with anything, he's in my office about it.

"But I *won't* tolerate him threatening you like that."

"Well, I appreciate it. I'd like to say that I could have taken him, but frankly, I'm not even sure *you* could have. That man is incredibly tall."

"Yeah, but you're scrappy," he grins at me, nudging me with his elbow. "I'm pretty sure you could take on anyone and win, Jareau."

"Is that right, Montgomery?" I tease back.

"Speaking of handling things…looks like your presence is needed." Lucas nods across the room to where two young boys are fighting over a bag of cookies.

Lucas trails behind me as I rush over. I arrive just as the bag breaks, sending cookie pieces scattering all over the floor. I try to hold my sigh in.

"Want to tell me what's going on?" I recognize at least one of them from the time I visited the school with Roan —the same day I officially met Lucas Montgomery.

"He started it," the boy points at his friend.

"No, I didn't," the second boy protests. They crumble into an argument, stamping their feet. In their total disregard for their whereabouts, they also crush the cookies.

"That's about enough," Lucas says, scooping up one of the boys and setting him down out of cookie-range. I follow suit and pick up the boy closest to me and move him behind me.

An older girl rushes over, apologizing as she lectures the boys.

"Their mothers will kill me," she shakes her head in dismay before leading the boys off, her face still white with horror over the scene her charges caused.

"I'll get the broom." I start walking toward the corner of the room where a broom and pan have been tucked away for an occasion just like this.

Lucas follows me, much like he had the day we met out in the schoolyard. Bending down, he scoops up the dustpan before I can reach for it.

"When have I ever not be there to clean up for you?" he asks with a sad smile.

"I suppose never," I reply, grabbing the broom. "You know how much I appreciate you, don't you, Lucas?"

I pause.

"I don't even know how many times you've saved my life," I add, realizing I have no idea what else he has done for me, "but I imagine it's more than I know."

"One day I'll tell you all about it, Jade," he winks at me, "and then I won't let you forget it."

I burst out laughing. "I'm sure you won't."

An addendum might need to be made to my little plan

if I wanted to find out those stories though. Saying goodbye to Lucas might be as tough as cutting off Roan and my father.

Lucas tugs the leg of his dress pants up a bit as he bends down to hold the dustpan while I sweep the cookie crumbs into it. When he stands, he drops the crumbs into the trash and we walk the broom back together.

As we walk away, he rolls up the sleeves on his dress shirt, showing off his forearms. Several women take notice as we pass them and it's all I can do not to point it out. Lucas obviously notices but pretends not to.

"You know you don't have to do that anymore, right?"

"Do what?" he genuinely asks me.

"Pretend not to notice. You don't have to stay hidden anymore," I quietly remind him.

"Maybe I like my anonymity. It's afforded me many quiet luxuries in this life. I stay under the radar and I know more things than you will ever know, Mrs. Commander-to-be."

"You can't honestly say you want to live this double life forever, Lucas."

Double life. *My mission.*

I had nearly let myself get distracted.

How is it possible that Lucas Montgomery could be so irritatingly distracting all of the time. Love him or hate him, no one stands a chance against his charms or his plans.

I look for a way to escape from Lucas, but for the next twenty minutes, he's glued to my side.

"Sophie always said you were one to notice things," he comments when he catches me taking stock of the room. "That's why I was so surprised you never noticed me lurking in the background."

"I was too busy looking over my shoulder for the monsters to notice the angels," I murmur, only realizing what I said after. "Besides, I thought the point was that you liked to not be noticed. Maybe this is less of a comment about *me* and more of one about *you*."

"I hardly think—"

"Take the win, Lucas." I interrupt. "I'm praising your sneaky prowess. I didn't notice you because you were so good at what you did."

"Sophie also said you were good at talking your way into and out of things," he chuckles. "I've come to know this as fact."

My chest tightened at hearing my aunt's name for the second time in less than a minute. I need to figure out where she is. I am desperate to shake free of Lucas and get outside.

"Lucas, can you check on Annie's side of the room? I'm going to check in with everyone over here."

He nods and walks away, sweeping around the tables on the far side of the room. He nods to me after each one, keeping tabs on me. *So much for escaping.*

I make up excuses to leave the room, running to find extra bags to pack purchases in, helping people to find the rest of the party, getting change for the different tables. I take any excuse that I can to disappear and then reappear.

Just as I planned on making my actual escape out of the building, I run into Erica. Over my shoulder, I can see Lucas walking my way. Roan is still at the registration table, checking people in, but he watches quietly.

"What do you need?" Erica asks quickly in a hushed voice. She must have read the panic in my eyes—I am out of time. She offers assistance without asking questions.

"Lucas. Distract him."

She nods and brushes past me, making her way to Lucas as I darted out the door.

I keep my head down outside, trying not to be noticed as people walked into the building. No one speaks to me as I move away from the school.

I can handle the Command building on Monday when I temporarily take over the Commander's office. Today I needed to search the surrounding areas.

Logically speaking, the Commander would keep Sophie where he feels comfortable and safe, which means she is likely nearby. Robert Diamond has a comfort zone, but he also has his secrets. It would need to be an area no one else has access to.

I slip along the streets, looking for secluded areas that might offer the shelter needed to hold a woman hostage, but that was distanced enough from people that outsiders wouldn't know she was there, nor could they accidentally stumble on her.

It's not like the country is bigger than a few towns put together, so it shouldn't be hard to deduce where the Commander could contain a woman of Sophie's skills, and yet, the answers elude me. I am completely clueless as to where Sophie could be.

She would need to be where he could get to her, should he need leverage, but he wouldn't be so bold as to keep her on his property, so likely not on the Diamond estate. He would only keep her in the Command building if he were certain no one would find her, and now that he is leaving us alone there, I doubt I'll find anything but clues once I return to work.

The sky is a peaceful blue—a stark contrast to the colors raging in my soul. I have a limited time to find Sophie and each step I'm not going in the right direction is one step closer to my grave.

Where would he keep my aunt?

Knowing he would stay away from crowded areas, I veer off, hoping I chose the right side of town. My first stop is the building project the Commander just finished. The work is done, but no one has moved in to work there yet.

The building is two stories high, casting a long shadow over me. It's cooler in the shade of the building but I can't step back out into the light now.

I creep up to the stone building which will eventually be used to store files and old projects and belongings of the Command. The door is closed, but I knew enough to come prepared. Reaching into my ponytail, I pull out a set of lock picks shaped like bobby pins. Mr. Eroh had given them to me within two months of starting my job with him.

By my fourth month working in Mr. Eroh's shop, I had become skilled at picking locks quietly behind the counter of his store where no prying eyes could see my well-trained hands.

It clicks under my movements and I turn the handle to walk inside.

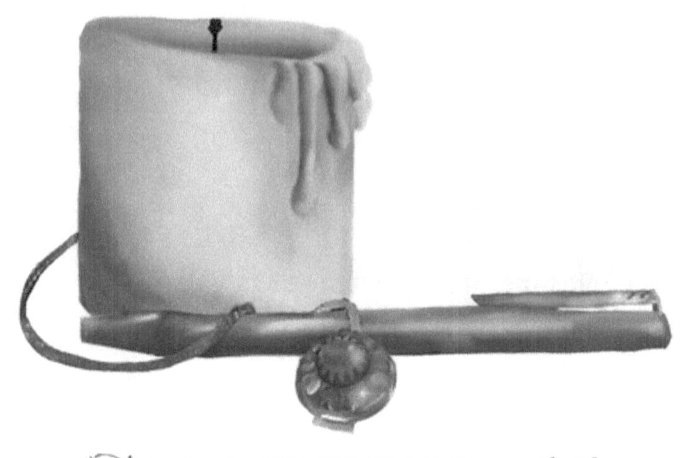

CHAPTER 11
JADE

he room smells empty and hollow, bits of dust contaminate the air even long after it settled. My footsteps echo, prompting me to walk on the outer edges of my soles. Muted light filters in the windows and bounces off the empty walls.

A few filing cabinets line one wall near the doorway, waiting to be moved to their proper home further inside the building. I follow their lead to the next room.

The second room is much larger. Desks litter the middle of the room, also out of place. Stairs at the far end of the room guide me toward the basement. If Sophie is here, she's down there.

I fiddle in my pocket, pulling out a tiny flashlight that Roan didn't see me slip into my dress right before we left. I click it on, using its surprisingly strong beam to illuminate my path down the stairs.

Covering the edge of the flashlight, I cut off the beam, allowing just a tiny bit of light to escape—just enough to see by. I have to assume Sophie is being guarded and I don't want to give away my presence too quickly. I also can't afford to walk in complete darkness.

Once at the bottom of the stairs, I take a moment to get my bearings. Much like any basement, it's littered with unnecessary items. The Commander has been busy hiding away his secrets down here.

The boxes form a maze, forcing me to pick my way through the winding paths. Papers sit on top of boxes, easily lifting in the breeze my movements are creating. My hand lashes out to save one from blowing off the top of the pile it is resting on, unleashing the full power of the flashlight until I slam it against my leg to block it. The warm end glows against my thigh.

A noise calls my attention across the room. *Dragging? No, shuffling.*

My body cries out for me to rush forward to my aunt, but I know it could still be a trap. Forcing myself still, I wait.

The noise doesn't stop.

I creep around a pile of boxes, fully prepared to find my aunt in chains.

Instead, I jump so quickly, that I topple a box from where it is precariously perched on two other boxes. It falls with such force that the sound it produces would frighten people all the way at the bake sale.

The rat runs at me, eyes glinting in the dark as they catch a bit of the beam from my flashlight. I contain my scream as it charges at me, pulling away only at the last second to hide behind a pile of boxes.

"Sophie?" I shout, unwilling to stay in the basement any longer.

No one answers.

I push forward, racing through the rest of the basement to ensure I haven't missed anything and then take off for the stairs. I have to get out of this basement, out of this building, out of this side of town and get back before they realize I'm gone. I've wasted my time on this adventure and now I may not get another chance.

The door, however, is locked. I shake the handle, trying to force my way out. It rattles beneath my fingers but stays together.

Digging my fingers back into my ponytail, I retrieve the lock picks. There is no lock to pick on this side of the door, but the screws can be undone, making me very grateful they chose to install an interior door lock without much practicality.

It takes time, much longer than I wanted, but I remove both screws enough to pull the handle away from the door, exposing the insides. With the second part of the tool, I force my way into the middle of the door lock, moving it around until I pop the lock inside. It clicks, allowing me to swing the door open.

I quickly jam the knob back together, tightening the screws back into place before bolting through the door and across the room. I only slow when I reach the exit to the street, and only because I know I need to check to make sure no one is outside first.

Once I make it back to a main road, I run as fast as I can without giving myself away, my wedges miraculously staying in place under my feet. I'm terrified that my ankle will turn out if I slip off my shoe, but time is of the essence and I can hide a limp easier than I can hide my absence.

I slow a block away from the school, willing my heart rate down. I wipe at the sweat on my face, eventually resorting to using my ponytail as a fan to cool myself.

Slipping in takes great skill, but I manage to blend in with a large extended family walking into the sale. I dart to the kitchen, praying no one is there. I scoop up a tray, quickly filling it with water to take to the volunteers.

I pile far too many waters on the tray and have to walk with slow, unsteady steps to get back to the gym. The moment I enter, tray wobbling at shoulder level,

Lucas spots me. He darts across the room, but Roan beats him.

"Let me help you, dear," he croons, taking the tray from me.

The influx of people has slowed, so we leave Janine to manage the table while Roan holds the tray for me to distribute the water to our volunteers.

"You've been busy," Lucas mutters as he nonchalantly walks past me as if he hadn't been gunning for me.

"I'm sure you have too," I mumble back with an eye roll.

"They sure have kept you hopping, haven't they, Jade?" Roan asks, pausing to smile at one of the volunteers as she thanks us for the drink.

"There's always lots to do at a fundraiser," I remind him, hoping my excuse will work. "Any idea how we're doing?"

"Just about everything is selling, and we've had some extra donations, so I'm going to guess we'll likely reach our goal in the next hour or so."

"Just in time to shut down," I smile, grateful the event is almost over. I can't stop picturing that black-eyed rat running at me and I shudder. "Did you tell everyone about the meeting tomorrow?"

"We did," he replies, adjusting his grip on the tray as I remove a glass of water and upset its balance. "I think we'll have a good turn out. People seem excited about it."

"That's good." I offer him a smile. "Now we just have to prove our point tomorrow."

"We'll be fine," he insists. "We're ready for this...and they already love you, Jade. You've got nothing to worry about."

That's what he *thinks.*

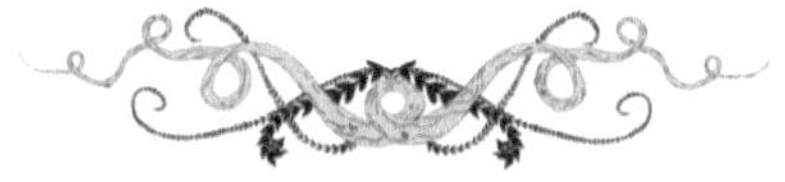

The walk home is quiet, my feet aching. I finally pull off my wedges and return to my normal height. Those shoes stood by me today and it is time to give them a break. I carry them the rest of the way home.

"You look exhausted," Roan teases.

"Well one of us had to be bright and cheery and talk to people and also pretend to be Maybelle and run around acting like a maid," I smirked. "Oh. Roan, what did Maybelle want today?"

I had nearly forgotten Maybelle had shown up at all.

"She wanted to talk about Dad," he says as we walk up to our door. Once inside, he continues. "She's been noticing him slipping out a lot. She was really upset about it."

"Why?" I asked, setting my shoes down, unable to carry them to my room to put away.

Roan grabs my elbow, guiding me to the couch where we collapse against each other like two rag dolls tossed on a shelf.

"The last time she noticed weird things and said nothing, you and I almost died. She didn't want that to happen again."

I look at him in horror.

"She knows about that?"

"No," he catches himself, "she doesn't know Dad and I were trying to hurt you. She just knows that I got poisoned and there's more to the story that she doesn't know."

He latches on to my hand when he comments about hurting me, ever-sorry for his role in my pain.

"Maybelle thinks something is going on and she doesn't want us to get hurt. Maybe Dad *is* acting weird—actually, I'm sure he *is*, but that's because he's trying to deal with walking away.

"Even so, though, I'm having Maybelle watch him for me. I'm going to start poking around to see what I can find. The last thing we need is for him to start stirring up more trouble."

I curl against him, tucking my feet up on the couch. I probably shouldn't after walking home barefoot, but I'm too tired to care. I'll wash them later. I really could use a shower after all that failed spy work today. I long to be under the warm water from the shower, but I regret even the very thought of trying to stand up.

My muscles protest against me as I try to get comfortable. Roan shifts, knowing I'm in pain, and wraps his arm around my shoulder.

"I should have let you sit at the table. I'm sorry."

"No, we were both exactly where we needed to be," I object. "Besides, pain means I had a productive day. It's like when you go for a run and you hurt, but it's a good kind of hurt—I worked hard today and I earned these aches."

"Let's see if you feel that way in the morning," he ducks his head to wink at me.

I close my eyes as I rest my head on his shoulder.

I barely feel Roan lifting me into the air as he carries me to my room.

Having fallen asleep so early, I find myself awake in the middle of the night. Roan must have stayed up and accidentally fallen asleep on the couch. I cover my husband with a blanket when I discover him on my way to get a glass of water.

Back in my room, I run through a list of possible other locations that the Commander could have hidden Sophie. I number things in order of likelihood, though I see no window of opportunity to check the areas. There has to be *somewhere* I haven't thought of yet.

Eventually, the sun starts to rise and the day officially begins.

I slip into the kitchen to make breakfast, waking Roan with the scent of food an inch from his face. When he opens his eyes, I'm sitting on the floor by the couch, tray in my lap as I wave a plate of eggs under his nose.

His eyes flutter open gently as he blinks me into focus.

"Good morning," he murmurs, his voice sounding gravelly. His growl makes my stomach leap into my ribcage.

"Good morning, gorgeous," I greet him. "I made breakfast."

"How long have you been up?" he stifles a yawn as he sits up.

Roan reaches down, pulling me up to the couch beside him. I shift the tray over to his lap as I pick up the fork and take a bite of the food.

"I fell asleep before it was dark, Roan, I've been up for awhile."

"Get anything productive done?" he asks, reaching for the juice sitting on the tray.

"You mean like building a bench out of stone by hand? No, Roan, I did not do anything productive."

"And just how long have you been sitting there watching me?" he teases, running his tongue across his lips viciously.

"I had to cook, remember? I haven't even been in here." I remind him playfully.

"You were staring when I woke up," he retorts.

"Check your food, *Roan*. Is it warm? *Yes?* Then *obviously* I just finished making it." I tease playfully. "If it was *cold*, you could accuse me of staring too long, but it's still hot, so you have no case."

"But you don't deny staring," he challenges.

"Oh, I never denied that," I say flirtatiously, batting my eye lashes. "I just said I haven't been sitting here *for a long time* staring at you."

"Too bad," he sighs, taking another bite.

"Hurry up," I pretend to lecture him. "We have to get ready for the open forum this afternoon."

"Oh, yes. That."

"Not looking forward to it?"

"Yes and no," he answers. "I think it's good for us, but I don't necessarily like being in the spotlight...but you know that."

"I do," I agree. "Oh, we should have Mr. Eroh sort our

questions for the forum. I know he's planning on being there today and I'm sure he'd happily do that for us."

"That's a good idea. Ask him when he gets there. I'm assuming he will be early?"

"Has he ever *not* been?"

"I'm pretty sure he's always around and we just don't know it," Roan laughs.

"I wouldn't put it past him." I dart forward, scooping the last bite of food onto my fork. Just as Roan starts to protest, I turn my fork and offer it to him. He stares at me quietly for a moment before accepting my small gift of the last bite of our meal.

I sit on the edge of the raised stage in the town hall, mere inches away from the place where I promised to devote my life to Roan Diamond. My husband paces behind me, waiting for people to arrive. Lucas casually leans against a chair the wrong way, looking far too effortless.

"Relax, son," my father encourages Roan to calm down.

"It will be fine, Roan. We've got it all figured out," Lucas adds.

"I'll make sure to find the most effective questions for you," Mr. Eroh adds from where he's sitting in the back to manage the questions box.

"This is a good first step," Mr. Zuckerman says, striding toward the stage. "The people trust you. They'll appreciate this gesture."

A few of the other politicians nod in agreement.

"Yes, I'm sure they will," the Commander's voice booms across the room as he enters. A cold wind follows him, though I'm fairly certain it should be much warmer.

"Dad?" Roan looks shocked. "What are you doing here?"

"I couldn't miss our open forum, could I?" He speaks in total innocence; as if the entire world would believe whatever story he spins. Several of his politician's smile and nod. *Our* colleagues do not.

"I thought you were sick, Commander," Lucas says flatly.

"Yes, shouldn't you be resting, Robert?" my father adds.

"I thought this was more important," the Commander waves his hand at my father. "Besides, I'll have a lot more time to rest soon."

"Why are you here?" Roan whispers as he walks up to

us, his voice nearly a growl. My father and Lucas close in, blocking the others from the conversation.

"I'm here to announce my retirement." His nostrils flare like a cat preparing to claw. "It's what you wanted, isn't it?"

"You can't keep changing the plan, Dad," Roan protests angrily.

"This is it, Roan. After this, you can do anything you want—you'll be in charge. This is the last you'll ever hear from me as Commander."

Roan ponders over his father's offering.

"What do you *really* want, Robert?" my father demands.

"To be done with you and your brat of a daughter," the Commander sneers, "but I guess that's too much to ask, isn't it?"

"You *do* realize we could out you right now, don't you?" Lucas challenges him. "Everyone will be here in a few minutes."

"And admit you've been lying to everyone?"

My heart jumps. If I tell them now, we could be rid of the Commander and we'd all be able to find Sophie together, all while protecting us from being accused of withholding information from the public about what really happened the night that Daniella died.

"Don't even think about it." Commander Diamond glances at me, ensuring I understand his reminder that I can't tell them about Sophie. A finger at his side quietly waves around him, suggesting that his people are watching. "Trust me, you don't want to see what will be said about that, but if you insist on hearing what *they* have to say, I can arrange that *tonight*, if you like."

Oh, perfect. He is threatening me *and* offering me a chance to speak with Sophie all in the same breath.

"Choose your next words wisely," he cautions.

"Fine, announce your retirement," I say louder than I meant to.

He turns to me, studying me for a moment, much like Roan did hours before.

"Good." He nods before smiling and turning back to his son. "So it's settled. Run your open forum, let me make my announcement, honor your people, and let Jade run your kingdom. It all works out in the end."

Roan cringes as his father mentions my name, prompting Mr. Eroh to lean to see what is going on from the far end of the room. Lucas quietly signals him that it's okay.

"You *only* announce your retirement. Nothing else," Roan instructs.

"Of course," his father nods, wrapping an arm around his son's shoulder as if they were best friends.

My father instinctively wraps his arm around my shoulders and pulls me close. If it were ever to come down to a battle between the two of them, I'm positive my father could bash the Commander's head in. Lucas would hold the crowd back and Roan wouldn't stop him.

My husband takes a deep breath, considering how to move on from the conversation.

"Mom's not here?" he finally asks, looking around.

"There's no need for her to be here for this," his father answers before removing his arm to greet Mr. Zuckerman as he intrudes on the conversations, stealthily coming to our rescue.

"Is this some kind of trap?" Lucas asks immediately.

Roan looks to my father for an answer.

"I don't know," Dad shakes his head. "I'm not sure how he could benefit from this."

I know, but if I want to talk to Sophie, I can't say anything.

"Oh," Mr. Eroh stirs from where he is sitting. Glancing behind him, he adds, "I think it's time."

"I guess we're just going to have to work with it," Lucas proclaims, turning to greet everyone.

Only a moment later, the door creaks open and the first few people tentatively step inside. More follow, slowly filling the room. I chat with Mrs. Thompson and her son for a few minutes until one of our neighbors comes over to say hello.

After twenty minutes, Roan brings the meeting to order.

"Thank you all for joining us today," he begins,

addressing the crowd as they take their seats. "Our plan with these open forums is to give you updates on what the Command is doing, answer your questions, and address your concerns.

"We're going to be hosting these open forums every week for the next few weeks and then scale back to once a month when we get the flow of the meetings more established.

"Please remember, this is a learning curve for us too. We want to take things slow for the first few meetings so we can see what will work best for everyone to have the most productive meetings possible without wasting any time. Please keep this in mind if things get a little complicated as we test these open forums out."

Roan stands tall in front of the stage, wanting to be on the same level as the people. They nod politely at his words.

"We'd like to start off with a few announcements before moving into the question segment of the meeting. If you have something you'd like addressed, there is a box in the back to submit your questions. We've asked Mr. Eroh to read through the questions and pull a few to be addressed tonight. The rest will be addressed over the course of the next few open forums, but like we said, we don't want to overwhelm everyone on the first meeting, so please bear with us as we try to keep the first few short until we can develop a better way to handling this during meetings."

"If you have questions and didn't have a chance to submit them yet, please feel free to do so now," Lucas adds. Roan smiles brightly at the people, encouraging them to follow Lucas' suggestion, had they not already done so.

"While you're doing that, let's get started with some announcements," Roan says.

The Commander jumps up out of his front-row seat, taking over.

"Thank you all for joining us tonight," he gloats. "We're so appreciative of your efforts to be involved in this community and in the work of the Command.

"It is with a heavy *and* joyous heart that I have an announcement to make."

I can feel the tension prickling behind me as the people wait in anticipation for what the Commander will say next. My mouth goes dry as I wait. His retirement means my execution.

"With great sadness, I must announce that I am retiring from my position as your leader, but it is with great pride and pleasure that I am announcing my son, Roan, as my successor. I know he will lead this country to do great things."

The audience claps—some in elation that Robert Diamond is finally stepping down, some in encouragement for Roan, and others in appreciation for their now-former leader and all the work he has done.

I feel sick.

"Yes, yes," he holds his hands up as if he's calming wild children. "I'm sad to be stepping down—and I'll miss *you* as much as you'll miss me—but this is a good thing, my friends. Roan will be a wonderful leader, and with his lovely wife, Jade, by his side, I know they will do great things for this country. I have every faith in them."

"And speaking of people we have faith in," Roan jumps in, trying to hijack the conversation, "There are a few people we should be recognizing.

"We have an incredible group of people supporting the Command—yourselves included—and as the leadership structure is changing, we want to give you and your representatives more of a voice in how things are done.

"That is why we would like to honor several outstanding members of the Command and give them more say in how things work around here."

The audience bursts into applause, approving of Roan's decision to remove some of the power from his role in the Command and give it to their representatives. Roan waits for them to quiet as my father tries to hide a smirk. He risks a glance at Robert Diamond who is quietly seething that James Jareau is getting exactly what he wanted all those years ago when this first started.

"The first person we would like to honor today is

Lucas Montgomery. Lucas has gone above and beyond for the Command and has worked tirelessly for all of you to make your lives better. We couldn't ask for a more trustworthy friend to the Command, which is why I'd like to offer Lucas my former role within the Command as I take over for my father."

Lucas looks shocked—he wasn't supposed to be elevated that high, but with the Commander's announcement, there's now a vacancy. He plasters his winning smile on his face and stands to accept the position.

As Lucas turns back to the crowd, Roan mumbles for him to stay—they are now a united front for the Command. Lucas settles back onto his heels, waiting for his turn to speak as Roan calls up the next honoree.

Mr. Zuckerman is next. Roan and Lucas sing his praises and tell the people a little about his updated job description that he also did not know was coming. Thankfully we had jobs planned out for everyone for after the transfer of power so we were ready with their new duties despite the Commander moving up the date. Roan and Lucas cycle through several more people before calling my father up.

He smiles graciously as Roan says lovely things, including how happy he is to have him as a father-in-law. It's sweet. I take in the scene, knowing I'll want to revisit it when things start getting hard. I truly believe they'll take care of each other after I die.

Roan and Lucas call a few more people up to expand their roles within the Command. Everyone applauds politely, murmuring nice things as each one is called.

When Roan turns to me, I can feel everyone staring at me. Maybe if they object to the Commander's wife having so much power, I can get out of this disaster...or at least delay it.

Roan calls me up.

CHAPTER 12
ROAN

Her light blue dress was a good choice —a *distracting* choice for *me*—but a good choice for the event.

"In the past," I start, "the Commander's wife has been in charge of hosting events and seeing to some of the more gentle things that needed to be taken care of in the Command. I grew up watching my mother do this for my father, and before that, for my grandfather after my grandmother passed away.

"But my wife, Jade, is unlike any other Commander's wife we've had. Jade has worked tirelessly to help her community. I myself have seen the way her side of town reacts when she walks into the café. Jade has spent an incredible amount of time helping me since we were married and she truly understands the way that the Command works.

"So at my father's suggestion," I add, making my father twitch, "we'd like to give Jade a position within the Command and expand her responsibilities."

I nod to the group to encourage them. My hesitation is unfounded.

"Yes!" Annie yells from somewhere in the back. I recognize her voice over the murmurs.

"Good idea!" someone else adds.

"Yes, Jade!" a girl our age cheers, clinging to her husband's arm. He looks excited too.

After a moment, Lucas quiets them all down.

"We're working on a specific job description for Jade this week and we'll be presenting that to you next week. She'll be given an office in the Command building and you'll have access to her like you do to us," Lucas waves his hand between the two of us.

The people are putting their faith in Jade. She's going to do amazing things for them—I can feel it in my bones. She's going to change the face of the Command.

I can't help but smile. I reach over to take Jade's hand in mine. It's warm and soft as I gently squeeze her fingers to tell her how proud I am of her. She reaches over with her other hand to cover mine, enclosing me in her grip. I am an incredibly lucky man.

"Thank you," she murmurs to the crowd.

"Now, we'd like to get this meeting wrapped up before too long, so with that in mind, we're going to answer a few questions selected from the box in the back," I conclude. Jade stays by my side, clinging to my hand.

Lucas navigates his way around the chairs to the back to get the questions Mr. Eroh has selected for us. He glances through the pieces of paper as he walks back to the front.

My father stares at Jade while everyone is quiet. He lowers an eyebrow at her and I squeeze her hand to get her to look away. She glances at me through her long locks that partially block her from me, but she offers me a small smile and squeezes my hand back to tell me she's okay.

When Lucas arrives back at the stage, he hands several of the questions to me to hold. I shuffle through them—Mr. Eroh picked good questions.

Lucas and I take turns answering the questions, pausing to address any additional concerns that come up in relation to the original question.

Lucas pauses dramatically before reading the last question.

"Jade, I think this is a good one for you to answer," he says, watching her closely. "This one is from Erica. She would like to know what other types of fundraisers we will be doing in the future. She would also like to know how the bake sale went and what we learned from it to use in the future."

Lucas definitely planted that one.

Jade smiles, pausing to think about her answer before speaking. She lets go of my hand, to turn to face part of the crowd where I assume the question asker is sitting in the back. My hand physically aches when she separates from me, leaving it cold.

"Let me answer that a bit out of order," Jade says graciously. I've never known a woman to be as effortlessly graceful as she is. Not even my mother or the wives of the higher officials in the Command are as genteel as she is. "I personally think the bake sale we had yesterday was very successful. We raised enough money to fix up the playground for the children."

She waits for the applause to die down.

"I'm looking forward to our next few fundraisers. We've been talking behind the scenes about what needs to be accomplished around here and I think we're on the path to a pretty good plan for fixing things up one at a time, but we also want your input on this.

"That said," she glances around the room, gaze sweeping to as many people as she can connect with, "I think these forums would be a great place to discuss Command needs and come up with plans to tackle them."

The group nods, encouraged by her words. Mr. Eroh is leaning against the table in the back, grinning at Jade. I try to keep my own smile in check to keep the spotlight on her and her work and not the fact that she's the Commander's wife and should be planning parties.

"We have a work day at the pond coming up on Wednesday and I'd love for you all to join us. The pond is an incredible place for us to swim and relax during the summer, but we all know there are certain things that need to be taken care of—like the dock—and we're hoping that by pitching in together, we can get it taken care of without having to raise a ton of funds to do it."

A few people start clapping as the group nods in appreciation for Jade's words. Winning them over to us may be easier than we thought.

"I feel like we *did* learn a few things from yesterday's experience—like how to make things run a little smoother—and I want to thank you all for coming out to support the cause—both helping *and* buying yummy treats. You all are wonderful!

"Once we get a few more of the forum meetings under our belts, I'd like to set up a core group of people to help run volunteer efforts. If that's something you might be interested in assisting with, I'd like to encourage you to think about donating your time over the next few weeks.

"Once we formally create the group, your job would

be to help these functions run more easily. You certainly won't be required to help run each event, but I think assisting with the organization of it will help to stream-line the process for the people that *do* run each individual fundraiser."

"I like that idea," someone near the front comments.

"I think it will help," Jade smiles back at them. "I feel like this would be a great topic to discuss next week, but if you're interested in joining the committee, feel free to talk with me after. I hope we'll see some of you at the pond on Wednesday." She turns and looks to me, waiting for me to end the meeting. James beams at his daughter, looking like he's going to jump out of his seat and hug her.

"And with that, thank you all for coming," I conclude. "We appreciate your participation and your under-standing as we try to find our footing with these open forums. We'll see you next week, but if you need us before then, you know where to find us."

"You'll have to forgive us though," Lucas adds, "as Roan and I get situated in our new offices this week—the Command building might not be as spotless as it usually is for a few days."

His grin makes a few of the younger girls swoon. Jade had better hurry up and find him a girlfriend before one of the younger girls decides to demand him as a husband.

"Have a good evening, everyone," I hold up my hand to wave.

Father jumps out of his seat, rushing toward the people to accept their well-wishes for his retirement. James quietly sidles up to his daughter.

"You did great," he says softly. "You all did."

He offers us a gentle smile.

Annie bustles up from the back of the crowd, dragging a girl by her wrist.

"Erica and I volunteer," she announces.

Jade giggles as Annie releases Erica.

"Well, thank you."

"Anything for you, Jade." Annie winks at her.

A few other woman Jade seems to know approach her, all volunteering to join the committee. Jade wanders a few steps away with them, chatting about what they might be able to accomplish. Every once in awhile, I hear a few words—I think they're discussing the workday at the pond.

"See? That wasn't so bad, now was it?" My father joins us after pulling himself away from his people.

"What's your angle, Robert?" James asks skeptically.

"Stop fussing, Jareau. You got what you wanted." He conceals his glare from the rest of the people, only allowing Lucas and me to see. "Now run along, I'd like a word with my son."

James looks to me for confirmation. I nod and he steps over to Jade to join her conversation.

"You too, Lucas." Father sneers. Lucas grits his teeth, but steps back a few feet.

"What?" I ask.

"Oh, nothing, I just didn't want to be around those two." Father waves his hand as if brushing them off. "You did well today, Roan. I'm impressed with how you handled yourself."

He doesn't usually speak to me like this when we aren't in public. It makes me wary.

"I can see your version of the Command is going to be different than mine. I don't think that's a bad thing."

The fact that he's making conversation with me is strange. I suppose most of my life, our conversations revolved around my training and his revenge mission. Now that it's over, the only topic left is work.

"You should come to dinner this week, Roan—your mother misses you."

"We'll see," I mumble as my father looks away.

"Ah, Marcy," he exclaims as he slithers backward to catch the young girl's arm and pull her over. "Roan, this is Janine's sister, Marcy. Marcy, this is my son, Roan."

Marcy extracts herself from my father's grip and reaches a hand out to me. She casually tips it up as she places it in my hand to shake it. It gave me the feeling I should be kissing her hand instead of shaking it.

"Hello," she smiles at me.

"Nice to meet you, Marcy. We're big fans of your sister over at work. She's been a great asset to us."

"I'm so glad," Marcy replies quietly.

"Marcy has just recently started working at the school, Roan. She's going to be a teacher there," my father announces.

"We're so grateful for your fundraiser yesterday. The children are really looking forward to the new playground update, and I, for one, am excited that I won't have to be so worried for their safety."

"We're happy to help," I say, glancing over at Jade as she talks to her group.

"Hello, Marcy," Lucas says, reaching out his hand to her as he interrupts the conversation. "I was wondering if I could steal you away for a moment? Now that I'm working with your sister, I was hoping you could give me a few ideas for making her less upset with me when I give her lots of projects to do and have to endlessly ask her for help finding things."

Marcy blushes at Lucas' grin.

"Of course." She turns back to me, batting her eyelashes. "It was nice to see you, Roan."

Lucas gives me a look over his shoulder as they step a few feet away to talk. My father doesn't notice as he swings back to face me.

"She's a lovely girl. We'll need to find a good

husband for that one." He smiles innocently at me. I honestly don't know how I put up with him for so long.

"Maybe you should head home to Mom," I suggest.

"In due time, son—"

"Commander," Mr. Zuckerman interrupts, before stopping to muse to himself. "I suppose I'll have to start referring to you as Robert now that you're retired. I was wondering if I could walk you out? I have an idea I'd like to run by you."

He clearly doesn't want to go, but knowing he has to play the part, Dad walks out with his colleague. When I turn, I find both Lucas and Jade escaping their conversations as well. They converge on me.

"Well, that went well," I offer.

"It did," Jade nods.

"I think so." Lucas looks as if he wants to sling his arm around Jade's shoulder, but he refrains. "Time for us all to go home. Apparently, I'm moving into a new office tomorrow."

He winks at Jade, making her smile.

"I think you'll be very good in that role," she admits.

"Thank you, Mrs. Commander." He nods at her, earning a smirk.

"Oh, gosh. We're Mr. and Mrs. Commander now..." I murmur.

I look at Jade to find mixed emotions on her face. I'm

sure she's not thrilled with the title, but I bet she's glad to finally be rid of my father.

"We are," she replies, taking my hand. "But *this* Commander's wife has some errands to run and people to talk to, so I'll see you later at home?"

I'm sure she has things to handle now that the plan got moved up, but I'd much rather spend the rest of the evening with her at home in the kitchen or cuddled on the couch.

"Sure, I'll see you at home." I lean over and give her a quick kiss.

"I'll be back in a few hours. You two behave your-selves," she says before slipping over to the door.

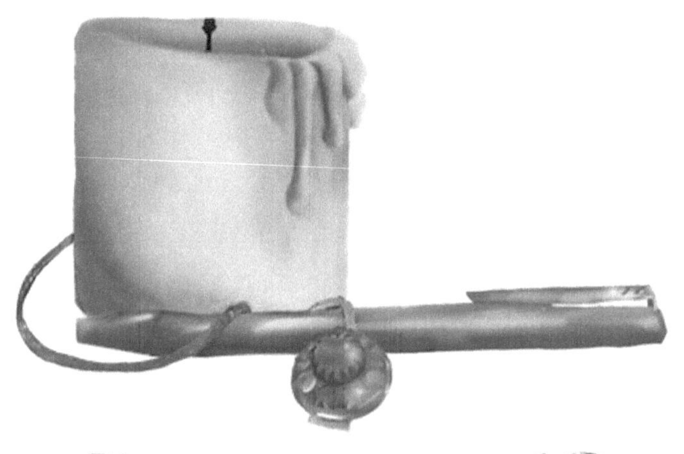

CHAPTER 13
JADE

trail the Commander down the street as he branches off from Mr. Zuckerman. I regret walking out the door but I also know this is my only chance to see proof that Sophie really is alive.

He doesn't look back, knowing I am following him. His eyes narrowed at me the moment he saw me walk through the door a few minutes ago.

I have no desire to catch up to him so I keep my distance. He breezes forward, never once showing any concern that I may lose him during one of the many times he darts around a building and turns.

When we reach the area where we could potentially

branch off toward Roan's parents' house, the Commander pivots, walking around their property. I speed up, unsure of where he is leading me.

Twilight is approaching as we near the edge of civilization. There's not much here this far away from town. When I see it, I realize I should have known all along—this is where the Commander staged the fake explosion to frame my father.

He slows as I catch up to him, quietly striding toward the building with his hands clasped behind his back.

"You don't have much time before Roan wonders where you are, so you'd better make this quick, *daughter*," he sneers, watching me from the corner of his eye. "She's downstairs...but she won't stay there for long, so don't worry about coming back."

He nods to a figure standing in the shadows just inside the entrance of the building. Whoever it is, they back away, keeping their face hidden from me as we enter.

The building is dark, tinted only with the dwindling light coming from the windows. I can still see the outlines of objects around the room with enough certainty to avoid tripping over anything, but making out detail is hard without straining my eyes.

I try to take in my surroundings, but if the Commander is telling the truth, Sophie won't be here for very long anyway. He guides me down a staircase to a lower level. It's lit brighter than upstairs.

I see no sign of my aunt until the pile of blankets moves in the corner. I see her eyes before I see anything else—the same eyes my mother had. They catch the light and reflect it back to me, drawing my attention to her.

"What are you doing here?" she gasps, struggling to her feet.

"Relax, Sophie," the Commander croons, "She's here for a visit."

He grins viciously at us, bobbing his head back and forth between us. My father-in-law certainly finds a great deal of things to delight in when it comes to the misery of others.

"What are you doing here?" Sophie whispers harshly.

"I needed to find out what was going on," I whisper back, knowing the Commander can clearly hear us. I walk quickly toward my aunt stretching my hands out to take hers. She pulls me close.

"You shouldn't be here. Go home and tell your husband and your father what is going on. Now," she insists as quietly as possible.

"He will kill you," I protest.

"Fine," Sophie responds quickly, "You need to go. *Now.*"

"I'm not going to let him hurt you to get to me.

Besides, he has people watching Dad. I don't know who they are, but they're close."

My aunt squeezes my hands, piercing her nails into me.

"Now you listen to me," she hisses. "You need to get out of here now. I'll be fine—so will your father—but you need to go."

"Tick, tock, ladies," the Commander interrupts. "Time to go, Jade."

I take a step back but Sophie latches on to my wrists.

"You've seen that she's alive," the Commander adds. "Now it's time to get back to work. Let's move along, *daughter.*"

"She's not your daughter," Sophie spits, glaring at the man.

"Oh, yes she is," he hisses back, taking a step toward us. "She's mine and she will do as I say because if she doesn't, you will die."

"Then kill me, you—"

"I'd love to, really," the Commander cuts her off. "Unfortunately, that will make it hard to control her. As long as I have you, Jade will do as I say, won't you, Jade?

"Besides," he adds, "You're easier to kill than James is...people will notice his absence. No one is looking for you, now are they, Ms. Donelly—one of the side effects of going dark to save your little niece for all these years."

I bite the inside of my cheek, trying not to draw blood while still controlling my anger.

"Your goal is to get back at our family, killing me will have the same affect as killing Jade. Why would you make your son suffer like that? He obviously loves her," Sophie protests angrily.

"She is a leech. She is not fit to be his wife and I'm already working on finding her replacement." His words hit me like an icicle that falls off of a roof when someone opens the door, smashing down to the ground as it nearly drives its icy point into its unwitting victim's skull. "My son needs to be rid of her…the sooner, the better."

Sophie's hand darts away from mine, clawing toward the Commander's face, but the chain around her ankle snaps her back with a ferocious metal clash. The skin around my eyes tightens as I gaze in horror at the restraint.

"Don't look at me like that, Jade," the Commander rolls his eyes, "I didn't put them on *you*."

"No, you just poisoned her," Sophie snaps.

"Too bad it didn't take," he glares at her before whipping around to face me. "Time to go."

"*Jade*," Sophie warns, clutching at my hand. Her nails dig into me.

"I'll be fine," I promise her. "Just stay safe."

"Don't do this," she says, eyes wild and desperate.

"Your parents and I didn't go through this just to have you—"

A slap to her face silences her. The Commander pulls his hand back, rubbing his knuckles quickly before grabbing my arm and spinning me. I'm too shocked to speak, though I probably shouldn't be.

"Jade, think of your mother" Sophie screams, begging me to come back.

"I'm sorry," I call over my shoulder. I would do anything to protect her, just like she was willing to do anything to protect me. She yells for me as the Commander drags me up the stairs.

"That was uncalled for," I reproach him.

"I told you it was time to go and you didn't listen, Jade," he hisses in my ear as we reach the nearly-dark upper floor. "I would have hit *you* but I didn't want Roan to notice. Now, move."

My mind struggles to remember Sophie's words. She mentioned something about my mother but what did my mother have to do with this?

The man upstairs backs away as we move deeper into the room toward the door. He's very intent on staying out of my line of sight. All I can see is the dark color of his hair.

"You have your proof," the Commander insists. "I held up my end of the deal. Assuming you play your part, Sophie can go free."

He eyes me warily.

"Before you ask, I know she will cooperate because once you're gone, I'll threaten your father—she won't risk him after losing you."

I liked it better when he was keeping his murder plans secret.

"This will all work out, Jade, stop fretting," he commands. "Be a good girl and play your part and this will all work out. I know it's a little bit harder this time, but you brought it on yourself."

He braces himself on the doorframe with his hand, leaning dangerously close to me.

"Go home, Jade. Roan will be looking for you and it's getting dark. I'll be in touch." He grins at me, looking me up and down—time to go.

I duck around him and step outside. The first star of the evening is in the dusky, cornflower blue night sky. It glitters, beckoning me toward it. The air has cooled down since I stepped inside to meet my aunt. I hold back a shiver.

"And, Jade," he calls after me. "Don't worry about coming back. We're moving her tonight. Sleep well, *daughter*."

I refuse to stop walking away, but I drop my shoulders, pushing my shoulder blades back at a sharp angle. He can't see me but I squint my eyes and tighten my jaw.

If Commander Diamond would like to go to war, a

war he shall have…or *would* have, if I didn't have to die first.

"You're back," Roan looks up as the door creaks shut behind me.

He sits on the couch, papers in hand. Roan stands to his feet, papers barely settling on the coffee table before he's moving toward me. His smile is so sweet it breaks my heart.

"You were magnificent today," he says, taking my hand in his. He guides me toward the kitchen. "Did you get everything taken care of?"

"Yes," I reply quickly, trying to keep my voice soft. I stop abruptly, making Roan nearly slam into me. "Oh!"

Across the kitchen, my father is filling his glass with water at the sink. His face lights up when he sees me. Roan's hand settles around my waist, telling me he's excited to have surprised me with my father's presence.

"You're back," he says, setting the glass down on the island as he walks around to hug me. I slip out of Roan's grasp and wrap my arms around my father. "Roan and I were just going through the other questions from today. Where have you been?"

"I met Sophie," I say, deciding to be honest to gauge his level of concern. His eyes widen.

"Oh, good, how is she? I haven't heard from her lately."

"You haven't?" I ignore his question.

"No, I was beginning to get worried. I'm glad she's all right. Want to come help us sort through the questions?" He turns to pick up his glass.

"We're trying to come up with the best order for addressing the concerns in," Roan informs me, walking behind the island. "Can I get you anything?"

He pulls a glass from the cupboard for me as my father waits.

"Did you eat while you were out?"

"No." My stomach decides to answer too, rumbling loud enough to make both men look at me.

"You need to eat more, Jade," my father playfully chides.

Roan hands the glass to me, motioning for us to go sit down while he fixes a plate for me. My father leads me to the living room, taking a seat across from me as I settle onto the couch where Roan had been moments before—this might be a good opportunity to figure out what Sophie meant about my mother if I can play my cards right.

"What have you done so far?" I ask, tucking my legs up under me on the couch. I arrange my skirt to cover as much of my legs as possible.

He hands me the list Roan had been working on and I glance over it—there are some good questions. When my husband returns, I trade him for my dinner and the two men continue to talk while I eat.

We work through the list for a while, organizing it into manageable sections so we could work through them over the course of the next few open forums. We weed out any duplicate or similar questions from the list, narrowing it down to the ones that will be the most productive use of our time.

"Well, now," my father turns a card around, smiling mischievously. "Here's one your mother could have answered."

My chance presents itself before I can figure out a way to bring her up. Roan leans forward, trying to read the card across the coffee table.

"Medical advice?" I ask prompting my father to nod. Having his answer, Roan leans back against the couch. I can tell he wants to lean toward me, but he keeps a respectful distance in my father's presence. "Should I even ask?"

"No," my father shakes his head with a laugh. "Although, it probably would be a good idea to address what you plan on doing to help our physicians out, Roan."

"That's a good point. Maybe we could work on that for next week or the following open forum?" Roan asks, taking my father's lead. Unlike his father, Roan is willing to take advice from those around him who are qualified to speak on such matters.

"What exactly are we going to be doing in relation to our physicians?" I ask, hoping for a stronger lead-in.

"Well, I think we could use more of them...*now*," my father's voice trails off.

"What do you mean?" I reply, sitting up.

"You saw how much work your mother did." He offers me a sad smile. "She certainly could have used rein-forcements."

"What did you mean by '*now*' though?" I persist. He pulls his attention back to us from wherever he drifted off.

"Now is a good time to build up our medical force, that's all," Father replies.

"That's not what you meant." I blink as Roan stirs uncomfortably next to me. I soften my tone. "What is it? Why now?"

He stares at us, reluctant to go on. Roan understands before I do.

"It's because we're in charge now and not my father,"

Roan quietly informs me. My father glances away, confirming it. "What did he do?"

Roan asks the question, getting me off the hook for figuring out how my mother is connected to this.

"It doesn't matter, son—"

"It does," Roan refuses to back down.

"It's not something you need to know," my father tries again to protect him.

"Sir, you know I respect you, but if this concerns my father, it concerns me. I need to know what he did," Roan says gently, not wanting to be disrespectful, but still wanting answers.

Still, my father hesitates.

"What is it, Dad?" I push gently.

"Nothing, it's just safer now." He shakes his head slightly, trying to warn us off but we won't shy away. Finally, he gives in with a sigh. "Your mother's father and uncle were physicians. They're the ones that trained Elizabeth."

I wait as he explains my mother's history to my husband in more detail than he did at dinner the other night.

"The Donnelly family was well known for their work in the medical field," he continues. "Your grandfather, Aloysius, had a great respect for them. That's why Elizabeth did so well once she started to train under her father and uncle.

"That's also why she worked so closely with your father."

"Mom worked with the Commander?" My knee nearly knocks the plate off the coffee table as I sit up straighter on the couch—he has my full attention now.

"I told you we met in the Command building. After we got married, she ended up doing a lot of work for the higher ranking officials in the Command." He glances at Roan.

"And this is where it gets bad," Roan leads.

"This is where it gets bad." My father nods. "Our families were close once."

This is shocking news to me. Judging by the look on Roan's face, it is to him too.

"Which is how you knew so much during the rebellion," Roan offers. How is he catching on to all of this faster than I am?

"It's the reason we nearly won," my father confirms, rubbing his neck uncomfortably. "The Donnelly family was well respected during the war and since, but Elizabeth got too close."

It is as if the room had soared in temperature. My clothes feel itchy and irritating against my skin. My tongue moves against the back of my teeth, preparing to brace myself for what I'm about to hear.

"I didn't know until after," Father continues. "I didn't

know what was happening because Elizabeth tried to protect us. Not even Sophie knew."

My rib cage closes around my lungs as my heart hammers against it—danger. *Run.*

"Your mother witnessed something," he gazes at me for a moment before confronting Roan with a soft stare. "The Commander had taken out a rival—I don't know the details—but Elizabeth saw the aftermath and somehow your father found out.

"She left letters explaining the situation to me," he swings back to face me. "That's where I found her letters to you, Jade."

He nods before turning back to Roan as if that were the only explanation I needed. It wasn't.

"That's when we decided the rebellion was necessary. The Diamonds had far too much unchecked power and they were making bad choices, I'm sorry, Roan," he apologizes. "Both your father and grandfather had taken out their opponents—we couldn't let that continue.

"We pretended like we believed Elizabeth's death was an accident until we had prepared enough to win the rebellion. Lucas' father and I—as well as some of the others—came up with the plan. Your father tried to trust Elizabeth, but he didn't count on her having a conscience. He had planned more. Elizabeth's letters gave us enough information to save us."

Too bad her letters can't save *me* now.

"Your father removed the threat, thinking no one else knew. When he caught us, he figured out that Elizabeth had tipped us off before she died."

Roan swallows as we both stare straight ahead. His father had a hand in my mother's death. Roan carefully reaches over to take my hand, snapping me out of my fog.

"You do not need to feel guilty for this," I quickly say, placing my free hand on top of his.

"I had never planned on telling either of you," my father interjects. "I didn't want you to carry that burden."

"It's better that we know," Roan assures my father. "I'm so sorry, James."

"It's not your fault, Roan, and you're not like him." My father reaches across the table to pat Roan's knee. "Elizabeth would have liked you."

My mind flashes to the letter I read to Roan in the cemetery a few months ago. I should see about getting some of my letters back from my father to read one more time before I follow through on the Commander's plan. Actually, that gives me an idea.

"Can I see her letters, Dad?" I request.

"Of course, Jade. Why don't you come over this week and take a look, but I don't think you'll find anything new in them that we haven't already found." He smiles sadly at me.

"I just want to see them, that's all."

That would give me a good excuse for being away

from Roan too since I have to push him away starting tomorrow. At least if I have to pull away from my husband and father, I can get closer to my mother.

"Well, come by this week. Maybe we can have dinner after work one night."

"Speaking of going home, we should probably wrap this up. It's dark out and you really should get home," I encourage him.

"You *arrived* after dark, Jade, there really is no avoiding it at this point," my father chuckles. "I'll be fine. No more monsters out there anymore."

He winks at me without realizing just how wrong he is. Monsters are real...and they're connected to me in more ways than I knew.

"You're right, though. I should be getting home if I want to be able to function for work tomorrow." He stands. "Thanks for dinner, Roan."

I walk him to the door, saying goodnight as he slips out into the darkness. When I turn, Roan is watching me.

The door clicks shut behind me as Roan slowly...*intentionally*...makes his way over to me. My hand is caught between my backside and the doorknob as I fumble to free myself in time to engage with Roan. He approaches me with eyes locked on me, ready to capture his prey. He grins.

"About time, Jade." His lopsided smile makes my heart

jump as he tangles his hand in my hair. He pulls me to his lips.

His shoulders rise up as he kisses me, moving me away from the door. Quietly, he guides me back to the couch. Roan catches me in his arms as I stumble from walking backward. He smirks against my lips in amusement as I try to wrap my arms around him without falling.

"You're not usually so jumpy, wife," he teases me.

"I usually see this coming," I correct him.

"Not tonight?" he asks between kisses.

"I might have been a little distracted," I murmur against his skin.

Roan kneels on the ground in front of me as I sit on the couch, having pushed back the coffee table. His hands rest on my knees, mine on his shoulders. He looks so gentle and perfect.

"I thought the rule was that *I'm* the only one allowed to distract you," he smiles patiently at me while I get my head in the game.

"Well, you *are* rather distracting," I agree, stroking his blond locks. "And I'd much rather be distracted by you, so…"

Roan breathes out as he reaches toward me, caressing my lips with his. It tickles my face as the air brushes past me. I giggle as his lips trail down my neck but then I realize what's happening and I can't allow it—I'm supposed to be pushing him away.

"Roan," I murmur softly, placing my hand on his shoulder. When he doesn't waiver, I say his name again, louder. "Roan."

He looks up at me as I push his shoulder back softly.

"I'm tired. I think we should go to bed. We've got a long day ahead of us tomorrow,"

It's earlier than we usually part ways for the night, but I need to start establishing some space between us—for both of our sakes.

"Oh," his eyes flash disappointment as his lips turn down slightly. He quickly smiles. "You're right, we should get some sleep. We should probably go in a little early tomorrow to get the offices moved around."

I nod as he stands, offering me his hand. Roan walks me to my door and we say goodnight.

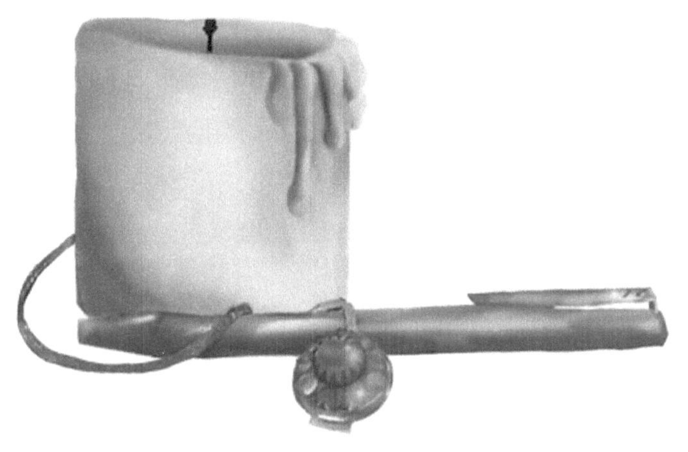

CHAPTER 14

JADE

orning is usually my friend. Morning means a new beginning, pretty sunlight, and quiet warmth.

Today it means darkness and devastation…for me, anyway. For Roan and Lucas, it means new office spaces.

"Good morning, Janine," I try to sound cheerful.

"Am I late?" She eyes me nervously as I carry a lamp from Roan's old office to his new one.

"No, you're early, like always." I smile at her. "We just didn't want to waste Command time switching the offices. Obviously, we didn't get as far as we thought, but we've been here for an hour, so that's an hour less that we'll have to take out of office work."

"Hi, Janine," Roan grins as he joins us. "Lucas should be here soon. Could you watch for the door in case he needs a hand? I think a few of the guys were going to help him get his stuff over here, but who knows what he might be carrying."

"Yes, sir," she replies, scurrying to the door.

I've been trying to avoid Roan this morning, making the trip opposite him so that we pass in the hallway but rarely end up in the same room together. I think he notices—he keeps watching me but doesn't say anything.

"Good morning, everyone," Lucas bellows from the doorway, his politician's voice on full display—we'll be seeing more of his professional side than his true personality within these walls, unfortunately. "Point me in the right direction."

Janine nearly melts to the floor as she points to Roan's former office. Maybe Janine would be a good fit for Lucas. He smiles, thanking her, and saunters toward the office.

"Maybe Jade should take this one and I'll take one of the other rooms," Lucas suggests to Roan as I approach them.

"No, you should have this one. I can take a different room if I need one," I protest, knowing I won't be around long enough to set up a working office space. I reach for the box of files in his arms. "This is where you belong, Lucas."

I brush by him, ducking into his new office and set the box on his desk. Several people fill the room, dropping some of Lucas' things off. I grab the last of Roan's items from his desk and carry them to his father's office.

I'm not sure how Roan won't see Daniella's death every time he walks into this room, but at least I wouldn't have to live with that for long. I drop Roan's things on the desk and glare at the family portrait on the wall.

"That's not staying." Roan surprises me, making me jump.

"Probably wise," I comment, keeping my back to him.

"Are we okay, Jade?" he asks softly.

"We're fine," I reply, offering him a tight smile. "Did you get everything out of Lucas' way?"

Roan frowns but accepts that I don't want to talk about us. He nods instead.

"Can you help me move the desk?" he asks, walking toward the far end of it.

Together, we lift it, repositioning it to face the door. We systematically work our way around the room, rearranging the furniture much as we had the day I decided to rearrange our house when I moved in—he is erasing any signs of his father's work and making it his own. Much like my work had frustrated Alice, this would infuriate his father. Similarly to that day, we also work in relative silence.

I keep my distance from him for the rest of the day.

I let Lucas force me to take one of the conference rooms in the Command Building as an office and spend the next day setting it up. We bring in a small desk and a few pieces of furniture which I can use when hosting meetings or receiving visitors. I avoid decorating, claiming that I'll do it when I have more time, though I make sure both Roan and Lucas have their offices set up to reflect their personal tastes before the end of the day—I'm not sure if they would do it once I'm gone and I'm sure Daniella would have had something to say about it.

Near the end of the day, I can't stand being in the building anymore.

"Hey," I say as I knock on Roan's office door. "I'm going over to my father's house to take a look at those letters. I'll be back later."

"I'll come with you," he offers quickly, jumping to his feet.

"No, you have work to do. I'll be fine." I shake my head.

"But—"

"I'm fine," I cut him off. "You stay. I'll be home later."

Before he can say anything else, I hurry away, nearly racing to the door. I feel like the rat that ran away from me in the basement.

"Janine, I'm leaving for the day. Have a good evening." I wave quickly before pushing the door open, giving her barely enough time to look up and acknowledge my presence.

When I reach the unmarked division between Roan's side of town and mine, I slow. The scents from the candle shop call out to me and I skirt around the building to avoid it. I feel bad every time I do it, but it's a matter of survival.

I catch my father just as he steps up to our house.

"Hi, Jade," he smiles, unlocking the door. "I didn't realize you were coming over today."

"I wanted to see mom's letters," I reply, sidling up to him as he turns the doorknob.

"Sure, sweetheart, come on in." He pushes the door open and lets me through first. The familiar scent of my home washes over me as he flips on the light. "Do you want to stay for dinner?"

"Sure," I say absentmindedly. I drop my jacket onto the arm of the couch. "Where are the letters?"

"You go start some water boiling and I'll get them for you." He pats my shoulder as he walks away, setting his own jacket on the hook by the door where he always put it like my mother trained him to do.

In the kitchen, I pull out a pot and fill it with water. Dad walks back in as I set it on the stove and turn it on.

"Here you go, my girl. I'll call you when the food is ready." He turns his back, giving me the freedom to take some space for myself to read through the letters.

I wander to my old room—he left it just the way it was the day I walked out for my wedding. The bed creeks when I sit on it, but my pillow feels exactly the same.

My father has carefully stored my mother's letters to me with his letters. I gently set them aside. I don't need to read them right now—I already have most of them memorized.

I get lost in the notes of Elizabeth Donnelly Jareau as she tracks the things she notices around the Command, including the information that got her killed. It was two months between the time she learned what my father-in-law had done and the time she died.

It was easy reading through her coded messages—my father had taught me to pick up the little things once he started preparing me to marry Roan. I knew all the tricks.

When I finally emerged from my room, dinner was on the table.

"It's still warm," my father smiles, motioning for me to join him.

"You didn't call me," I reply as I pick up my napkin.

"I thought you could use a few extra minutes." He passes the food to me before gently asking, "So, what did you find?"

"How did she die? I know she was sick."

"Robert made it look like an accident. I don't know who it was or how it happened, but they gave her something that made her ill. We never got specific details on it, but she told me what was happening to her."

The pasta tastes amazing. I don't know how my father makes something as ordinary as pasta taste so much better than mine, but he does it every time without fail.

"But we're sure it was the Commander's doing?" I focus on my plate.

"Yes, we were both very sure. We don't know who it was or how it happened but your mother was very good about preparing me for what was coming and helping us to be able to move on." He fixes his eyes on his table in front of him. "We thought once we took power away from Robert that we could put him on trial to find justice for his sins, but I would rather let him get away with all of this than to let him hurt you."

"Do you mind if I take the letters home? I'd like to read them over again," I quickly change the subject.

"Of course, you can keep them if you like," he offers, looking up.

"Oh no, I think they're better off here, I just want to read them over again, that's all."

"Whatever you think is best, sweetheart." He pats the back of my hand before returning to our food.

"Speaking of things at home, how is Roan doing after last night?"

"He's okay, I think." Not that I would know—avoiding him makes it hard to know these things.

"I worry that he's trying to take on responsibility for the sins of his father. I'm sure you're taking care of him though." His fork clinks against the plate. "I hope he's taking care of you too."

"He is, Dad."

"Good. The boy is starting to grow on me." My father winks at me as I try to suppress my grin. I'm pleased they're starting to get along better. I think they will be good for each other.

We talk quietly while we finish our meal.

I lay sideways on my bed, leaning on one elbow as I

read one of my mother's letters to me. My fingers stretch out under the pillow where I have the other letters stored so that I don't knock them off the bed when I twist to get more comfortable. It's as safe a place as any.

The paper crinkles under my fingertips, though the noise is dulled by the fabric of the pillow. Tears burn at my eyes, but I keep them in check as I read my mother's words as she writes about what our life might have looked like had she lived.

She and I are more alike than I realized.

The house is quiet...empty. Only the sound of wrinkling paper and my own breathing fills my room as I pour through every letter I had from my mother. My distaste for the Commander grows with each word but I can clearly see how my mother feared for our well-being while she was dying from whatever the Commander had exposed her to in order to silence her. He was wise to make it look like she had been sick, but we knew the truth.

After a while, my head sinks down to the mattress, resting quietly just below the pillow where I have the letters stored. I drift in and out of sleep, still half awake as I wait for Roan to return home.

CHAPTER 15
ROAN

"**M**aybe she just needs some space," Maybelle says as she stands up. I arrange the hot pads on the counter.

"I don't know, it's pretty bad," I mumble.

She sets the steaming glass pan on the counter and puts her hands on her hips.

"Well, I may not know what's going on, but I do know you two. You and Jade will be fine."

I lean forward onto the counter, resting on my elbows.

"I hope so."

Maybelle mimics me, leaning across the counter to pat my hand.

"Jade is a very reasonable girl. Whatever happened, you just need to give her time to process it. Roan," she pauses, leaning in to whisper, "is this connected to what we talked about the other day?"

The pan next to us sizzles, making us both turn. I feel my mother's presence before I hear the clicking of her shoes on the hardwood floor. Maybelle pulls back.

"Dinner is almost ready." She turns back to the oven and closes the door.

"Hi, Mom," I turn in my chair to greet her.

"What's going on here?" she asks, a hint of confusion in her voice. She looks back and forth between our maid and me.

"I came over to see how you were taking the news of Dad's retirement," I offer as Maybelle sets a stack of plates on the counter next to the cooling food behind me.

"I don't really have much of a say in that, now do I?" my mother asks, brushing a piece of hair behind her ear.

In truth, I came to talk to Maybelle, but checking in on my mother doesn't hurt either.

"Are you okay with it?" I ask.

"I'm not worried about *you*, Roan," she rushes to say. "I'm just confused on why your father left so abruptly. He wasn't supposed to retire so early in his career."

"I'm sure he just needs a break, Mom. Everything

that's happened in the last few months has really taken a toll on him."

"I'm sure he's ready for a break," Maybelle interjects only to be faced with an annoyed glance from my mother. "He's done so much for the Command, it's only natural he would want to spend a little more time with you. It must be nice not to have to worry about taking care of the entire country every single day and we all know Roan is more than capable of doing the work."

Her voice trails off as she turns to finish preparing dinner, taking the glare as her dismissal from the conversation. She clinks the glasses together louder than usual in what I assume is a sign to me that she's still here and listening.

"Did you hear we're working at the pond on Jade's side of town tomorrow? We're trying to make it a bit safer for the kids that swim there."

My mother wrinkles her nose at the idea of us working in the water.

"I hope it goes well."

"You know, you could get involved in some of our projects, Mom. You don't have to just watch us do them. I'm sure it must be hard on you because Dad's retirement also means *your* retirement, but you can still do any projects that you like."

"Where is Jade tonight?" she changes the subject.

"She had to go to her father's tonight."

"You didn't go?" she questions, glancing at the bread Maybelle set on the counter.

"No, she had to leave early to get over there, and I had some work to do so I thought I'd pop in here for a bit since she'll be there for awhile."

"So we only get to see you when *she's* busy?"

"*You* can see us whenever you'd like. You're always welcome to come over, but you know Dad has made it very uncomfortable for us here. I won't expose my wife to the way he treats her," I reply. I'd rather be forced to endure all of the endless conversations of a Command party every day of my life than to let my father near my wife again. "If you would like to see us, you're welcome to."

"Are we going to dinner at Roan's?" My blood runs cold as my father speaks.

"No," my mother and I say at the same time.

"Why are you here, Roan?" His voice goes icy.

"I came to see Mom and tell her how we redecorated your office." I force myself to suppress my grin when his face twitches. I had hoped to let him discover it when he walked in one day but I needed something to throw at him in the moment, and it was the best thing I could think of that didn't involve throwing Jade into his line of fire.

"You redecorated?" she asks in a small voice.

I swing around to face her. She had a hand in decorating my father's office, so it is understandable that she would feel a bit of a loss if I changed it.

"We just moved some of the furniture around to make it easier for me to see who is coming and going from the office, that's all."

"A word, son?" My father veers away, walking out of the kitchen. I catch up to him in his study.

"You changed the office?" he snarls.

"Yes, it was kind of hard to focus when I had to watch Daniella die every time I walked in there. Besides, now that I can see the lobby door from my office, I know when my enemies are showing up." I give him a pointed look. His face flushes red.

"How is Janine doing these days? It certainly was nice to meet her sister, Marcy, the other day, wasn't it?"

"What are you doing with your free time now, Dad?" I take a little dig at him. His shoulders rise up to meet his ears for a moment as his nostrils flare. He's never restrained himself so much around me—now that I've sided with Jade and James, I'm someone he has to "manage" rather than yell at. It's not the worst switch.

"I've been very busy fielding meetings with some of the Command members. They don't want me to retire, of course," he pauses dramatically. "That's not a comment on you, son, but rather one that they'll miss me."

He grins wickedly at me. I can see why Jade dislikes him so much.

"But once I'm done with all of that, I *will* have to find something to occupy all my new free time. I was thinking of coming to the pond event tomorrow—"

"No," I cut him off. "This is Jade's. You will not be involved."

"But I—" he tries again from behind his desk.

"I said no."

"Fine," my father scowls. "But you can't stop me from coming to the open forum this weekend."

"You can sit in the back," I snap.

"Jade did well this weekend." He tips his head as he speaks, looking out at me from under his brow.

"Of course she did, she was magnificent."

"You should think about giving her a little more responsibility."

"Just why do you want Jade to have more freedom?" I demand.

"More rope to tie around her neck, Roan. I'm a fan of the noose she's making for herself."

"If Jade goes down, I go down too, and I'm taking you with us, so watch your step." I lean against the back of the chair mimicking his pose as he balances his weight on the desk.

"You should give her a little project to keep her out of your hair is all I'm saying. I mean aside from that silly little charity workgroup she started last week." He straightens, jutting his chin toward the door, changing the subject. "Don't upset your mother again."

He struts out of the office. I follow behind him.

"Alice, we're trying to think of a project for Jade to work on. Thoughts?" my father bellows across the house.

We take seats around the dining room table as Maybelle sets the last of the trays out. She makes eye contact with me before walking away.

"Thank you, Maybelle," I call after her.

I listen as my parents discuss possible projects for my wife, but I barely speak. Maybelle hovers in the hallway just out of my parents' sight. I nod to let her know I'll meet her as soon as we're done. She motions with her arms as if she were swimming—the pool house.

"Roan, what is going on?" Maybelle insists as she fiddles with the lever to turn on the waterfall.

"Have you learned anything else, Maybelle?" I redirect her.

The waterfall springs to life, adding a tiny bit of cover

for our conversation. The air is damp and warm inside the pool house.

"Your father hasn't left since the open forum over the weekend. He didn't come back until very late according to your mother. I had already gone home for the day."

That doesn't make sense.

"Maybelle, he left long before I did. He should have been home before you left for the day."

She glances around nervously. She holds a small bag of chemicals to add to the pool when we're done speaking.

"Roan, you have to tell me what's happening here, *please*," she sounds desperate.

"I honestly don't know, Maybelle. Maybe it's something, maybe it's nothing." I'm beginning to think its *something* rather than *nothing*. "Have you noticed anything else, Maybelle?"

"He's been having meetings but nothing out of the ordinary."

"With who?" I question.

"I don't know, Roan. Your father always brings them in himself. I never get a look at them."

That can't be good.

The water sputters off to the side, likely from some air in the line leading to the waterfall. We both turn, but Maybelle catches my wrist.

"We should go," she murmurs. "Roan, I need you to trust me with this. Just think about it."

She tosses the content of the bag into the pool before she scurries around me toward the door.

"Thank you for your help with the waterfall," she says louder. "Oh, Commander."

My father steps out of the shadows in the yard into the light of the pool house.

"I thought I saw you two come out here."

Maybe belle smiles brightly, brushing her hands against her skirt.

"Roan was helping me with the waterfall. I'm cleaning the pool tonight and the filter sounded a little off to me the last few days, so I wanted him to listen to it—he has the best set of ears I've ever known."

"And what's the verdict?" my father asks, crossing his arms as he leans against the doorframe.

"I didn't notice anything, but I'd keep an eye on it for the next few days anyway." I shrug. My father grunts, adding a nod, before letting us out of the door.

"Thank you again, Roan." Maybelle brushes against my arm as we walk, pressing something into my hand as she pats my arm for my father's benefit. "Commander, can I get you anything before I finish up for the night?"

He dismisses her for the evening and I follow behind her after taking a few minutes to say goodbye to my mother.

I try not to wake Jade up when I quietly open her door. She didn't shut it all the way so she could listen for me but fell asleep while she was waiting. Ordinarily, I would never enter her space without being asked but ever since she locked Lucas and I out to run off to her death, I've needed to see that she was safe.

Her body rises and falls with deep, gentle breaths. I'm tempted to walk in and read the letter in her hand—I'd love the opportunity to get to know her mother better. She's always been so important to Jade.

I close the door, deciding not to wake my wife. If she's sleeping this early, she probably needs the rest. Tomorrow I'll ask her about the letters before we go to the pond.

In the kitchen, I read the note Maybelle handed off to me and set to work making food to take with us tomorrow so we don't have to assemble it in the morning.

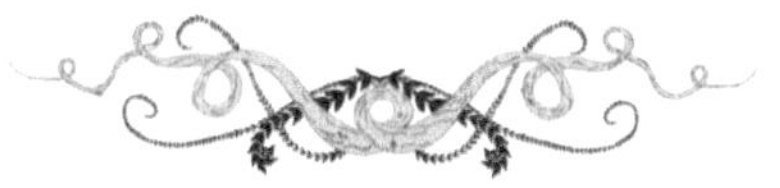

"Ready to go?" I ask, setting a pack with our lunches on the counter.

"Yes," Jade says, brushing back her hair. She has it up in a ponytail, but it still reaches all the way down her back. "Did you make lunch for us?"

"Last night when I got home. How was your dad's?"

"Good," her eyes dart around uncomfortably. "You weren't home when I got back."

"No, I went over to see my mom and Maybelle."

"Oh." She looks like she wants to say more but stops herself. "We should go."

I frown but follow her to the door. We make it all the way to the line dividing our sides of the town before I break the silence.

"Jade, did I do something?"

She glances up at me.

"No," her words are casual, but I can tell they're calculated.

Before I can push, she notices someone up ahead.

"Oh, it's Erica, we should walk with her." Jade pulls ahead, rushing to catch the girl. "Erica!"

They greet one another and chat the entire walk to the pond. At some point, Lucas joins us.

"This is interesting," he murmurs, coming up behind us. The girls don't notice as they walk a few feet ahead. "How come you're way back here?"

"I think Jade's mad at me…"

Lucas straightens next to me. He turns his face sharply to look at me.

"What did you do?"

It strikes me how strange it is to see him in casual clothing. He looks put together even without his suit and tie—I know for a fact I don't look nearly that mature without work clothing. He could run the country in slippers if he wanted, I'm sure.

"Nothing," I insist. "Calm down, would you?"

I guess we know whose side he will be on if it ever comes down to that. I roll my eyes, dropping my voice.

"We had dinner with James the other night and found out that Jade's mother discovered information about my father before she died and it might not have been as innocent of a death as we thought."

"Your father killed Elizabeth Jareau?" Lucas looks furious, brow twitching.

"Elizabeth seemed to think so. James isn't blaming me but Jade's been a bit distant."

"It's understandable," Lucas comments.

"It is. I just don't know how to make it better."

"This isn't exactly something you can make better, *Commander*."

"Lucas?" Jade and Erica turn around at the same time.

He beams at them, lengthening his steps.

"Ladies." He steps between them, entering their conversation. "Don't you two look lovely today? I assume you're pretending you're mermaids while we work?"

"You know us so well," Jade jokes. "Or did Mr. Eroh give you that line?"

"I might have found it in one of the books in his shop," Lucas teases. "Doesn't mean I know you any less."

"Good point, Sir Stalker," Jade laughs.

The conversation devolves into the two of them throwing jokes back and forth while Erica slips back next to me.

"Commander," she nods quietly.

"You don't have to call me that," I reply. "Roan is fine."

"You don't have to worry about those two. She clearly loves you."

"I'm not worried about them."

"You don't need to be jealous of their connection," she corrects herself. "She's yours, and nothing is going to change that."

Erica pretends not to notice things, but I can tell she knows more than she's letting on. She's incredibly perceptive. I'll have to keep an eye on her.

"I appreciate that."

"I've known Jade from a distance for a long time. I trust whatever decisions she is making. Oh look," she says, motioning ahead. "We're here."

The pond glitters, each ripple catching the light and bounces it back at us even in the early hours. All I can think of for a moment is painting it for Jade, but we have work to do.

"Where do you want to set up?" I ask loud enough to break Lucas and Jade out of conversation.

"Over here is probably a good place to set everything while we give out assignments." Jade motions to a grassy area. Several people wave hello as we approach.

Once everyone has arrived, I take my place next to Jade and she thanks everyone for volunteering to help before handing out the assignments for the day. I make my remarks when she turns to me but otherwise, my goal is to back her up. My father is right, Jade needs to be seen as a leader because I don't want her to be discounted like my mother was.

When she's done speaking, people jump into the water, splashing along the shore as they begin digging up weeds and removing bigger rocks that are in the way along the edge. A team takes their equipment to the edge of the dock, prepared to remove the dangers under it. Yet another group works on fixing the loose boards on the different docks around the water's edge.

Jade keeps her distance the majority of the day. I try to focus on my work as I build benches for parents to sit on as their children play in the shallow end of the water.

I try to align myself to work near Jade but she expertly sidesteps my every advance. At some point, I'll need to tell her about the note Maybelle shoved in my hand last night but apparently it won't be while we're working.

"Roan," a voice startles me.

I turn around to find my father-in-law walking toward me.

"Can I help with that?"

"I thought you were diving with Lucas and the others today," I comment, stepping back to allow him space at the other end of the bench. Charlie steps away, finding another bench to help with to give us some space.

"We're taking a break. You can only hold your breath for so long before you end up making yourself lightheaded." He chuckles. "We switched off with another team for a bit. How are the benches going?"

"Fine, I think we've got most of them up at this point. Jade is going to have to give us another job soon."

"She seems to be doing well today," he grins with pride but keeps his eyes focused on the bench.

"They love her," I smile back.

"I'm glad she has this opportunity. She's going to thrive here."

A loud crack sounds near the water, disrupting the conversation. When we turn, we discover that the dock has broken, as if one of the poles supporting it has given out. It tips into the water, quickly knocking half of the people on it into the water.

"The divers!" someone shouts.

James and I run to the water.

CHAPTER 16
JADE

eople scramble off of the dock, pushing to get as many of them to land as possible. Some bob in the water, having fallen in to the waves. The dock submerges, pieces sinking.

We have a team below, working on pulling the dangerous items out from under the platform that once trapped Roan and gave parents many worried experiences. Panic courses through me as I dart toward the water.

"Stay," my father and Roan command at the same time as they rush past me. Erica jerks me back.

"Over here," she says, forcing me toward the people

that just dismounted the dock's incline. We help them to their feet, pulling them further onto the embankment.

"What happened?" Lucas bellows as he runs by us.

"It collapsed," I barely manage to get out before he splashes into the water. My eyes search the water for signs of our people. "Where are they?"

Someone pops out of the water, gasping for air. Another figure emerges from below the surface.

"We're fine," the first man yells.

"They're just checking, but no one is hurt," the second calls, brushing his hair out of his eyes.

More people reach the surface and I do a quick head count. My father and Roan materialize at the same time. The group swims back to shore as they evaluate what happened.

"It looks like one of the pieces of machinery shifted too close to the pole supporting the dock," my father informs us, dripping wet. "We were working from the outside in to remove things. It got too close and when they moved it, it took the pole down with it. I think we should replace them all if it happened that easily."

Roan nods in agreement, trying to catch my eye. I've done so well avoiding him all day that I don't want to give in now. He demands my attention though, and I can't help but be drawn in by his eyes. He looks so different than the day I untangled him from under the dock—he's more confident.

"Is everyone all right?" I shout, pulling away from his gaze.

People nod, murmuring responses. I pause as my father reorganizes the work party, giving new instructions so we can get the dock fixed before the end of the day. Eventually everyone splits off.

Roan gives me a long look before tearing himself away, still dripping. I remain with Erica.

"Everything okay?" she asks.

"Yes," I reply without thinking.

"You're shaking, Jade."

I glance down and discover my legs are trembling. My eyes grow wide. I attempt to tighten my muscles, trying to force them into submission.

It doesn't work.

"Maybe we should sit." Erica grabs my elbow and guides me to a bench. "You and I need to have a little talk anyway."

My eyes shift to the right to see her. Her soft demeanor is gone momentarily. I haven't seen this side of her before.

"Where did you go during the bake sale?"

"I had to take care of some things."

"What things?"

My lips part slightly, unsure of what to say.

"Jade, where is Sophie?"

"I don't—"

"No, you probably don't," she cuts me off. "Sophie has always been good at hiding, but I haven't seen her recently and that means something is going on, and *you're* acting weird. Suddenly you're pulling disappearing acts and roping me into assisting you? No. You need to tell me what is happening, Jade."

If her goal was to get me to stop shaking over my worry for Roan and my father, it worked. I'm stunned into motionlessness.

"Are you all right, Jade?" Mr. Eroh's voice rescues me from having to explain my actions to Erica. She smiles at me politely, patting my arm—she's not done with me.

"Jade?" Mr. Eroh asks again.

"I'm fine," I shake my head, gathering myself. "I was just worried about everyone, that's all. When did you get here?"

"I've been here for forty minutes or so. Annie just arrived with some snacks for everyone too," he informs me. "I've busied myself with some smaller projects."

He winks at me.

"How is it going?"

We spend the next few minutes going over what the group has accomplished and working out what was most important to finish before the end of the day since it is unlikely we'll get it all done before we have to quit for the day.

"Jade," a voice calls as we clean up for the day. "A word?"

I step away from the group packing up tools and supplies toward the dark-haired young man. He smiles casually as he pulls me aside.

"Hey, Sean." Roan raises his hand to wave as he moves a heavy tool into a cart with Charlie and a few other men a few feet away.

My body goes cold as Sean smiles and waves back. He looks back at me innocently.

"What do you want?" I hiss, knowing he has been sent by the Commander.

"Oh, don't need the act then, I see. Great." He holds only the corners of a smile on his face, just enough to keep onlookers from suspecting anything other than a nice conversation.

"What does *he* want?" I punctuate my words.

Sean's hair glistens with the remnants of water he must have just been in—he's been with us all day and I had no idea. He casually brushes his bangs away from his face, flicking droplets of water at me.

"I just wanted to thank you for all of your hard work,"

he grabs my hand, pumping it up and down. "I'm so impressed by how you have stepped up. I anticipate great things from you, ma'am."

He smiles, waving at a group passing by, making sure they see us. He looks back at me, eyes icy.

"I'm here to support you in any way you need. I have worked with your husband and father-in-law for a long time and I'm happy to assist you however I can."

I grumble under my breath.

"Oh, I think you're husband is looking for you," he points with one hand, digging his nails into mine with the other. "I should be going too. Have a nice night, ma'am."

He leaves me with a piece of paper in my hand and far too many questions.

"Ready to go?" Roan asks. He looks like he wants to take my bag from me, sling his arm around my shoulders, and guide me home. Instead, he drops his voice to a whisper. "Want to swing by the art house?"

Yes.

"No," I say instead. "We should get home. We're both exhausted after everything today and tomorrow is a normal work day so..."

He looks disappointed as I trail off but doesn't protest.

The walk home seems excruciatingly long as we walk in relative silence with the explanation of a note

Maybelle left with Roan with a list of times the Commander wasn't in the house reminding me of my own secret note.

My mind tosses me back and forth between Sean and Erica as we continue our quiet walk home. Erica is already starting to suspect something is going on with Sophie which means she could insert herself and get in the way of the Commander's plan. Sean is working for my father-in-law which is bad news all around. His note burns through the bag I'm carrying, searing into me as it calls to be read.

Roan makes us an easy dinner when we get home. I really should be the one doing it since I did less physical work than he did today, but I'm so drained that I perch myself on an island stool and rest my head in my hand until he sets a plate in front of me.

After we eat, he walks me to my room to say good-night early. Instinctually, I lean forward and kiss his lips but I don't linger.

"Good night," he says as I close the door.

The room offers me some solace and I immediately perk up as I grab my bag. I dig the note out. Sitting on the bed, I unfold it until I discover a very detailed plan.

I will be creating a community garden. I'm to bring it up at the next open forum as one of my big projects. Once I have their attention with the opportunity to create a sustainable food source that everyone can contribute to and benefit from, I have to impose rules and regulations that will limit access by certain groups. The Commander's plan is for me to force a class system and take away rights from certain people while favoring others.

It's an excellent start to his plan.

Every detail is planned out for me right down to suggested lines to say at the open forum. Robert Diamond has been working hard on this for the last two days.

His writing twists and transforms from angry, to calm and powerful, back to vengeful. I can read his emotions through his barely-legible script.

I pull out paper and a pen. I'll have to begin working on "my" proposal tonight if I want to be ready in time for the meeting. I'll follow his little game, but I'll add in some things he's not prepared for that will actually help the people and allow Roan to get things back on track should the proposal go through by some miracle.

I have three days to get this right.

I work much later than I should.

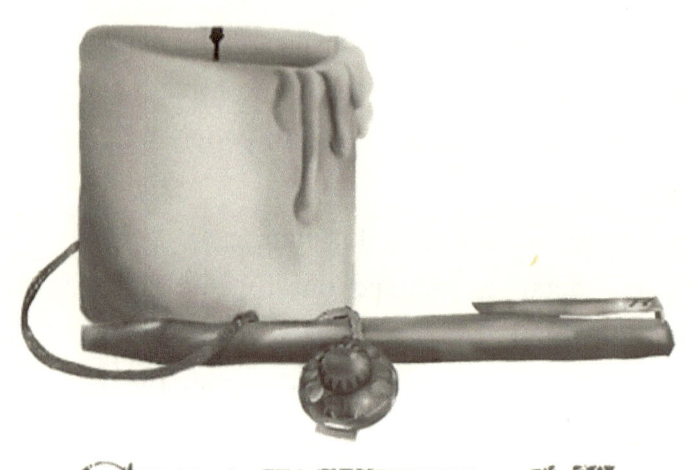

CHAPTER 17
JADE

I spend the next three days working on the Commander's proposal at work and writing letters to the people I love in the evening to explain my actions. I hide them among my mother's letters in case they should be found. My husband spends his time working on some secret project of his own, giving us both reasons to keep our distance.

Roan and I talk quietly through meals. I try not to make it too awkward while still maintaining some distance from him. By the end of the week, we've settled into a place that doesn't seem too off balance for us. We even manage to cook a meal or two together and enjoy our time with each other.

I hope he will be able to forgive me for what I'm about to do.

"With that job description, Mrs. Diamond has a proposal for us," Lucas announces, wrapping up the previous part of the open forum. "Jade?"

I take a deep breath and step forward, pushing away from the edge of the platform with papers in my hand, wishing we could go back to talking about Roan's plan for creating a stronger force of physicians for the country.

"I would like to set forth a proposal for the Command," I begin. "I've been thinking about what might benefit our country and help our people, and after much research, I think I've found something I'd like to take on sooner rather than later—especially given the time of year."

Everyone leans forward slightly, waiting to hear what I'm about to suggest to them. The Commander sits in the back on the opposite side of the room as Mr. Eroh—I imagine so my former boss won't be able to notice my father-in-law's glee when I cause my own destruction.

Roan and Lucas already know I'm about to propose the community garden but they don't know any of the details—those will come as a shock to them. Before that though, I have to build it up.

A wild look spreads over the Commander's face reminding me a bit of the man I saw at my wedding. It's fitting, I suppose, since we're back in the same room.

"I would like to start a community garden, one in which we can all work together to grow different crops and all benefit from."

The crowd starts murmuring, pleased with the suggestion. The more I speak, the more excited the people get. Roan and Lucas make comments when needed, applauding the virtues of the garden as they bolster support.

They trust me so they never think to ask what is in the proposal. They simply go along with it when we tell them it is happening.

The Commander practically jumps out of his seat when I break the news that there would need to be limits on how and when people could access the crops from the gardens. Roan turns to me in shock.

Lucas leans around him, trying to catch my attention but I blatantly ignore him. From the corner of my eye, I notice my father leaning forward in his chair, lips parted in an unspoken question. I avoid his gaze too.

"Jade makes a good point about needing some regulations," Roan jumps in, trying to calm the crowd before they turn on me. "I think this would be a great thing for us to continue to develop as we talk through this to make it fair and reasonable for everyone."

"A great deal of research went into this, Roan," I protest. I don't mention it was his father's research that I was talking about and not my own. "This is the way it needs to be for everything to work out."

"I think this is something we should talk about later, Jade," he says quietly, desperately trying to help me out of what is clearly a bad situation.

"No, now." I turn to the group and continue to push the Commander's agenda, explaining why I'm trying to regress the country to a class system. Even Annie looks nervous as I glance around the crowd, offering them my most sincere smile.

They all smile nervously back at me—it's hard to argue with someone who is being so nice about it. I flawlessly act as if I think this is the best idea in the world to the point where I may have some of them convinced to join me.

The back of my throat burns. Heat creeps into my temples as I try to control my breathing. At least my legs aren't shaking this time—I'd never be able to control it and I'd give myself away.

Eventually, Lucas manipulates the conversation away from the community gardens and onto a report from the pond workday. He and Roan expertly point out all of my hard work from the event as they try to make the crowd forget my errant ways from only moments before.

They come close to succeeding.

The two men take a few questions from the list, promising to open up the forum to new question as soon as we got through the ones already submitted to us. Eventually, the group wanders off, leaving the sanctuary of the open forum.

"Jade," my father's voice is a warning.

I turn, smiling at him. *Play the part, play the part, play the part.*

"Can you tell me what just happened there?"

He closes in on me with Roan, Lucas, and Mr. Eroh all taking up a place next to me as well. My husband is clearly concerned. Lucas looks furious. Mr. Eroh keeps his emotions hidden until he hears more from me but there is a distinct look of betrayal on my father's face.

"What do you mean?" I ask lightly.

"With the gardens," he prompts me.

"Isn't it a wonderful idea?" I say, far too chipper. "We can create a sustainable food source and everyone gets access to it. Roan and Lucas thought it was a great idea when I told them."

"We didn't know you were controlling how much access everyone had to it, Jade," Lucas snaps at me.

"We *have* to control it or it will be over before it's started, Lucas," I bite back. "If everyone just comes in and cleans it out, there will be nothing left. We have to be strategic about it."

Rotating crops and regulating when things could be

picked is a good idea…it's the limitations set on specific people that are the problem.

There is nothing fair about the system I was proposing. It was designed to make me look biased toward specific people—*my* people.

"Jade, you can't honestly think the system you outlined is fair," my father quietly says. "Honey, we can fix this."

"It's already done. It's all in the proposal," I challenge him. "Roan and Lucas already signed off on it."

My father looks like I slapped him—I am standing for everything he hated in this moment and it radiates across his face.

"I think this is perhaps something we should discuss another day," Mr. Eroh mercifully suggests, seeing that I'm on the verge of tears. "Why don't we all go home for the evening and we can prepare for the next open forum later this week."

He tugs on my father's arm.

"Jade, come by the shop this week, I have something for you."

I know its code for "we have to have a talk" so I simply nod, knowing I can't get out of it.

He turns, allowing my father to walk with him to the door. The two will walk all the way to Mr. Eroh's home together like they always do.

"Don't," I cut Lucas off before he can speak, holding

up a finger.

"You need to tell me what is going on here, Jade. This isn't you," he says anyway.

The Commander isn't standing in the back as I assumed he would be, fanning the flames of my destruction. In fact, he's nowhere to be found.

"Enough," Roan interjects, stepping between Lucas and me. "I think it's time for us all to go home."

He gives a pointed look to Lucas to let him know they'll be discussing me later. He's going to try to handle me on his own first. Roan takes my hand and tucks it around his arm so that I'm holding his elbow.

"Let's go home," he says softly. I nod and he leads us toward the door.

Outside, Erica catches my eye but she doesn't stray from where she's standing with Annie and Mrs. Thompson. Another girl with shoulder length, dark hair comes running up to us.

"Community gardens are a lovely idea," she smiles quickly at me before turning to Roan. She gazes at him as if it had been his idea. "If there's anything I can do, of course, let me know."

"Jade, this is Janine's sister, Marcy," Roan turns to me to introduce us.

"Hello," I say, trying to keep my voice even. She doesn't even glance at me.

"I just wanted to let you know that you have my

support in whatever way that you need it. I should go find my sister now. Have a lovely evening." She backs away, slowly walking off to the left.

"That was…unusual," I comment and we fall back into step.

"Dad introduced us last week after the meeting. She's more outgoing than her sister, apparently."

It clicks—she is my replacement. Roan just doesn't know it.

I try not to hate the girl.

My hand is warm tucked between Roan's body and arm as we walk toward our home. I hover a step behind him so he can't get a good look at me from the corner of his eye.

He holds the door open as I step inside. It clicks shut behind us as I wait for him to start into me about my actions at the open forum.

"Are you hungry?" he asks.

Shocked, it takes me a moment to answer.

"Um, yes. I could eat."

We walk to the kitchen where he motions to a stool. I sit as he prepares to start some food for us. He works quietly, pulling out materials to make sandwiches.

I'm silent as he works, watching the muscles in his arms move every time he leans over to move something closer to us. I desperately want to guide the conversation away from what happened earlier, but it will be far too obvious if I try. I wait, letting him initiate our dialogue.

"I think the gardens are a very good idea, Jade," he says before we eat.

I take a bite of my food. He follows suit.

I expect him to continue, but we make it half way through our meal without anything more.

"That's it?" I finally question when I can't stand waiting any longer. He's learned my technique of waiting and is using it against me to get more information—I can see it in the sparkle of his eyes when he connects with me.

"That's it." He offers me a soft closed-lip smile, but there's a challenge in it.

"Well, thank you for the support," I don't rise to the bait. His face twitches slightly, but he continues to play the game.

I pick up my sandwich, taking another bite. He watches me as I chew, yet somehow it doesn't make me uncomfortable. I lower my hands so that my wrists rest against the edge of the table as I swallow. Slowly, I reach for my glass of water, all the while letting him observe me.

"What do you want to do tonight?" Roan carefully asks.

"I was thinking about reading a little," I say cautiously. I don't want to invite him to do anything with me, but I'd also like to be in his presence if I can.

"That sounds like a nice idea," he says casually. I can tell he wants to suggest we do it together. I contemplate my next move.

"It's still light out…maybe I'll read in the back yard for a bit."

"That could be nice," Roan muses. "Maybe I'll go get a little yard work done while you're out there if you don't mind, of course."

"No, that's fine." I smile at him, trying to soften the edges of the game we're clearly playing.

We clean up from our meal, Roan hovering just far enough away to keep from bumping me as we work, before heading outside.

I perch myself on the stone bench Roan built for me, tucking my legs up under me while my skirt hangs down the front of the stonework. Roan quietly works a few feet away, pulling up weeds so that I don't have to.

Roan changed into a navy blue tee shirt before coming outside to work, but I hadn't bothered changing.

I take a moment to appreciate the way the color looks on him. I might need to remember that for the future, should I have time to buy him any new clothing between now and the funeral.

When he looks back over his shoulder, I look down. It feels like those first few days with him when we watched each other surreptitiously over our reading materials from the library. I had no idea what my books said then and I have no idea what it says now.

"How is it going, wife?" he asks playfully as he turns back around to pull out another weed.

"Fine. How is the yard work going?" I reply.

"You tell me," he turns back to me and grins coyly. "I noticed that you've been watching me."

"Which tells me," I glance back down as if I don't care, "that you've been watching *me* too."

"Did you think that I wouldn't?" He spins on his heels, turning all the way around to face me. He duck-walks toward the bench, spade in hand. "I think I've made it pretty clear what being married to you means to me, and if I want to stare at the gorgeous woman I share a house with, then I will."

I accidentally snort as I try to keep in my laughter as he waddles toward me, still crouching low to the ground. His face lights up. When he reaches the bench, he puts his hand on the stone to steady himself.

"Jade." My name comes out as a sigh. "What is going

on? I know something is up, but I'm just so confused. Is this about what your dad told us the other night?"

"What?" I ask abruptly. I hadn't seen the change in conversation coming. "No, it's not about your dad killing my mom. You don't need to worry about that."

"But I do, Jade," he says, leaning forward just the slightest bit. "I worry about that very much."

"I'm just distracted, that's all. I have a lot going on between all the volunteer work, and moving into the new office, and picking up responsibilities now that your dad is gone. There's just a lot for me to handle right now and I'm distracted, that's all."

A piece of his hair drifts into his face, covering one eye. Roan adjusts his feet so he has better balance, stabilizing himself against the corner of the bench. He's close enough that I could lean forward and kiss him.

"I just worry that it might have some bearing on what happened today," he says softly. "Please don't punish the people because of my father."

"I'm not punishing anyone, Roan." His words shock me, though they make sense. "I'm just trying to create the most effective way of running the gardens, that's all."

I stand up, nearly knocking him over.

"I want to back you up, Jade, I really do, but isn't creating a class system exactly what we're trying to avoid?"

I storm away. My dress swishes in my wake. I hear

Roan stand up behind me, but he doesn't follow. The edge of the spade taps against the rock of my bench as he pauses in defeat. I want to go back to him and tell him it's his father's plan, but the division it's creating between us will only serve to make things easier for him. I have to lean into the moments the Commander's plan offers me to make this easier on both of us to say goodbye, or it will break me before it's over.

After an hour, Roan knocks on my door, calling a gentle goodnight.

"We have to fix this," his voice travels out of the office, wrapping around to mine. Lucas isn't happy.

"I know," Roan tries to calm him.

We've all arrived early enough that Janine hasn't shown up yet. The Command building is empty save for the three of us.

"If she keeps pushing this, they're going to turn on her. We can't let that happen."

"They won't turn on her," Roan says in a steady voice. How he's not more upset than Lucas, I'm not sure.

"Roan—"

"Lucas, this isn't helping. We both agree that the garden is a good plan. We just have to tweak the execution of it a little."

I rearrange the papers on my desk, pretending not to hear them in Lucas' office. I've already moved the papers three times—there is no new place to set them on my desk.

"Good morning, Janine," Roan says suddenly, making me look up. Unlike my husband, I don't have a view of the lobby from where my desk is situated.

I quietly walk to the door, grateful my office has carpeting to absorb the sound of my footsteps. I press my back against the wooden door, allowing the back of my hand to rest against the doorframe near my eye...*as if* it would help me hear better.

"Good morning," Janine replies as she noisily sets her things on her desk. "I saw Mr. Artemus on the way in this morning. He said he would like a meeting with you. He's on his way over but had a stop to make first. Your schedule looked clear when I left before the weekend so I told him that would probably be fine."

"That's fine, Janine, thank you. Send him in when he arrives, please."

"What do you think he wants?" Lucas says quietly. He and Roan nearly slam into me as they walk around the corner, surprising me. Lucas smirks when he sees the shock on my face. "Spying, Jade?"

"Well, I didn't think you wanted to see me just yet," I huff at him as he analyzes me.

Janine's heels click against the lobby floor before anyone else can speak.

"Sir, Mr. Artemus is here," she says behind the boys.

"That was fast," Roan mutters.

"I didn't know he could move that quickly," Janine mumbles. Her eyes grow wide when she realizes she said it out loud. I chuckle to let her know it is okay. She spins away quickly, motioning the older man toward Roan's office from across the lobby.

"I guess I'll be back," Roan mutters, pulling back from the door. He adopts his politician's smile—*they all have one*—and walks toward his office.

Lucas steps inside and closes the door. He motions to the small couch near the coffee table similar to the one Roan had in his office that now sits in Lucas' space.

"You understand that he's here to talk about you, right?"

Direct.

"Your point?" I challenge him.

"This isn't you, Jade, so what's the deal? You would never do this."

"I would and I did, Lucas," I pretend to try to persuade him. "It's important."

"I know taking care of people is important, Jade," his voice gets quiet. "Believe me, I get it. But this isn't the right way and you know that. What is this really about? If you're trying to get revenge on the Commander, there are other ways of doing that—believe me, your husband has been investigating him."

He reaches over and takes my hand.

"I've watched you since you and I were young, Jade. You're the little girl who always helped people."

"I'm trying to help them, Lucas. I believe this is the best way."

The best way to keep people alive at least.

Lucas sits back against the arm of the couch, nestling himself in the corner. I can see him eye the coffee table, but he keeps his foot on the ground.

"Our lives would have been so different, wouldn't they have, if all this hadn't happened?" He watches me intently. "If the Commander hadn't put you in his sights, none of this would be like this."

"I certainly wouldn't be here," I respond, leaning back to mimic his pose in my own corner of the couch. "You probably wouldn't either."

"I doubt that very much." He rubs a hand across his chin thoughtfully.

"Where would you be?" I ask.

"I don't have any idea, truthfully. It's always been about the mission for me, just like it was for you and Roan."

"There must be *something* you've always wanted to do,"

I try to guide him. I might have to pull away, but that doesn't mean I can't work a little magic behind the scenes to give them a bit of happiness somewhere along the way.

He looks smugly at me, bobbing his head just a touch before he speaks.

"Really? What other job would I get to wear a suit like this for? I took this job for a reason and it was because I get to look fabulous."

"Oh? Here I thought it was to save me. My mistake," I tease him.

"Happy accident," he banters.

"Yes, well, while you're looking so fabulous over there, maybe we should talk about how no one notices it." I bat my eyelashes at him playfully.

"Hey! I resent that," he pretends to be horrified by my comment.

"I mean, really, Lucas, with a face like that and those 'fancy clothes' how is it possible that not one girl has noticed you?" I inquire.

"Janine seems quite taken with me," he retorts, lifting his arm to rest on the back of the couch.

"She's taken with anyone who wasn't directly connected to this office before the Commander's retirement," I throw back at him.

"Point taken." He lifts his leg up and stretches it alongside of me on the couch, conscious of keeping his shoes off the cushions. Lucas lounges, staring back at me.

"You need a girlfriend, Lucas."

"I'm fine, Jade."

"So am I," I reply immediately.

He looks shocked for a moment, taking in my point.

"Fine, if that's how you want to play it—"

"It is," I cut him off.

"Find me a girlfriend."

I do a double take.

"Excuse me?"

"You back off on this class system thing and I'll let you pick out my girlfriend." He looks calmly at me, waiting for me to agree.

"As simple as that, huh?"

"I'd rather have you avoid the lynch mob if I can, Jade, and if that means I have to go on a harmless date to achieve that, so be it."

"Oh, and what if I picked someone less-than-sane?"

"I gave up my whole life to protect you. If you're going to do something stupid, I'm going to throw myself in front of you again…or do you need to see my scars to prove I'm willing to suffer a bit for you and your husband?"

The matchmaker in me springs to life, demanding I take his offer, but the Commander's voice rings in my head, forbidding it. Sophie would pay the price, and Lucas had already paid it once—it's my turn now.

"No deal, but nice try."

He watches me for a moment as he decides what to say.

"I was close though, wasn't I?" he asks seriously. I roll my eyes and look away as I grin.

"Maybe."

"You're not going to give up on this, are you?" he asks reluctantly.

"Have I ever?" I remind him, tucking a piece of my hair behind me. I instinctually reach for the hair comb that isn't there, my fingers only brushing against my mane.

"Okay," he resigns himself. "I trust you."

"Thank you."

"And I'll help you out of whatever mess you find your-self in when this is all over."

I sincerely doubt he can help me out of a casket.

CHAPTER 18

ROAN

M r. Artemus spends most of the day in my office before he's finally satisfied enough to leave. Overrun with paperwork, I barely have time to check on Jade and Lucas before the end of the day, opting to eat my lunch at my desk. Both Lucas and Jade are buried in their own work, so none of us are too disappointed when we spend the day apart.

The office is quiet for the remainder of the day. The hours fly by as we work. I wait for Jade to sneak out early again but she doesn't.

"Ready to head home?" I stand in her doorway, waiting for her to gather her things.

"Yes," she says, not bothering to look up as she slips some folders into her bag.

"Did you get a lot done today?" I ask.

"I did. Did you?"

"I did." I step back into the open lobby space, leaning forward to wave into Lucas' office as he finishes up for the day. "Good night, Lucas."

"Good night," he waves me off like Jade did without ever looking up.

"Lynn?" Jade calls around me.

"No." Lucas doesn't sound impressed.

I raise an eyebrow at Jade.

"I'm finding him a girlfriend," she informs me.

"No, she's not. She knows what the deal is," Lucas calls loudly.

"Should I ask?" I interrupt their banter.

"Probably not," Jade smiles softly. "Let's go."

We're halfway home before either of us tries to start up a conversation.

"I thought maybe you'd go see Mr. Eroh today," I remark as Jade trails ahead of me. She slows down a step to wait for me.

"I was planning on going tomorrow. I needed to see Annie about something anyway."

"Oh." I couldn't think of anything else to say so I tried

Jade's trick of being silent so the other person would give up more information again. It worked the other day…sort of.

"What are you doing tomorrow?" she finally asks.

"I have a few meetings about the project I'm working on."

"I see." Her hands dangle around her as she walks, softly swaying with the movement of her body. "Anything I can help with?"

"Not just yet but soon."

We fall into light conversation about how to spend the rest of the evening. Once we reach our house, we have dinner together and spend the evening reading in our separate corners of the living room before saying good night.

Once inside, I settle down against my pillows and kick my feet up on the mattress with my papers in hand. It will be a little bit until the pool is built, filled with water, and ready for public use but tonight I'm working on the final designs for the mural we'll be adding to the walls protecting small children from walking into the pool area unattended.

I've secured the builders and commissioned a few of the people from the art house to work on the sculptures built into the façade. They'll start building it soon. Once everything is assembled, I'll show it to Jade before letting the public know it's available to them at an open forum meeting. The team I've contracted has been wonderful about working on the project covertly.

My fingers swirl on the page as I sketch the design for the mural. My goal is to use this as a way to open the arts back up to the country so that we won't have to hide in the art house anymore, though I'm positive we'll all still use it as our own personal retreats as often as possible.

Eventually, my eyes grow heavy. With my pad of paper tucked safely away in my drawer, I climb back into bed and pull the sheets over me. My mind drifts forward in time to the day I can reveal my gift to my wife, the waterfalls of the pool springing to life as we enter the first public pool our country has seen in a very long time.

Not even the birds are up when I get out of bed. Darkness still consumes the country, the first glimmer of day barely a speck in the distant sky. I slip on old shoes and make my way quietly out of the house.

The jog to the art house isn't bad, though the dew drenches my feet, soaking my pants all the way up to my knees by the time I arrive.

From the outside, you'd never know there was light

inside. They covered the windows knowing the meeting was private.

"You look good," Charlie smirks, catching sight of my less-than-professional attire.

"You try looking good after running through wet grass," I retort. He makes a face and looks down.

"I did and I do, *Commander.*"

"Helpful," I mumble.

A number of people stand around the room—not everyone that uses the art house, but enough.

"Was everyone able to secure the time to work on the project?" I ask as I look at the people surrounding me. They nod. "Good. If anyone gives you any trouble when the time comes, just tell them you're working on a special project for the Command. I'll speak to your supervisors if necessary."

I hand out papers to everyone with their assignments. I've given each person free reign over one area to create as they please, but we'll all be working on the large mural together. I'm not sure how I personally will find time without getting caught, but maybe I can use a bit of Command time during my lunch hour to lend my hands to the wall.

"Roan," Duncan holds me back once everyone is dismissed. "Are you sure it's a good idea introducing this so quickly? Your father *just* stepped down and you have so much to handle now that you're in charge. This isn't something that has to happen overnight."

"It won't happen over night, I'm sure," I reply, trying to give him my most convincing smile. It's times like these that I wish I had a little more of Lucas' charm. "This is a good introduction. It's a way to open up the doors for people to start taking notice and it gives them the freedom to start considering things outside of our usual way.

"I know my grandfather wanted us to focus on the future and not be distracted, but we're settled now. We're progressing. We're not living in a dire, post-war situation. We have more freedom now and as we branch out to give people more of a voice, I want to be able to offer this to them too."

"I understand," he nods, "But try not to get your hopes up too high on this, Roan. It's a good first step."

"Perhaps once we make it through this, you could sit down with me and help me make a plan for reintroducing the arts back to the country, Duncan," I suggest hopefully.

"When all is said and done, I'd like to help with that. Thank you for asking me, Roan."

"Of course." I really do appreciate everything Duncan has done for me over the years. He mentored me from a young age and I don't respect many opinions more than I respect his.

"We're going to keep this place private though, right?" he asks nervously.

"Absolutely. This is just for us," I motion around to the door where people linger outside. "This is *our* home. No matter how accepting and involved the community gets, this is and always will be just for us."

"Good." He looks satisfied with my answer. He takes a deep breath before patting my shoulder as we walk toward the door so I can rush home to have breakfast ready before Jade wakes up.

"Now about this butterfly…"

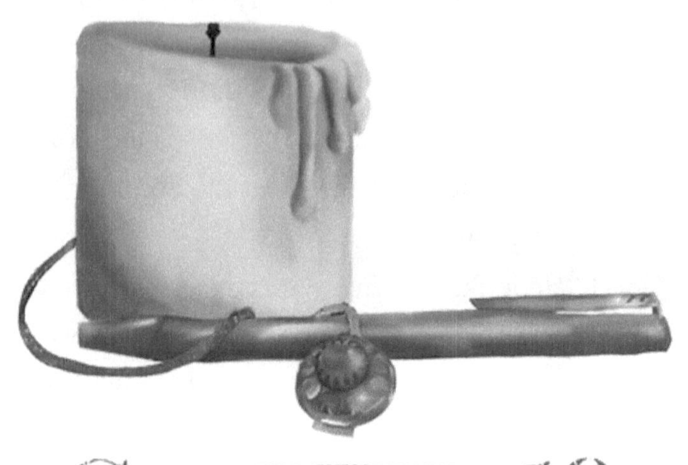

CHAPTER 19
JADE

urprisingly, the smell of bacon and pancakes rouses me from my bed. I stumbled out of my room, still clothed in my pajamas to find Roan grinning at me from over the kitchen island.

"Good morning, sweetheart," he chirps.

"Good morning," I answer. "What's all this?"

"I know you're headed to Mr. Eroh's today and I'm sure you have a lot of other things to do on that side of town, so I wanted you to have a good breakfast to start your day."

"That was sweet of you," I murmur as I slide onto the island stool.

A white pitcher with syrup slides in front of me as it scrapes along the counter's surface. Roan moves to add bacon to my plate. When he turns back, he sets it in front of me.

"Are you planning on coming into the office today?" Roan asks as we finish our food.

"We'll see how things go," I hesitate. "I've got a lot to do today."

"Well, maybe give me a warning before you walk into my office today because I'm working on that project."

"Are you ever going to tell me what it is?" I nudge him. I'd like to find out what this top-secret undertaking is before I die.

"Soon, wife." His eyes sparkle as he winks at me. "I'm going to head out early. Have a good day with Mr. Eroh."

He slips around the island and kisses my temple before hurrying off to his room to change for work. He slips out while I'm washing the dishes.

I quickly change and get ready to set out for Mr. Eroh's shop. The walk is calming and gives me time to plan my next move. If the Commander's goal is to have me dead within two weeks, he must be planning something else too because the garden disaster isn't enough to make people that angry with me.

"Pay attention," someone says as they race by me.

I turn to find the back of a man running away from me, his feet kicking up behind him as he continues his early morning jog. I hadn't been in his path, but maybe he's just an aggressive runner.

I skirt around Erica's shop as I reach the town line, hoping to avoid another conversation with her. The smell of Annie's bakery calls me. I nearly keep going, but food might help whatever conversation I'm going to be having with my mentor.

"Jade!" Annie bellows as I walk in. "You're out early."

She bustles over to me, hair back in pigtails, still holding a tray of danishes she was about to set out before I interrupted her. She holds it out to me, nodding to the cheese one.

"Staying or going?" she asks.

"I'm headed over to Mr. Eroh's so two to go, please."

"Coming right up."

She scurries over to her counter, slipping behind the glass cases housing her pastries. Annie opens up a brown bag and begins filling it with more treats than I asked for to take to my mentor.

"So the other day was fun." Her words are light, but I know Annie enough to know she's demanding an answer about my behavior at the open forum.

I ignore her.

"Those look good," I point to a cinnamon crumble muffin.

She lets out a bored sigh before reaching for the muffins for me.

"Taking some home for Roan?" She allows me to avoid answering.

"Please," I answer, knowing I needed to support her, especially if she wasn't going to push me on this.

She sets the first bag down, reaching for a second. When she's done, she tapes it shut so I can tell the difference. Annie knows exactly what everyone likes, and Mr. Eroh's treats are not to be confused with the ones for Roan.

"Thank you, Annie," I say, picking up the bags after I pay for the food.

"Careful out there today, Jade," Annie says from behind the counter. "You've got some unhappy people out there who might want to ask some questions today."

"I'll be fine, thanks, Annie." I wave at the door, balancing both bags in one arm.

"Jade?" her voice makes me pause. "Go see your father today. I slipped a cinnamon bun in there for him."

Annie always adds extra things to my orders when I take food out. She's taken care of me for a long time.

"Have a good day," I call, shaking my head as I exit.

"Good morning, Jade," Mrs. Thompson says politely as she passes me, slipping in through the bakery door with her son. He nods to me.

I deviate from my course, opting to visit my father first. I make my way down the familiar path to the former library that has been transformed into offices for the town's representatives.

The office that formerly belonged to Lucas is now dark as it waits for his replacement to be chosen. The secretary looks up from her desk on the left side of the lobby.

"Can I help you?" she says automatically. When she realizes it's me, she adds, "He's in his office."

She looks back down after giving me a quick smile, continuing her work. In my peripheral vision, I see an aid walks up to the desk next to hers and sets some papers down before touching her shoulder. I hear her shoes clicking away as I turn to walk toward my father's office.

"Pay attention, Jade," he stresses each word as if they were a complete sentence.

I turn back, noticing the man's features for the first time.

"Sean," I growl as viciously as the Commander usually does.

"Pay…attention," he repeats, smirking at me.

"Why are you here?" I demand, wishing I could cross my arms, but the bags of treats prevent me from doing so.

"I work here," he answers. "*Right* here."

"I thought you were a representative's aid," I challenge.

"I am. We work here in this building…right where I

have a great view of," he pauses dramatically, "your father."

"Why are you doing this?" I lean forward, snarling. I have no reason to hide my distaste for the man.

He smiles at me, knowing he holds all the cards.

"I'll be taking over Lucas' office soon and after that, I'll be well on my way to the Command Building."

"You honestly think my husband is going to welcome you into the Command Building?"

"With open arms. The Commander has his ways and his son will fall in line. I'm more than happy to help until then."

He's in it for the power. Leave it to Robert Diamond to find someone just like himself to dangle privilege in front of for manipulation.

"So you're here to…what? Threaten me?"

"Threaten your father, yes."

He shifts papers around on the desk to make it look like he's working if anyone should pass by and notice. If I weren't holding my food, I'd lean intimidatingly against his desk and see how much ground I could gain with the conversation.

"What do you want from me?"

"I told you," he glances up but quickly looks back down, cutting off his thought as he whispers, "Pay attention."

"Jade?" My father's voice fills the lobby, bouncing off the ceiling and walls. "I see you've met Sean."

"We've met," I mumble. "Annie sent some things over. Let's go to your office."

I hold the bags up as I turn away from Sean. He staples something loudly behind me, punctuating our conversation.

"Nice to meet you, Jade," he calls after me.

I quickly take a seat at my father's desk and dig out his cinnamon bun from the bakery. I wrap it in a napkin that Annie supplied and set it in front of him.

He studies me for a moment but resigns himself to eat before we have our serious talk.

"Annie sent this over, huh?" he muses quietly.

"Yeah, I'm on my way to see Mr. Eroh."

"That's good," he takes another bite.

I dig around in the bag, looking for something small I can snack on until I arrive at the shop where I used to work. A corner of a scone breaks off in my hand, so I take advantage of my careless moment.

"How is Annie today?" he asks.

It's not usually this hard to talk to my father but neither of us knows what to say yet to move forward from my moment at the open forum. The conversation feels heavy and awkward as we try to proceed.

"You know I'll always love you, even if we don't see eye-to-eye, but Jade—"

"Sir, we just received word that the Commander would like to see you," Sean stands in the doorway, leering over me. The corner of his lip ticks up when I make eye contact with him as if he's proving that he has won something.

When I turn back to my father, his brow wrinkles in confusion.

"Why does Roan want to see me?"

"The *former* Commander, sir," Sean corrects.

My neck prickles. A burst of tingling energy starts in my lower chest and radiates quickly up my spine to the front of my shoulders and down my hips to where my legs connect to my body.

"Thank you, Sean," my father answers, his voice low.

We share a glance as he stands. He puts the last bite of his treat in his mouth and brushes off his hands.

"Well, this can't be pleasant," he mumbles.

I'm sure it's a message to me.

"Sean," my father calls into the lobby. "Did he say where I'm supposed to meet him?"

I follow him into the large foyer, nearly stepping on his feet as I trail him.

"Oh, sorry, sir. Lucinda sent me to tell you," Sean pretends to stumble over his words.

The secretary glances up from her desk.

"His home, James," she nods politely to my father.

"The messenger he sent said you would know what it was about?"

She poses her last sentence as if it were a question. We play along.

"Of course, thank you, Lucinda." He guides me back to his office and waits for me to gather the bags from Annie. "Go to the shop."

His instructions are clear—go somewhere that I trust.

"What is this about?" I ask.

"I have no idea." He shakes his head. "Just go to the shop and then go home. I'll reach out when I know what's going on."

"Should you really be going over there by yourself?" I question.

"It will be fine, sweetheart. Don't worry about me."

With his hand on my back, he ushers me out the door and locks his office behind him. We wave to Lucinda as she works at her desk. Sean is nowhere to be seen. He's probably lurking around the corner somewhere.

"I'll talk to you later," my father promises, branching off before I can protest.

"See how easy that was?" Sean slips next to me once my father is out of sight. "Any place, anytime. And it's not just me—there are others too, all looking to advance their placement in this world. I just happen to be the favorite."

It's a competition. Lovely.

"Run along, Jade. I have work to do. The Commander will be in touch soon."

He turns away as quickly as he arrived, leaving me to continue the walk to Mr. Eroh's shop on my own. A few streets away, the shop waits for me.

The bell jingles as I enter. Mr. Eroh nods as I round the counter and set the bags down on a stool against the back wall. I wait for him to finish with a customer.

"I'm glad you're here," he says when we're alone.

"The Commander just demanded a meeting with my father," I interrupt him. I can't hide the worry in my voice.

"What?"

"I was just at his office and the Commander summoned him."

"Do we know why? Or at least what he *claimed* it was about?"

"There was no information given, just that he had to go to Commander Diamond's house."

"Well, I don't like the sounds of that." He rests his hand on the counter, not moving toward the food I had brought.

"I think I need to go check on them, I'm sorry," I say, rushing around the corner.

"Wait," Mr. Eroh's sharp voice stops me. "Take your food and I expect you back here in the next forty-eight hours, young lady."

He turns behind him and picks up a backpack. Dropping the sealed bag of food inside, he hands it to me.

"Don't do anything foolish," my former boss calls after me. I have no doubt he'll be following along behind me at some point. He has a habit of being in the right place at the right time.

I try not to rush through the busy parts of town. Drawing attention to myself won't help my cause. When I reach the outskirts of town, I break into a run, thankful I'm wearing flats.

I use my time to look for signs of Sophie, though nothing stands out to me. I slow when I reach areas where people might notice my haste. Eventually, the Diamond estate looms before me.

I loop around, entering from the back of the property near the pool house. The house seems still from the outside—though I'm sure it always does—it was built to keep its secrets *inside*.

Slipping in is easier than I anticipated. I quietly sneak by the kitchen where Maybelle is working and head toward the Commander's office when I discover they aren't in the living room. Muffled voices confirm my choice.

I keep a watchful eye out for the women of the house as I listen to the Commander lecturing my father.

"Why?" My father's voice is threatening and dark as he addresses his former leader.

"If I can make it harder for you to exist here, James, I'm going to," the Commander says smugly.

"Then go after me, but leave Jade out of this—that only hurts your son too."

I lean forward trying to hear more clearly by putting my ear to the door.

"Jade is making her own decisions, we're just leaning into it," the Commander lies. "You have a choice here, James. Perpetuate your daughter's mistakes and Sophie will be safe—eventually—or I'll leverage Sophie against Jade and see what games I can play there. It's up to you. I came to you first so the choice is yours.

"Yes, you and your daughter will be seen as the villains here, but I get the satisfaction of the country knowing your little rebellion was for naught all those years ago and the pleasure of them never trusting you again, while firmly placing my son as the one and only authority over this country once again. *You* get the comfort of knowing you're taking the fall with your daughter, because I'm sure you'll convince the people that she was just following your orders—who knows, maybe you can even clear her name."

"Jade?" Alice whispers from the end of the hallway.

My jaw drops. I had stopped paying attention when I got involved in the conversation inside the office.

"Fine," I hear my father say as I pull away from the door.

Alice's eyes shift toward the door—she's going to call me out.

I shake my head, terrified.

"Please don't," I whisper.

She reaches me just in time for the doorknob to turn as my father and the Commander prepare to exit the study. Alice shoves me into a closet and closes the door, leaving me in the dark.

"Alice?" my father-in-law asks in confusion as he sees his wife.

"Oh," she says calmly. "Hello, dear."

She pauses a moment before adding a grunt of disgust I assume was meant for my father.

She puts her back to the wall, brushing against the closet door, trapping me inside. I swallow hard as my father walks away. The feeling I had on my wedding day when my father and I couldn't protect each other washes over me as he steps out of hearing range.

Alice doesn't move, blocking me inside. For a moment, I'm terrified she's holding me there until her husband comes back to reprimand me. When the door finally opens, I find her alone.

"Why are you here?" she demands.

"He called my father." I don't think before I speak.

"And you just decided to show up?" she inquires. She waits while I stare at her, still standing inside the closet.

Alice looks over her shoulder before grabbing my

wrist. My mother-in-law pulls me out of the closet and down the hall.

I rush around a small sitting couch as Alice turns to close the door behind her, giving me only a moment out of her sight.

She raises an eyebrow at me. Light from the window filters into the sitting room, bathing it in a soft white glow. I've been in the room before and want nothing more than to wrap myself in the thick floor-to-ceiling drapes covering part of the windows and hide from Alice Diamond.

"What is going on, Jade?"

"You will tell me what is happening around here, even if my own family won't," she huffs. "I am tired of the secrets, now speak."

"What do you know?" I ask cautiously.

"Apparently nothing. Now, tell me what is happening."

"Your husband wants my father to help destroy my name," I reply. "And my father's."

"Why?" She crosses her arms. I've never seen her so forceful before.

"He wants to destroy our reputation before I die."

"Die?" Alice's eyebrows shoot up. "What do you mean *die?*"

She doesn't know.

I try to calm my heart rate as every organ in my body

pulsates against my skin. I have a lot to explain—Roan won't be happy his mother knows.

"Your husband is trying to kill me again," I inform her.

"Again?" Alice nearly shrieks. She manages to hold the last note down, ensuring the Commander doesn't over-hear our conversation.

I quickly explain what happened a few months ago leaving out the more dramatic parts of Roan's near-death experience to spare her the horror. Her nostrils flare as she processes the information, trying to keep her eyes from growing wide. Alice clutches at the pearls around her neck.

She's less concerned about the parts of the story revolving around me, but that is to be expected, since she's always hated me. She asks the occasional question as I speak.

"So he's given you a month to live?"

"I'm down to just over two weeks now, yes," I confirm.

"All of this just to get back at you for messing up his first plan. *This* is why we don't let men make the plans, Jade—they always over complicate things. This could have been so much easier if he had just let me in on all of this."

My blood goes cold as I realize Alice Diamond is about to enter into planning my execution.

"Where is your aunt?" Her question surprises me.

"I don't know." I don't want to answer her, but there's no point in holding back now.

"Go home, Jade. I'll try to reign my husband in."

I blink in confusion.

"Why are you helping me?"

"Why are you questioning me?" Alice looks unamused.

"You hate me," I remind her.

"I hate what you did to my son. I hate what he had to become in order to deal with my husband's vendetta against your father. Whether it was you or some other girl, I would hate anyone who put my son in that position —it just so happened to be you.

"For some insane reason, Roan actually loves you. Robert might not have seen the switch but a mother always knows.

"I don't care what happens to you, Jade, but it would break Roan's heart if you die, so I'm going to do what I can to protect my son. In order to do that, I need to help you. Now, go before I change my mind."

She opens the door and looks into the hallway before exiting. I carefully follow behind her as she watches for Maybelle and the Commander.

I slip out the back door, making my way past the pool house and out onto the isolated road that leads to the main street that will take me back to town. Once I'm out of sight, I pause behind a wall of hedges where I crumble.

Alice's promise gives me false hope. She holds no real power and she can't stop Robert Diamond from doing anything. At least she knows the truth now. She miraculously held it together when I told her about who had really poisoned her son and why—she's stronger than people give her credit for, truthfully.

When I catch my breath, I straighten from where I was bent over, hands on my knees. Angry tears drip from my cheeks. Alice can't save me—no one can this time.

Part way home I notice a figure walking slowly ahead of me. My father's shoulders slump as he contemplates his choices. He will try to accept the fall for me as I take freedom away from our people, yet it will do no good.

My instinct is to catch up to him and comfort him, but telling him *anything* only endangers him and Sophie even more—he can't know I'm here. I follow behind him, lingering far enough away that I can still see him without easily being noticed. He never turns around.

I barely make it inside my house when there's a knock at the door. I walk back through the kitchen without the glass of water I was going for to find Commander Diamond at my door.

CHAPTER 20
JADE

ou followed me?" I ask in disgust.

"One of the guards saw you skulking around in back of the house," he informs me, pushing me out of the way as he enters my home. "Why were you there?"

"You summoned my father," I cross my arms, glaring at him.

"I didn't call for *you*," he reminds me.

"You couldn't just leave him out of it, could you?" I hold my ground, spinning on my heels as he walks deeper into my home. I wish Roan were home to help.

"Good news, daughter—your father is about to help

make your mission a little easier."

"Leave my father alone!" I shout.

Too bad the poison isn't still in the couch cushions.

"He already knows about Sophie. This way you *both* get to make sure she doesn't die for you."

This is getting old hat.

"Funny enough, she was just down the road from the house this morning. I had her outside long enough to prove to your father that I really had her. I had only just returned home when I heard you had paid us a little visit.

"Imagine my surprise when I caught up to you walking back here."

He grins viciously at me. My skin prickles.

"What *were* you doing all morning, Ms. Jareau?"

"It's *Mrs. Diamond,*" I snap.

"You were never one of us, dear."

He stumbles backward, crashing into the couch. My hand stings as I look down, realizing that I had slapped him.

His hand flies to his cheek, eyes wide as he stares at me in shock. Almost as quickly, rage fills his face. The Commander jumps up, one foot accidentally catching the leg of the coffee table. He shudders forward as it snags him.

Without thinking, I take advantage of the moment, raising my leg to push him backward with a foot to his stomach. He falls, crashing once more onto the cushions.

"Stay down," I threaten.

"That's a very unwise thing to have done, Jade," he snarls at me.

"Why?" I challenge. "You can't do anything to me yet. If you do, your plan is all over."

His eyes narrow as he realizes I'm correct.

"But Sophie can pay for this."

"She won't because if she does, I'll disappear. People will notice if the Commander's wife goes missing, you know. They'll start looking for me, and all the clues will lead to you.

"You can't have a dead girl if she's missing, now can you? If you want one of your little lackeys to take me out, I have to be in the public eye, otherwise Roan and everyone else will turn to you for the blame."

The Commander sits up calmly, eyes focused on me with checked, burning rage. He leans forward, resting his elbows on his knees.

"You always have to stick your nose in other people's business, don't you? You can't just make this easy."

He leaps forward, flipping the coffee table. It crashes into the chair, bumping the side table. The lamp teeters, threatening to fall.

My father-in-law walks steadily toward me but I hold my ground.

"I should string you up from the rafters right now. Leave a note saying you couldn't take the pressure of being the Commander's wife and after your failure-of-an-open-forum, you just couldn't handle it."

He glances up, looking at the ceiling.

"Roan would never believe that."

"You think I can't have a note written in your script before he gets home? It's not that hard, Jade."

"You'd let him find me like that?"

"He has to get over you at some point, Jade," he comments. "Besides, it's not that hard. It's not like he's watching you die this time."

"You mean like my father had to watch my mother die?"

He reels back as if I slapped him again.

"I'm very aware of what you did, Commander," I inform him. "I know every little detail. She made sure of it. I have proof."

My threat is thin but effective.

"Your mother was in the wrong place at the wrong time and, unfortunately, I couldn't trust her. I tried, don't get me wrong. I gave her every opportunity to work with me, but she had to go and act like you and your father. Your entire family is full of foolish, idealistic people.

"That's not the way the world works, Jade." He sneers.

"My mother wouldn't help you conceal a murder. There's nothing about that scenario that could be considered acceptable. You have been removing your enemies from the game board and making it look like accidents all along—something I assume you learned from your father —and then you tried to pass that along to your son. At least he was smart enough not to fall into your trap."

"He was well on his way before *you* got involved," he seethes. "My father taught me well. He led this country with greatness and I did the same. You may have cut my power short, but Roan is and always will be an extension of the Diamond family. He will act accordingly.

"James Jareau, Asher Montgomery, Elizabeth Donnelly, not even you and my son can take me down. The Diamond family was created and shaped to oversee the Command. *We* are the ones who won the war and protected all of you. *We* are the ones capable of making decisions for you. And *you* will not stop that.

"My father told me time and time again to protect power at all costs, because those who don't have power, die. We watched it before, and we've watched it since. Bad things happen to people who are taken out of power."

He steps forward. Reaching around me, he picks up the lamp on the end table. It crashes to the ground, shattering in large, jagged pieces.

"You took my son from me. I want him back."

"That's *his* choice."

"I know you think that, but it's really not."

A knock sounds at the door. Great, he brought reinforcements.

We both glance toward the sound but the Commander quickly looks back at me.

"You'll hear from me tomorrow," he hisses before retreating to the back door. He closes it quietly so as not to alert the person at the front door.

I could go after him, but what good would that do?

Picking my way around the broken ceramic pieces of the lamp on the floor, I make my way to the front door.

I'm shaking again. This is becoming a habit.

"Who is it?" I call as I look through the small hole to check for guests.

"It's me," Mr. Eroh's voice filters through the closed door.

I throw it open, nearly slamming it into the wall. I try to cover up my distress but he clearly notices it.

"The lamp broke," I motion behind me, hoping he will accept it as a valid excuse.

"How did that happen?" Mr. Eroh mumbles as he steps inside.

"Why are you here?" I ask softly, attempting to keep my voice from trembling.

"You have a very nice house, Jade." He walks into the living room and slowly bends down to start picking up the shattered remnants of the lamp.

I hurry to the kitchen to get a bag to put the broken pieces in and a vacuum to catch the smaller bits. When I return, Mr. Eroh has several pieces resting in his hand as he leans forward to pick up more. He sets them inside the bag when I place it beside him.

"You know, lamps are so easily shattered. They're kind of like life in that way. In some cases, you can put them back together—lamps *and* life—but there will always be those cracks left over. It's easier for people to forget they exist in life than in lamps though, don't you think? Sometimes it's harder to see the cracks in a person."

He sits upright, rocking back onto his heels.

"Come sit with me, Jade." He extends his hand so I can help him up off the floor.

We take a seat on the couch, leaving the rest of the lamp on the floor. He takes a deep breath while studying me.

"He has Sophie, doesn't he?"

My jaw drops.

"He does," Mr. Eroh confirms my reaction. "He has your aunt and he's holding her against you. Why?"

When I don't answer, he squints at me.

"He's trying to hurt you again, isn't he?"

"How do you know about Sophie?" I've never been nervous to ask Mr. Eroh questions before.

"Jade," he looks at me as if I should already know the answer. "Do you honestly think that I believed this would all end after that mess with the secretary? I've been keeping tabs on everyone. Sophie hasn't been around for weeks. She doesn't usually check in often, but some of us have noticed her absence."

"I've seen her," I offer, pulling my knee up to my chest. "She's alive."

"But the Commander is threatening her. I'm going to guess your little plan for the garden was his doing too, wasn't it?"

I nod miserably.

"How long has this been going on?"

"Since they opened the offices in the library." My fingers run the length of my leg nervously.

"I see," he nods. "And how does your father fit in with all of this."

"I snuck into the Diamonds' house today. The Commander told him he has Sophie. He's supposed to make it look like he and I are trying to get power but he doesn't know that the Commander has threatened me too. He told Dad that I was making bad choices and he was just pushing it to be worse."

"Your father knows. Probably not the extent of it, but Robert Diamond doesn't have a piece on the game board without playing it from all angles."

"I slapped him."

"You *what*?" Mr. Eroh's face goes white.

I bite my lip, letting my eyes travel to the carpet until my gaze reaches the lamp pieces. I shouldn't have struck him—it's only going to make things worse.

"We can't tell the others," I finally say. "*You're* not even supposed to know."

"I figured it out on my own. The Commander doesn't give me enough credit. He also doesn't know that I have just as many spies as *he* does running around this country." He finally takes credit for his work. I *knew* he had more people working for him than he let on.

"I'm supposed to die in two weeks."

"That gives us two weeks to find Sophie and end this," he retorts. "I don't like that you've given up so easily, Jade. I know you're trying to protect people, but—"

"He has people inside my father's office," I interject sadly. "He has a group of them that he's promised power to if they help with this. If I don't cooperate, they're in a position to hurt Dad and Sophie. Probably even you and Lucas, to be honest."

"Don't you worry about us, Jade."

"He has a new wife picked out for Roan," I add sadly. "He introduced them already."

"You're not being replaced, Jade," he says sharply. "Look at me. You keep acting like you're playing along. Let me work on finding Sophie. I'll handle your father and we'll tell Roan and Lucas as soon as we can."

"I don't think we should tell them," I counter. "You know those two will charge in and try to fix things. Roan can't hide anything from his father and Lucas will just end up getting himself hurt again. That's the last thing we need."

"So you want to keep it to just your father and me? Is that what you're saying?"

"The three of us are already involved. This is going to come down on us one way or another. Besides, the people need someone to turn to when this is all over. If we can protect Roan and Lucas, at least they can still lead the country."

"All right. If that's what you want." He rubs his chin. "Jade, you don't have to die for this any more than you did the last time. Let us help you. We'll find Sophie and we'll find a way to expose Robert."

"He's been moving her," I confess, realizing I hadn't mentioned that fact yet. "She was at the site of the explosion the Commander faked when I saw her and I know today she was near the Commander's house."

"How do you know that?"

"The Commander told me. He was here when you knocked."

Mr. Eroh's eyes grow wide as he realizes he saved me. His eyes dart to the shattered lamp.

"On that note, you should be suspicious of anything written in my hand writing from now on."

He nods.

We spend the rest of the morning and afternoon developing a plan.

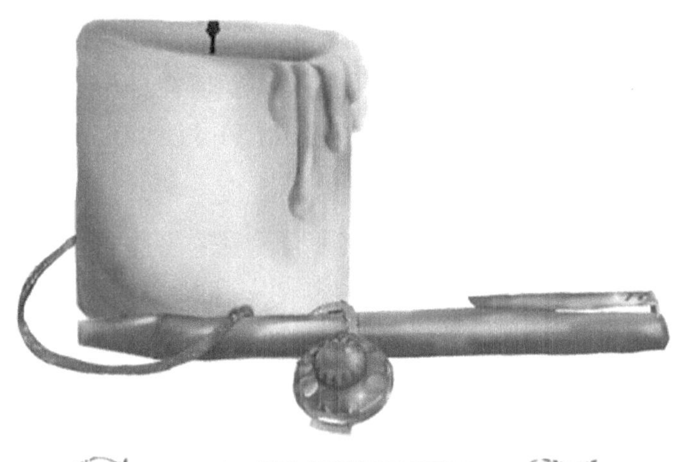

CHAPTER 21
JADE

 tug on the drawer of my desk. It bangs loudly, refusing to open. Angling it, I try again, hoping to catch the track at the right angle so that it will slide open easily. Wiggling it does no good.

"Jade," Janine says, standing in the doorway. "I have those papers for you."

She looks calmer than she does most days. Her hair is swept back, opening up her face whereas she usually hides behind her locks—something I myself have been known to do.

"There's a list of seeds available to us on top." She

hands them to me. "Also, my sister, Marcy, would like to volunteer to oversee the schedule of one of the gardens."

She sounds like she has rehearsed that last bit.

"That's very kind of her, Janine. I'll keep that in mind, thank you."

She retreats, venturing back to her desk. I return to my drawer trying to open it, but the top page of the papers our secretary handed me catches my eye.

Janine's research is impeccable and I spend the next hour sifting through all of her notes. If I plan this strategically, Roan will be able to work around the Commander's plans later on.

When I finally set the paperwork aside, I'm faced with the formidable challenge of opening the top drawer of my desk. After a great battle, it finally pops open with a loud thud. I catch it before it drops out entirely.

Reaching back, I find a few things have been jammed in the wheel on the tracks of the drawer. I fish them out, ripping one in the process. I keep my desk drawers immaculate—unlike my drawers at home—which leaves me confused as to how it could have shifted so much the last time I closed it.

I riffle through the bent papers I pulled out until I come to one in my father's handwriting. It's a letter to me, detailing part of a plan to take over control of the Command. Several more follow, the last of which is in my writing detailing a response to his last letter.

I didn't write this and I know my father didn't write the others.

The Commander had them put here.

"Jade?" Janine's voice echoes like an explosion around the room, making me jump. I hurriedly throw the papers back in the drawer and slam it shut. "Oh, I'm sorry."

She takes a step back, retreating from my movements.

"No, it's okay, Janine. You just frightened me, that's all. What is it?"

"Your father sent a message over. He said he needed to move your meeting up."

I was planning on seeing my father today, but he didn't know that. Now that I've seen those letters, I'm not even sure if it's from him or the Commander. Either way, I have to go.

"Thank you," I smile brightly as I take the note from her. I look for some kind of clue about whom it's really from, but find nothing.

I gather my things to leave, but can't get the drawer open once again. After several minutes of fighting with it, I resign myself to leaving them locked away until later. I've seen them and can report back to my father and Mr. Eroh without having them in hand.

"Roan," I say in his doorway. "I have a meeting to go to, I'll see you at home later."

"Okay," he replies quickly. He's awfully eager to see me go…or maybe he's just busy.

"Okay," I repeat as I turn to go. I say goodbye to Janine —who may or may not be working with the Commander at this point, since I don't know how the letters got into my desk—and scurry out the door.

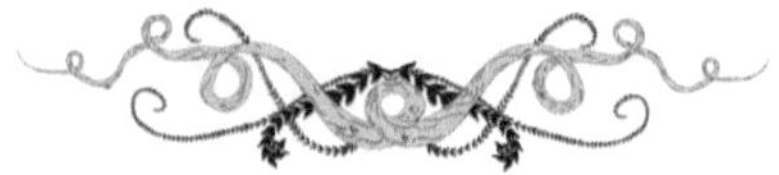

"So you *didn't* send that note?" I clarify.

"No," my father shakes his head.

"But you're both here." My brow furrows just enough that my eyebrows hover in my field of vision. "Do you think he knew and set this up?"

"I'm not sure," Mr. Eroh replies, leaning forward in his chair. "I myself didn't know I was coming over until right before I left so I doubt that. By the time he had a note created and sent over, I assume he had planned it just for the two of you."

"What are we supposed to do now?"

"He's setting us both up. He wants us to take the fall for trying to take over power of the Command," my father muses. "This meeting only lends itself to that scenario, but we're here now so we might as well make the best of it."

"Any sign of Sophie yet?" I direct my question to Mr. Eroh.

"I was just telling your father before you came in that we haven't located her yet. I have my people on it though. If anyone can find her, it's them." He nods, proud of his contacts.

I take a seat next to Mr. Eroh, crossing my legs as I lean to the side. My father's office feels inviting, yet gives me an overwhelming sense of strength. I wish I had brought my mother's letters along with me to return to my father, but I didn't know I would be making the trip across town today.

"What are we going to do once we locate Sophie?" I inquire, looking to my father for an answer.

"I think it depends on where we find her and how quickly we can move," he muses. "We need to get her back safely without endangering anyone else."

"After that, though. What are we going to do about the Commander?"

"I think we need to expose him," Mr. Eroh chimes in on the conversation.

"Won't that get us in trouble for covering up Daniella's death?" I whisper despite the door being closed.

"Isn't it better to remove him from power?" Mr. Eroh questions.

"We need to be aware of the state of the country once

they find out. They may no longer trust Roan to lead. I have faith that it won't turn into a riot, but I'm not sure how safe it will be for us here once that information gets out. Truthfully, what reasons would they have to trust us?" My father reminds us. "I saw the fall out after the rebellion happened. Not everyone settled back into everyday life easily. We might find ourselves in a bad situation."

"They're going to feel like we've betrayed them by keeping the truth from them," I mutter.

"I imagine they will, Jade," my father agrees. "We'll come up with something."

"Maybe *you* should be in charge, Mr. Eroh," I suggest. "You didn't have anything to do with the cover-up."

"Just every other one in this country," he chuckles as my father smirks. At least we're finding the humor in this. "Now that we know, we can be strategic about this."

"And Jade doesn't have to do this alone." My father looks like he wants to leap over the desk and hug me. "I understand we're not telling Roan?"

"I think we should protect Roan and Lucas from this," I respond. "Especially since it's one less thing for them to be blamed for being secretive about later when this all comes to light."

We spend the next hour discussing locations to search for Sophie and work on ways to keep the country from starting another uprising when they learn about what the Commander has been doing.

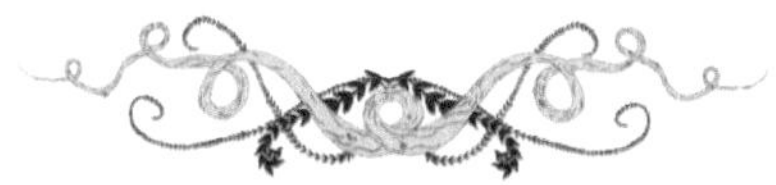

I take a deep breath. Despite being prepared, I don't want to do this.

The wind created when I opened the door jostles a small set of chimes across the room, making them tingle as they dance at the end of their strings.

"Hello," Erica greets me from behind her counter, face in a book. Her eyebrow quirks up when she looks up and sees me. "Oh, hello, Jade."

Her greeting is friendly enough but I can tell she wants to talk to me.

"Hello," I smile back at her. "May I set this down while I look around?"

I lift my bag up slightly. She nods, allowing me to step forward and set it on her counter. The top conveniently flips open, allowing Erica access to the note Mr. Eroh has instructed I give her.

I meander around the store as I attempt to hold my breath. Shallow breathing only serves to make me light headed as I brave the scented candles I'm so allergic to.

I ignore her when she sucks in a deep breath across the room.

"Anything in particular you're looking for?" she asks.

"I was hoping to find some unscented candles. I'm planning a fancy dinner for my husband, but I'm allergic."

"Of course. I have some in the back. Why don't you come pick a few out?" Erica turns, walking into the back room.

I skirt the counter and follow her back. The room is dimly lit. Shelves line every wall. The room is strongly scented, much more noticeably than the sales room.

"Apologies," Erica mumbles. "This is where I make my candles."

The door swings shut behind us. We make our way past thermometers and large steel vats. Jars line one wall, the rounded glass corners reflecting the little light in the room. Erica flips a switch to turn on another light.

"Watch the pouring pitchers, please."

I tuck my elbow in as I slip around the table. My throat burns from the mixture of scents swirling around the room, engulfing everything.

"I think there's some back here," she motions me further into the room.

When we reach the back wall, she turns to me, quietly placing a hand on a candle.

"I knew Sophie was missing," she says bluntly. Erica hands me a candle. "You should have told me."

"I didn't tell anyone," I reply as she hands me a second glass jar with a cream colored candle in it. I'd have to trust her that they were unscented because in a room this saturated with chemically produced scents, I can barely think, let alone discern if something is scented.

"It says I can't tell Lucas," she comments, piling more candles into my arms. The glass jars are heavy and I worry I won't be able to balance them now that my equilibrium is being tested from all of the scents in the room. I blink, trying to keep my focus.

"Come on," she says, noticing me sway. She points to a large container of flakes on the counter. "That's my wax. I use that to make the candles."

Next to it sits a box full of wicks. Clothespins lay scattered on the table next to an arrangement of glass jars and lids.

The main room is a relief, even though it's still enough to make me feel like waves from the lake are running over my body. I bite down, clamping my jaw together to stay focused until I can escape.

"Do you have your card?" she asks. It takes me a moment to realize she's asking for the card she once gave me to earn free candles.

"Oh."

She totals my purchase. She handed me so many that I don't know what I'm going to do with all of them. My total is significantly less than I expected it to be, but I accept it and place as many of the candles in my bag as I can fit before taking a paper bag for the rest. My shoulders ache by the time I reach the house.

I rub the muscles in my shoulder with one hand as I pull the candles out of the bag with the other. My fingers catch the metal chain of Sophie's necklace around my collarbone making it twist under my thumb.

Inside the paper bag, I discover Erica added something extra.

CHAPTER 22

ROAN

"**S**he's gone," I lean into my old office where Lucas sits behind my old desk.

He leaps to his feet, pushing his chair back. I turn to the lobby to get Janine's attention.

"Janine, there's a pile of papers on my desk. Would you be able to take them downstairs to file, please?" I point toward my office.

"Yes, sir." She promptly stops what she was working on and scurries to my office. I smile and wave when she pops back out, turning on her heels to go to the filing room.

"That will keep her busy for at least an hour."

"That pile was so big she could barely carry it, Roan. Don't you think you should have helped?" Lucas scolds.

"Probably, but we really don't have a lot of time to waste," I chide, leading the way to Jade's office. "I told you something was up."

"Yeah, I noticed," Lucas replies, closing the door behind us. "I'd like to say I take issue with going through Jade's office, but I really don't at this point."

"Noted," I say, going straight for her desk.

Lucas steps across the room, scanning her bookshelves. Jade doesn't have much in her office, which will save us a lot of trouble as we search, but I make a note to force her to personalize it the way she once forced me to update my own workspace.

"I really don't know why she has these books," Lucas mumbles. "None of these even apply to her work here."

"I think they're more for show. She's gone out of her way not to have any personal touches here."

"I noticed that too," Lucas sighs, pulling more books off the shelf to check behind them and inside the pages.

"The lamp was broken, Lucas. In all the time that I've known her, I've never even seen her trip, much less do something like accidentally knock a lamp over." I shuffle through the papers on top of her desk before moving on to the right-hand drawers.

"I saw her fall once. It was the most graceful thing I've

ever seen. Her leg kicked out in front of her and she glided down on one knee. She was holding a tray and it never even waivered. She just slid down, held onto the tray with both hands, and then without ever letting go, she rocked forward and stood back up before anyone else even had time to notice. She walked away completely unfazed," he pauses. "I sincerely doubt we're going to find anything here. Jade has always been good about hiding things. I doubt she'll just leave a clue around in her office."

I shuffle through the desk drawers, not finding anything on the right side. I shift to the left as Lucas starts checking around the furniture.

"She's hiding something," I say, struggling with her top drawer. "You and I both know something isn't right here."

"I agree—she's keeping something from us."

Lucas shuffles around the couch, pushing his hands between the cushions. When he gives up, he moves on to the closet. It creeks just enough to be noticeable.

"We should fix this for her later," he mumbles.

I throw my weight into opening the drawer, moving the entire desk toward me several inches.

"What are you doing?" Lucas lectures, turning to see why I'm knocking things over.

"It won't open," I inform him.

"Is it locked?" he asks, coming over to investigate.

"It doesn't have a lock. It must be jammed."

"Let me see," Lucas gets down on the floor, waving me away.

He fumbles with the drawer, mumbling under his breath.

"See?" I roll my eyes at him unceremoniously.

"This is ridiculous, what did she do?"

"It's probably papers or something," I respond, taking another turn at the drawer.

After a few minutes, we manage to work the drawer open enough to reach in and move some of the papers around. It finally pops open, nearly dropping into our laps. We scramble to catch it.

"All right, what's in here?" Lucas murmurs as he hands me half the papers.

I start to shuffle through them.

"Nope, I have the right pile," he says immediately.

I set my stack of papers down, not having found anything valuable anyway, and lean over to read.

"I don't understand, what is this?"

"It's from James." Lucas doesn't stop bouncing his head back and forth as he reads the lines on the page. "But I'm willing to bet this doesn't have anything to do with James Jareau at all."

"What do you mean?"

"You haven't spent a lot of time with James, but I have. This is his hand writing but there's no way he wrote this."

I skim the page Lucas is still holding.

"These are plans to take over the Command…" my voice trails off.

I looked down at the papers I set down a moment ago. None of them are connected. Lucas hands me the bottom of his stack.

More pages from James detail out the take over of the Command, giving specific points of how Lucas and I will be manipulated, what he plans on doing to restrict power, and how he plans to undo my father's work.

I gasp when I see the last page.

"What?" Lucas shifts to see.

"It's Jade's writing," I say, tipping the paper toward him.

He snatches it from my hands to examine it.

"How is this possible?"

"Well Jade certainly isn't involved," I reply. "Why does she have these?"

"This doesn't make any sense. There's no reason for these to exist unless someone is trying to set Jade and James up."

"Who would want to do….oh," I realize I don't need to finish asking that question. "How could he possibly think this is a good idea? Or that we wouldn't find out?"

"Your father is a deranged man," Lucas replies. "He's probably trying to get back at Jade for foiling his last plan."

"Why didn't Jade tell us about these?"

"She would have," Lucas gathers the papers up, "*Unless* he has some kind of leverage preventing it. Where did Jade just run off to?"

"A meeting with her father." My eyes roam around the room, searching for an answer it will not offer me.

"Now why is she meeting with James?" Lucas puts the papers back in the drawer. "Maybe she's telling him about the papers?"

"Why are you putting them back?" I ask.

Lucas turns to me.

"She can't know that we know. No one can. We have to figure out what Robert is holding over her first. We can't watch her if she knows that we are aware of what is going on."

"Good point." I wait for him to close the drawer. "Will she be suspicious when the drawer opens normally?"

"We really can't jam that thing again," Lucas shakes his head. "Chances are that she doesn't even know it was stuck."

"Let's hope."

"Now that we know your father is involved, maybe we can shed a little light on everything else that has been going on around here," Lucas adds.

"The lamp," I breathe. "You don't think that had anything to do with him, do you?"

"Do I think your father caused Jade to break a lamp? Yes, yes I do, Roan."

"Mr. Eroh was at the house yesterday. He's never been to our house. Do you think he knows what's going on too?"

"Amos Eroh knows *everything*. I don't think that's even a question," Lucas stares at me blankly before turning toward the door.

He touches the handle quietly, opening the door just enough to check to make sure no one is in the lobby. He steps back, opening the door into the room.

"Why does everyone know but us?"

"I don't know why they kept us in the dark, but there must be a reason. I'll reach out to some of my contacts and see what they know."

Lucas steps into the lobby.

I really need to find my own contacts.

"So where do we go from here?" I question.

"We go back to our offices. You make sure you handle the stuff here and I'll use this afternoon to see what I can find out. Jade will be gone all day, so we'll make our plan before we leave, but chances are that you're going to have to try to get some information from your father without him realizing what you're doing."

Great. The last thing I want to do is go back to my parents' house and deal with my father. That might be a mission for another day. At least Maybelle is on my side.

It might be necessary to bring her in on all of this if my father really is up to his old tricks.

We split up, going toward our separate offices just as Janine wanders back into the lobby.

"Are you all done, Janine?" I stop, turning to face her.

"No, sir," she replies. "I just had a question. It looks like this file is mislabeled."

When a quick glance confirms she is correct, I give her the accurate information and send her back to continue her work.

"That could have been a disaster," Lucas comments, reappearing in his doorway. He leans one shoulder casually against the frame, his foot kicked across the other, only his toe touching the ground.

It amazes me how effortless Lucas makes life look. I sincerely doubt he feels like it's effortless, knowing how hard he works to preserve this image, but I'm still jealous of how flawlessly he plays his part without ever flinching.

"You don't think she works for my father, do you?"

"I think we need to be suspicious of everyone at this point."

"Great," I mutter. "That's just what I wanted to hear."

Jade doesn't suspect anything when she returns to the office. Lucas and I keep our heads down, waiting for her to notice the drawer but she doesn't say anything.

By the time we leave, we feel secure that we got away with our unscheduled search of her office—I'll apologize when all is said and done—but for now, I'd rather keep her out of harm's way.

The evening passes quickly and it isn't long before I drop her at her door and say good night.

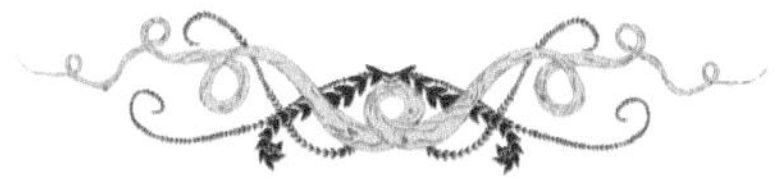

Morning comes with a hint of a pink sunrise. Sharp golden angles fill the floor of my room as I get ready for work courtesy of my curtains.

I finish the knot in my tie and meet Jade in the living room.

"Ready?" I ask as I offer her my arm.

She gives me a small smile and slips her hand around my elbow—I can see her trying to protect me so clearly now as she tries to draw a line between us. Distance may be *her* friend, but it isn't mine.

I take my free hand and pull hers away from my elbow. Withdrawing my arm, I wrap myself around her, pulling her close to my side. She can't do anything to stop me once we're outside in public.

I suppress my smirk as I hold her close the entire way to the office. Jade pulls away as soon as we get inside, rushing to her own space.

"How quaint," Lucas ribs me.

"You saw how she pulled away." I lift my bag over my head, temporarily setting it on Janine's empty desk. "She doesn't know that I know, but I'm not letting her get away with that."

"Good. You shouldn't," Lucas agrees.

We go our separate ways, settling into our work for the day.

"Janine, where have you been?" I ask as kindly as possible an hour later.

"Jade had left some papers for me to deliver on my desk this morning. I went right out," she answers as she sets down her clutch.

"What papers?" I ask skeptically.

"I'm not sure, sir. I didn't read them; I just delivered them. I figured it was none of my business. There's a copy in your box but it might be toward the bottom of the pile."

I rush back to my office, calling a thank you over my shoulder.

Inside my office, I discover a packet of papers with Jade's signature on them. The papers detail a number of new proposals—all, I assume, created by my father—that will infuriate the community.

"Janine, who were these sent to?"

"Most of the politicians. I gave most of them to our delivery people, but I took the local ones myself."

"Thank you," I mumble, turning to my friend's office.

I throw the pile of papers on his desk.

"Read those," I say shortly. "I'm going to my father's house. I need to see what Maybelle knows. This is getting ridiculous. And watch Jade while I'm gone."

I leave before he has a chance to answer me.

Once I reach my old house, I realize I should slow down. I can't just march in for my father to see me. I slip around back, avoiding the guards in the front.

Once inside, I look for Maybelle. There's no avoiding telling her now. She needs to know the man she works for. I don't want her in this situation any longer than she needs to be. If I have to hire her on as my personal secretary in the Command Building, I will. Maybe I could even hire her on as Jade's assistant once this is all over.

Her shoes click against the floor behind me as I stand in the kitchen.

"We need to talk."

"Roan?" My mother's voice greets me instead of Maybelle's.

"Mom?"

"What are you doing here?" she asks as I turn. My

mother shakes her head. "Never mind, we need to talk. Come with me."

Without a choice, I follow behind her all the way to my old room.

"Your father isn't home, but I know what's going on," she begins.

"What do you mean?" I try to gauge how much she knows.

"Jade was here two days ago spying on your father and James Jareau. I caught her and managed to hide her before your father found her."

"Why was James here?"

"I don't know," she huffs. Her hands make their way to her hips. "I don't know why any of this is happening. You two have kept me in the dark this whole time."

"Mom, I—"

"No," she cuts me off. "It doesn't matter. All I know is that Jade is supposed to die and I can't let that happen because it would crush you."

My heart feels like it has hit the floor, bounced back up, and slammed into the floor again. Jade's impending death has a way of doing that to my internal organs.

"I'm not going to let her die."

I will publicly expose my father and take whatever punishment the people see fit for lying to them about Daniella's death before I let anyone hurt Jade again.

"I'm aware," she looks at me in dismay. "I don't know

how to stop this. I tried to talk to your father yesterday but he wouldn't say anything."

"Mom," I whisper. "We can't let him hurt her."

She sighs, unsure of what to do with herself as tears spring to my eyes.

Before she can decide if she should try to hug me or not, Maybelle opens the door and enters with the vacuum, gasping when she sees us.

"Roan?" her voice is high-pitched.

"Come in, Maybelle." I wave her into the room as my mother shoots me an incredulous look. "You need to know too."

My mother shakes her head vehemently.

"She already knows something is going on. We have to tell her so she can make her own choices."

Maybelle blanches. When she realizes that my eyes are still watery from the near-tears, she promptly takes a place by my side, staring my mother down. If forced to choose, Maybelle will publicly align herself with *me* over my family.

"What is going on?" Maybelle asks, staring at her boss.

"Maybelle," I say softly. She turns to look at me. "My father has spent many years being very angry at James Jareau."

Maybelle cringes at his name.

"James did nothing wrong but my father wanted to punish him, which is why I was supposed to marry Jade but I'm pretty sure you knew that," I explain. "He tried to hurt Jade a few months ago. We managed to stop him but now he's going after her again. I don't know what he's holding over her, but it's bad enough that she's willing to sacrifice herself—*again*—to appease him and stop whatever he is planning."

Maybelle quietly takes my hand as I speak. Miraculously, she manages to hold her expressions still. I imagine she's used that trick many times over the years.

"Who poisoned you, Roan?" she finally asks, blinking.

My mother makes a strangled noise.

"I knew he was trying to hurt Jade so I took the poison to prevent her from taking it," I admit.

Maybelle looks to my mother. Something passes between the women—an unspoken agreement—before they look back at me.

"What do you need us to do?" Maybelle asks.

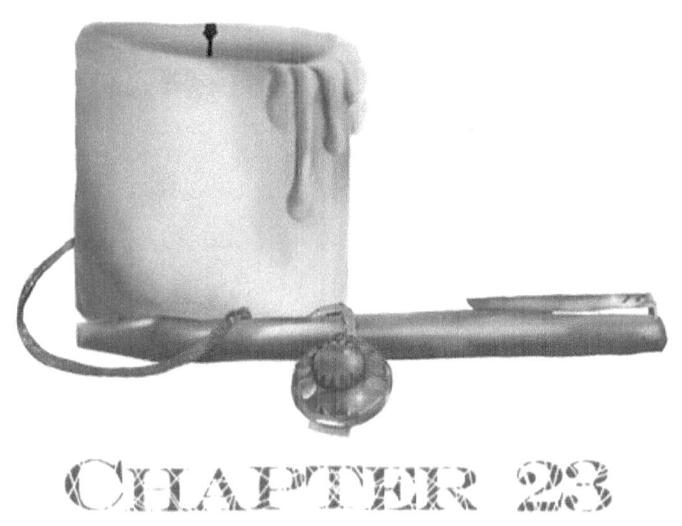

CHAPTER 23

JADE

Roan is oblivious to the tension mounting in the Command. Everywhere I go, I see people scowling at me.

The last day of the workweek flies by as I stay chained to my desk, trying to avoid the outside world. I have to play the part until we can find Sophie, but so far we haven't had any luck.

Without any word from my father or Mr. Eroh, all I can do is wait.

Roan stays unnervingly close to me until I say good-night to him.

Saturday morning greets me with a slight temperature drop. I brave the backyard anyway with a blanket wrapped around my shoulders.

I have the smallest bit of hope that I might actually survive this.

Eventually Roan joins me, breakfast tray in hand. He curls up against me as he hands me the tray. It rests in my lap and Roan runs the tip of his nose against my neck making me flinch.

Now is not the time for kissing.

Maybe soon though.

I manage to talk him into focusing on breakfast. He reluctantly gives in, giving me a bit of space on the stone bench. Roan plays with the fringe on the blanket wrapped around my shoulders, staring wistfully at me.

Hope is an interesting thing. It tricks perfectly rational people into believing the insane is possible. Can I really be happy? Can I actually survive? Will I get to do this again and this time not turn him away?

Hope is the one thing I can't afford to linger on now.

Lucas arrives before long. We take the day to plan out the open forum. Surprisingly, neither of them argues too forcefully about the plans for the community garden.

The open forum is a lynch mob. Documents had been spread to the politicians detailing proposals the Commander has constructed to frame me. Roan and Lucas have trouble keeping the crowd at bay. Both of them step between the group and me to protect me from their words.

It's the first time I'm hearing of these plans but I try to play along and not act surprised.

Copies of some of the papers fly in the air, none close enough for me to catch and read. My father shifts in his seat, ready to defend me should someone come at me.

Suddenly I feel like I'm in my black dress again, about to drink the Commander's poison. Just like that day, my father, Roan, and Lucas all work to stop me from accepting my fate.

Lucas shuts the meeting down when one of the Commander's minions stands in the back and accuses my father and I of being in on it together. He stirs the people up, explaining how James Jareau and his daughter have clearly infiltrated the Command in order to take over leadership.

"Enough!" Lucas shouts. "We will investigate this matter. Go home. We'll meet with you all next week."

His furry finally forces people to their feet. Annie and Mr. Eroh assist in clearing out the room and keeping civility. People argue both for and against my father and I.

"We'll clear your names," Roan murmurs as the people walk out. "It's all going to be okay."

"We may have a problem," Mr. Zuckerman ambles up to us. "I just heard a number of people say that they spoke with your father yesterday."

"What do you mean?" Roan asks. "Why?"

"Apparently several people met with your father," he explains. "They said he tried to calm them down, but I think we all know what that means."

He said he would do this.

"I'm sure Robert is using the situation to his advantage," my father jumps in. "Clearly Jade and I aren't trying to take control of the Command, but we'll just have to convince the people that we don't intend to take anything away from them.

"I think perhaps it would be best for us to all go home tonight and work on this tomorrow," he concludes.

"I think that's wise," Mr. Eroh jumps in, knowing the plan is to distance Roan and Lucas from this.

"Roan, take Jade home," my father instructs. He casts a worried glance at me—we hadn't anticipated things getting this volatile this quickly.

"Yes, sir," Roan responds, guiding me toward the door. I dig my heels in for a moment, wanting to stay, but I catch Mr. Eroh flick his wrist at me to wave me off—there's a plan in motion.

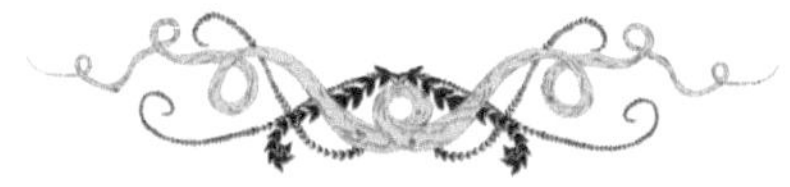

"We know," Lucas confronts me.

"Don't deny it, Jade," Roan crosses his arms to match Lucas as we stand in our living room. "Why have you been keeping this from us?"

Warmth spreads through my body, mixed with tension and regret. My cheeks blaze, but there's nothing I can do.

"I talked to my mother," Roan admits.

My jaw falls open.

"But—"

"She told me everything," Roan informs me. "Maybelle knows too. My father had your father at my house the other day."

"Yes," I confirm.

"Who else knows?" Lucas asks.

"Mr. Eroh and some of his people." I take a breath. "Erica figured it out too. I'm pretty sure Annie has a decent idea too."

"*Erica* knows?" Lucas nearly shouts before lowering his voice to a whisper as he talks to himself. "She didn't say anything to me."

"Wait, all of those people knew and you thought *we* wouldn't figure it out?" Roan asks in horror.

He makes a valid point.

"I was trying to protect you," I protest, hoping for a little mercy at my trial by peers.

"What does he have on you? Is he threatening your father again?" Roan asks.

I twist my fingers.

"Not *what. Who*," I correct. "He has Sophie. I've seen her. My father has too."

"Where is she?" Lucas looks like he's been punched in the stomach.

"We don't know. We're trying to locate her."

Roan takes my hand and guides me to the couch.

"What do we need to know?" he asks kindly.

"You don't need to know anything," I reply. "You two need to stay out of this. The Commander is working to turn everyone in the Command against me and if you get caught up in this, you won't be able to pull everything back together. Let us handle Sophie and you two handle the country."

"I don't like this," Lucas replies.

"Neither do I," Roan protests.

"Stop," I say, holding a hand up. "Listen to me. We have my dad, Mr. Eroh, and his entire team working to find Sophie. We're playing along with your father's games for now, but if it takes awhile to find Sophie, the people still need to be able to look to someone who isn't caught up in this. If they believe my father and I are trying to take over, and they think you're a part of it, we'll never get their trust back."

"Those papers?" Lucas asks.

"Forged. I don't know how he did it, but he matched our handwriting."

"The garden disaster?" Roan inquires running his finger over my knuckles as he continues to hold my hand.

"The Commander…though I like the overall idea."

"How long has this been going on?"

I pause. I don't want to answer but know there's no way of avoiding it.

"Since the offices opened up in the old library," I reply. I swing to face Lucas. "The day you moved in, the Commander cornered me in your office and gave me Sophie's necklace."

Both men suck in a breath.

"Dad and Mr. Eroh only just found out last week."

"We all knew something was up at the open forum meeting where you lost your mind and tried to send us back to the pre-war cast system," Lucas mumbles, running his hands through his hair.

"Can you both just trust me on this?" I beg. "We need you to focus on the *country* so *we* can focus on Sophie. Your father can't win now—we all know what's going on

—so we need to play the game, find Sophie and then take your father down."

My leg starts to twitch under our hands. Roan notices and scoots closer to me.

"I'm assuming the broken lamp has to do with all of this?" he asks quietly.

"He was here."

"What?" they both demand at the same time. Lucas jumps out of his chair and Roan hovers just above the cushion, refusing to leave my side.

When he relaxes back onto the couch, I continue.

"He was here. One of the guards saw me when I snuck into your parents' house while he was with my father. He came to find me and threaten me after."

"Threaten how?"

"With my father," I look down, trying to avoid his gaze.

"And?" Roan presses.

"And with the rafters," I whisper.

"The rafters?" Roan echoes quizzically.

"He was going to string her up, Roan. He threatened to hang her," Lucas supplies.

Roan's grip on my hand tightens so much that I yelp. It snaps him out of it. He shakes his head before gathering both of my hands in his.

"Jade," he whispers.

"I'm fine. He broke the lamp, that's all. Mr. Eroh arrived and scared him off."

"Amos Eroh saves the day again," Lucas says with a rueful smile. "That man has a gift."

"So maybe we could let him work his magic and you two can stay out of this," I suggest a little too harshly. "I'd rather not see you die, Lucas."

"Robert Diamond hasn't been able to kill me yet, Jade," Lucas boasts, giving me the smarmiest grin I've ever seen.

I roll my eyes dramatically, biting back a smirk.

"So if we can't help save you and Sophie, what are we supposed to do? We're not just going to sit around and wait," Lucas presses.

"We're going to come up with a plan to take down my father once and for all," Roan says diplomatically. "As soon as they find Sophie, my father goes on trial."

"Preferably without *us* burning as well," I add. I look away and blink a few times before Roan realizes how overwhelmed I am.

"But that's something we can work on tomorrow," Roan murmurs. "I think Jade could use some rest right now. Tomorrow, Lucas and I will start putting a case together for the trial and you can go back to Sophie-hunting…and by that I mean, you will wait for Mr. Eroh's people to find her while you're safely within twenty feet of me at all times."

I give him a patronizing look, but he doesn't care.

Lucas twitches at the idea of being thrown out, but he complies.

"Whatever you need," he kneels down in front of me and takes my hand as Roan towers over us, waiting to walk him to the door, "we are here for you. You and Sophie and even your dad will be all right. I promise."

He watches me for a moment before standing back up.

"Thank you, Lucas. Your loyalty means the world to me."

I watch the two men walk to the door as I sink back against the back of the couch. Exhaustion waves over me.

"Are you okay?" Roan asks, approaching me gently.

"I don't know, Roan. He has Sophie. I've been searching for weeks."

"You were doing it on your own. Now you have a team of people helping you." He picks up my hand and kisses it. "And the best news is that you don't have to keep up this silly act of trying to pull away from me."

He grins at me.

"Roan Diamond, my life is falling apart and all you can think about is kissing me?" I playfully chide.

"Jade Jareau Diamond...yes," he teases back.

"You, sir, need to prioritize better," I remark, pulling my hand away.

"And you, my wife, need to eat something so that you stop shaking."

I look down and realize my legs are bouncing up and down again. He reaches out his hand to pull me up.

"By the way, Marcy—that girl you met at the forum? She's supposed to be your new wife."

Roan nearly slams into the wall as he turns to look at me in shock. I smile and prod him to keep moving toward the kitchen.

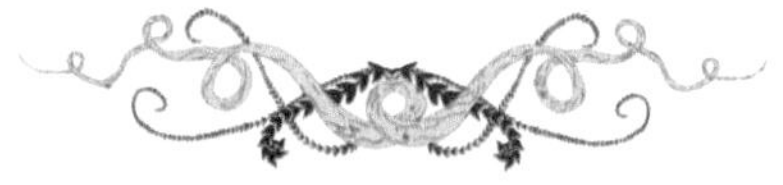

I'm up early the next day. Sleep was elusive as I poured over ideas to get through the outcry at the open forum. The only thing I was sure of was that I needed to see my father and Mr. Eroh.

I inform Roan where I'm going and slip out. The streets are mostly empty as I make my way to my side of town.

Erica stands in the doorway of the candle shop putting up her open sign. She looks at me for a long time before nodding once. Tucking her hair behind her ear, she turns away from me.

Annie catches me on my way through town as she is

returning form her early morning deliveries. She waves me inside.

"You want to tell me what that was about yesterday?"

"You know I can't do that," I mumble, not wanting to talk about the open forum.

"I *knew* it," she scowls. "Fine. Who do I need to talk to? Eroh? Lucas?"

"You don't need to get involved this time, Annie," I protest, hoping to keep her safe.

"You don't get a say in this," she glares at me. She means well.

People start crowding into the bakery for their breakfast. They all stop talking when they see me.

"Time to go, honey," Annie grabs the nearest tray of scones and dumps them into a bag as she shoves me out the door.

She blocks a few annoyed glares sent in my direction, welcoming her patrons while clearly putting herself between them and me.

Mr. Eroh's shop is probably the safer decision at the moment, especially if people believe the accusations about the Jareaus. I duck inside the shop without checking.

Mr. Eroh nods to the back room and continues helping someone I don't recognize. I pace in the darkly lit room, paper bag still in hand. Minutes pass before Mr. Eroh finally enters.

"This doesn't seem like the best call, Jade."

"I realize that now," I purse my lips. "Have we found anything out about Sophie yet?"

"Not yet, I'm afraid." His lips pull back in a tight line. "We're still looking. I got my hands on some of the proposals though. Let me go get them."

I look around for the chairs we keep in the back. Dragging them out, I situate them near the light Mr. Eroh flipped on when he entered.

"Roan and Lucas know. Alice told them and apparently they snooped in my desk at the office and found the fake notes."

"They're staying out of it?" Mr. Eroh inquires, crossing his ankles as he sits.

"They've agreed to work on bringing the Commander down while we locate Sophie."

"Good," he nods. "I know you were worried about them."

"I just came from Annie's," I explain the scene I just left.

"Hmm. I was worried about that. Perhaps it's best for you to stay at home for a while. I don't like you walking around on your own."

"Why, you can't follow me around with a cart all day, every day?" I joke, thinking back to the time he prevented a fake mugging designed to end in my accidental murder.

He laughs.

"Not if you want me to locate your aunt. You know," Mr. Eroh pauses. "I trained your aunt too. Right after your mother died. Sophie and your father saw the writing on the wall and came up with a plan to separate you."

"It makes sense that you were the one to train her."

"It wasn't just me, dear, but I had a hand in it." He reaches over to pat my leg. "She'll be fine."

I pray he's right.

"Now, my dear Jade, it's time for one more lesson and a little more talk about how to use those rumors and comments from the bakery to our advantage...and the Commander's downfall."

He leans forward and grins at me—my studies under his watchful eye continue.

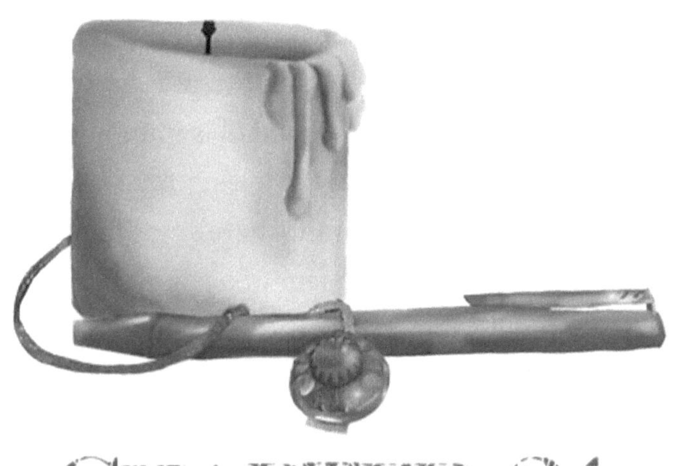

CHAPTER 24
JADE

hroughout the course of my life, pieces of paper have changed the direction of my fate. The letters from my mother, so carefully scripted out for me, helped to rescue me from my husband when he planned to kill me. Pages in books saved me my entire childhood when I was isolated away from the world to prevent it from being hurt simply by being connected to me. Papers from the Commander, shoved carelessly in a drawer sealed my fate as a traitor just days ago.

Now a note—one simple piece of cream colored, linen textured paper—is changing my life once again. Sophie is alive and we know where she is.

A simple sketch in the bottom right-hand corner of the hair comb Mr. Eroh once gave me is enough to confirm the source is true. Sophie really is within our grasp and the Commander's downfall is imminent.

I hold the paper in my hand, letting my skin soak up the texture. I memorize it until there's nothing more to know about this simple fragment of a page.

When I finally stand up, I tuck the note away in my bag and make my way to my husband's office.

"We found her."

He looks up from his paperwork.

"Where?"

"I don't know. The rescue is tomorrow," I inform him.

"That makes sense since it's going to be dark soon."

I don't know where the day has gone.

"Lucas and I are making headway on creating a case. I'll be ready to leave in a few minutes," Roan nods for me to take a seat on the couch.

He scratches out words on a document in front of him, mumbling to me as he works.

"Roan," I say his name suddenly, causing him to look up sharply. "You're going to have to force me to stay tomorrow."

He smiles.

"Already ahead of you on that one, wife. Don't forget, I know you. I'm perfectly well aware that you're going to want to go on that rescue mission, and I also know you have a talent for sneaking out."

Roan looks back down, writing on the documents in front of him.

"Tomorrow," he continues without looking up, "Lucas and I have some work to do on the case. I'm going to need you to run things around here so we can focus. Is that okay?"

"Giving me a task to keep me occupied?" I tease.

"Yes…but we also actually need the time to work on this, so…"

"Okay, I can handle that," I agree.

"Good. Did you tell Lucas? I know he's been worried about Sophie."

"No, I came to you first."

"Maybe you should go tell him while I finish up. He's still here I believe."

"Tell me what?"

"Right on time." I swing around to look at Roan, giving him an I-saw-that-coming look.

I wave Lucas in and hand him the note from my bag. His face lights up momentarily before his entire body deflates as if he had been waiting all this time to let out the breath he was holding until we located Sophie.

"And you're sure we can't be a part of this?" Lucas asks.

"We're the distraction." Roan sounds like he's tired of trying to convince us to stay put.

"Fine, as long as I get to have my say at the trial, I can play along."

"I have a feeling we're *all* going to get our say."

Waiting for news of Sophie's rescue isn't easy, but Alice Diamond sitting in Roan's office serves as quite the distraction.

She sits on the couch nervously, eyes darting around the room.

"I'm still not sure why I'm here," Alice finally says.

I would have to remember to thank Roan for this later. Perhaps an ice cube down the back of his shirt would be sufficient.

"I'm sorry, I didn't know Roan had sent for you. I think he's trying to use you as our alibi."

"For what?"

"Hi, Mom," Roan greets her as he walks around the corner into his office. "Thanks for coming."

"Why am I here, Roan?" She stands to her feet. Alice gracefully clasps her hands in front of her.

"We've located Jade's aunt. Our people are attempting a rescue today."

"Yes, but why am *I* here?"

"Mainly, because I need to explain to you what is about to happen with Dad." He guides her back to the couch and sits with her. "We also need him to know you were here, and that Jade was here too. Once Sophie is free, he has to still believe that Jade is falling in line."

"How do you expect him to believe Jade had nothing to do with it if that woman disappears?" Alice questions.

"They're going to make it look like she escaped, which is why you need to be here to confirm that Jade was here today. Dad will believe you."

"I don't like lying to your father," Alice huffs quietly.

"You're not lying—Jade is here. You're just not admitting that you know what happened to her aunt. Honestly, Dad hasn't even told you that he abducted Sophie in the first place so it's not like he's going to bring it up, Mom." Roan takes a moment to prepare himself. "But there is something else."

He spends the next hour explaining the charges that will be brought against his father once Sophie is free while Lucas works on scripting the charges and I manage the Command Building work. By the end of the mother-and-son discussion, Alice is finally convinced not to interfere with our plans.

Evening comes and goes without any word about Sophie. Twilight fades into evening. The stars make their first appearances in the night sky. My confidence wanes.

Every what-if that jumps to my lips is soothed by Roan, assuring me that it will be all right. I fall asleep on his shoulder as I stare at the clock on the wall.

We wander to the office the next day, hoping for news. My neck hurts from where I slept against Roan's shoulder.

I bury myself in work on the couch in Lucas' office. He works quietly on the case against the Commander.

To keep up appearances, Roan keeps a meeting he has across town, leaving the two of us to run the building. Janine keeps a watchful eye on us through the open door.

Roan looks a little worse for the wear when he returns at the end of the day. His clothing has bits of dust and dirt on them. The sleeves on his shirt are wrinkled from being rolled up and his hair looks like he's been standing in a windstorm.

"What happened to you, Diamond?" Lucas smirks.

"I stopped to do a little yard work along the way," he answers making my heart melt.

"Like you don't do enough of that at home." I shake my head.

"Speaking of which, we should probably head home," Roan says, glancing at the clock.

Another day and still no answers.

I stop dead in my tracks the next morning when I see it sitting on my kitchen island.

"Roan," I call.

I hear him stirring in his room but he's not moving fast enough.

"Roan!"

My shout awakens him fully and he throws the door open, racing to my side. He lets out a deep sigh when he sees the message waiting in our kitchen.

"That's good, right?"

"I think so," I reply, resting my hand on the back of the stool pushed against the island.

Roan reaches out to pick up the hair comb. He pushes the long end meant to contain the poison back into place. The comb is dry and free from toxins. Inscribed into the design is a pattern similar to Sophie's necklace—I wonder how long Mr. Eroh has been holding on to this piece.

Roan turns it over in his hands before offering it to me.

"What does this mean?"

"It means that I need to go see Mr. Eroh," I reply. "And that we need better locks for this house."

I hurry to get ready.

Roan and I walk to the Command Building, trying not to rush. We don't want to tip anyone off too early. With Sophie safely hidden away somewhere, we have today and tomorrow to prepare for the open forum where we will expose Robert Diamond for what he truly is.

I look for any excuse to make my way to the other side of town to check into the shop. But Janine keeps me incredibly busy with paperwork she needs handled for the community garden project. By the time I finally finish, Erica is bustling in the lobby door.

"Erica?" I try to get her attention.

"Good morning," she nods politely as she steps quickly across the lobby. "Is my boyfriend in?"

She gives me a hard smile, clearly telling me to play along. I smile back, unsure of what to do.

Without stopping, Erica walks to Lucas' office, closing the door behind her.

"Was that Erica?" Roan whispers, stepping along side of me.

"Yes." I try to raise my eyebrows to their normal positions but my face seems frozen in a state of shock and confusion.

"Why is she here?"

I shake my head.

"She had a basket of candles and she asked if her *boyfriend* was in," I whisper back.

"I'm really not sure what to say about this," Roan stares at the closed door. I tug at his arm.

"Come on."

I knock on the door, waiting only a moment before opening it. If I were trying to be respectful of my friend, I would have waited for him to answer.

Lucas and Erica stand by his desk. Her basket of candles sits near his paperwork. Lucas nods for us to join them. Roan closes the door behind us, blocking the conversation from Janine's sight.

"They got her out," Erica informs us, hand reaching back to steady herself against the desk. "She's hidden."

She turns to me.

"You can't go, Jade."

"They sent you to warn me off?" I feel like rolling my eyes.

"Someone had to," she replies. "We don't want you accidentally tipping the Commander off on her location. We made it look like she broke out on her own so he's definitely trying to find where she is before she can get to us. He will be watching you.

"Now that we have Sophie, when are you planning on exposing your father?" She directs her question to Roan.

"At the open forum."

"Two days," she nods. "We can protect her until then."

She turns, nearly bumping into Lucas. He steps back, giving her space.

Erica places a finger on the top of the basket handle and looks at me.

"Just sprinkle these around the building. They're all unscented so they won't bother you." She quickly turns back toward Lucas. "I won't be back. Just lay low until the meeting. We'll be ready."

Roan and I split apart, stepping back as Erica moves toward the door. Lucas follows after her, motioning for us to wait in the office.

He walks her to the main door, pausing to pull her into his arms to complete the boyfriend angle Erica so expertly planted in front of Janine as an explanation for her presence in the building.

Lucas takes it a little too far when he kisses her.

She untangles herself from his arms and slips outside. Lucas turns slowly and realizes we've been watching him from the open office. He flushes red, stalking quickly back to us.

"That was commitment," Roan mutters before Lucas reaches us.

Our friend closes the door behind him, forcing us deeper into the room. He ducks his head as he bites his lip.

"The dating angle is interesting," Roan comments.

"Had to get her in the door somehow," Lucas mutters.

"Did you really have to kiss her though?" Roan squirms.

No, no he did not have to *do anything.*

"How long?" I cross my arms, keeping my voice as deadpan as possible.

My former protector glances at me.

"Lucas Montgomery, how long?" I can't keep the grin off my face.

"Recent," he finally admits.

I punch his shoulder playfully.

"At least you saved me the trouble of having to find you someone."

Roan marvels at how well they hid their relationship. While he and I were busy pretending to be a couple, Lucas and Erica were pretending *not* to be.

The rest of the day consists of finalizing plans for the

open forum and mercilessly teasing Lucas about the wedding we were going to plan for him.

Saturday is supposed to be a day off for us, so Roan and I choose to take a walk around town. I use the basket Erica had brought the candles in yesterday to collect different items from the farmer's market in town.

People keep their distance from us, not wanting to be connected until they can figure out if we're friends or enemies. I can't say I blame them with all of the rumors swirling around.

We gather enough supplies to make a pie once we return home.

Between kissing and actually making the peach pie, we manage to fill the rest of the afternoon. Even if our town isn't welcoming at the moment, Roan knows how to make me feel right at home.

It's warm inside the building. I feel like I'm suffocating, though that may have nothing to do with the heat.

Lucas puts on a brave face but I can tell he's nervous. His fingers twitch nervously just outside of his pockets as he loops his thumb there. My father sits quietly in his chair, rehearsing every possible scenario in his mind like he does every time we find ourselves in a tricky situation.

The Commander waltzes in before the people start to arrive.

"Well, today should be interesting," he sings. "I have had people in to see me all week. Now, don't worry, I calmed them down, but I'd say you have a lot of damage control to do."

He chuckles as he takes a seat in the back.

The Commander glares at me for a moment, trying to decide if I know where my aunt is. I'm surprised he's not frantically searching for her, but perhaps he thinks the damage is already done and I can't escape the people's retribution.

Once everyone files in, we start the meeting as we typically would, addressing a few main points before moving on to the place where we should be addressing questions from the box.

I held my ground moments ago as the crowd grumbled when I spoke briefly with an update about the community garden, but now my brain runs over every word I spoke again and again as I wait for my husband to change the direction of the conversation.

Alice is nowhere to be found. I was afraid she would insist on coming, knowing what would be happening, despite never having attended an open forum before. That certainly would have tipped her husband off.

Sean sits in the back on the left side of the room. He looks impatient, constantly looking around the room. I'll be happy for the day we can throw him out of office too.

Timothy looks ready to pick a fight off in the corner of the room. Not that he particularly stands out from the angry masses at the moment, but his height does give him an advantage.

Mr. Eroh has strategically planted two large men in the aisle seats in the very back so they can block the Commander, should he try to leave. They wait patiently for their signal.

"I know last week we had some things come up during the forum that we told you would be investigated and addressed," Mr. Zuckerman starts. Everyone leans forward. "I want you to know we have taken that seriously and an investigation has been set into motion."

The Commander's jaw twitches as he locks eyes with me. He doesn't realize that Mr. Zuckerman is on our side.

"I have been tasked with investigating the claims made last week, and while it may take time to complete our review, we do have an update for you," Mr. Zuckerman continues.

"A number of documents have come to light this week," Lucas says as if he's struggling to act like he isn't upset by the findings—a show purely for the Commander's benefit. "Commander Diamond, would you join us?"

Lucas watches as Roan stands and walks over to the table. He swings his gaze over to the Commander as he waits in the back of the room. Lucas gives him a grin that would frighten me to the bone if I were the recipient.

"We've been working very hard to uncover the source of several documents that have recently come into question and I'd like to thank you all for the opportunity to bring this to light." He slowly sets several papers on the table, laying them out for inspection. Roan's eyes run over them even though he already knows the plan. "You all know I have recently taken a new position within the Command that has given me access to new parts of the government as second in command.

"What you *don't* know is that I've been investigating our leadership for a long time and have worked my way up to the highest access I could get to find this information." He slips into his politician-persona. "It is with great remorse that I bring these charges against our Commander."

Everyone looks to Roan. His jaw tightens but he doesn't move.

We've scripted a power play to make it look like Lucas is about to bring Roan, my father, and I down. He plays his part beautifully.

"I'm certain once you all see this proof, you'll agree that it is time to take back the power from this leadership and focus on a new direction—a stronger direction—and our leadership should reflect this."

The Commander's face goes white as he begins to realize what Lucas is supposedly doing. If Lucas weren't so loyal to my family, I could see him playing the role of a villain.

"We've studied the documentation," Mr. Zuckerman picks up the dialogue. He also glances at Roan. "We believe that there is enough evidence to charge Commander Diamond for a number of crimes."

"The office of Commander has been held in the highest esteem since our country has been formed, but when our leaders have gone against the rules of our country, something must be done." Lucas looks convincingly at the crowd. "It is with heavy heart that I must bring these charges against my friend and leader—"

"My son had nothing to do with this," Robert Diamond leaps up from his chair and storms to the front of the room in an effort to clear the Diamond name.

"You've seen the charges brought against James Jareau and his daughter. They've planted evidence to make Roan look bad. I promise you he had nothing to do with this—he would never tarnish the Diamond name."

The Commander spins to face the people, flecks of spit flying from his lips as he speaks.

"Oh. No," Lucas says slowly. "We know Roan didn't have anything to do with this. The charges we're bringing are against *you, Commander.*"

The crowd erupts in conversation as the Commander's eyes grow wide.

"You wouldn't dare," he whispers.

"We would," Roan replies. His father whips around to face him.

"Keep your head, Robert, if you want a chance to talk your way out of this," my father says calmly from his place in the front row, loud enough for his former boss to hear him.

The Commander begins to shake. Part of the crowd looks distressed while the rest lean back in their chairs to watch the show.

"This is ridiculous," the Commander addresses the crowd. "But I welcome the opportunity to see our justice system prove my innocence, just as it will prove the guilt or innocence of James Jareau and his daughter."

"In light of the evidence we've been collecting," Mr.

Zuckerman interjects, "we will be holding this trial as one *of the people*. We can not rely on the leadership put into places of power specifically to side with the Command, therefore our typical cabinet will be released of their duties and a committee will be selected by the people to preside over this hearing."

The Commander flushes the deepest red I've ever seen. He clenches his fists at his side, unable to control himself.

"You see, ladies and gentlemen," I start, knowing it won't end well for me, "The Commander has been putting people in place to do his bidding all these years—"

Before I can finish, the Commander is racing at me, tackling me to the floor. I squirm under his weight as he tries to recover from the fall. Noise explodes around me as people leap from their seats to see what is happening.

My father hauls the Commander off of me. Lucas helps to hold him back as Roan scoops me off of the floor.

"You knew he was going to do that," he hisses in my ear.

"I was making a point," I whisper back. The back of my head throbs from slamming into the floor.

"You have nothing against him," I recognize Sean's voice shouting over the crowd. A number of people echo his sentiment.

"Oh, but they do," Sophie's voice fills the room. Everyone turns to look at her. "If nothing else, *I* bring the charges of kidnapping and murder against Commander Robert Diamond."

She marches down the center of the room, looking like she's been beaten. The cuts on her face are healing but the bruises boast a deep purple tone.

"I was recently rescued after being held captive for weeks by this man," she points at him.

Several people protest.

"I helped rescue her," Mr. Eroh stands in the back. "I saw the conditions where she was being held. It's all true."

The majority of the people in the Command know or at least respect Amos Eroh and his words hold great weight for them.

"We have evidence of this. But more than that," Sophie continues. "I am charging Robert Diamond with the murder of my sister, Elizabeth Donnelly Jareau. I have evidence of this too."

"In fact," Lucas continues. "We have evidence of several murders, falsified evidence, and multiple counts of wrongful prosecution."

"Furthermore," Sophie raises her voice. "He's been working to frame his daughter-in-law and implicate her in crimes she didn't commit and *never would* commit.

"For the record, the only reason she made all those suggestions last week at this meeting was because the

Commander was holding my safety against her. Her name will be cleared once the trial is over. She was protecting me and she was protecting all of you—many of you were threatened as well."

The people murmur, eyes darting between everyone standing in the front of the room.

"The trial begins tomorrow," Mr. Zuckerman announces. "It will take place here, at which time we will be choosing our committee. No one will know which people are involved in making the final judgment and sentencing. You're all expected to join us. The trial will last for the next several days. If you have evidence either for or against, you may bring it tomorrow and submit it. We start first thing in the morning."

We dismiss the group, taking the Commander into custody. His people slink away with the rest of the crowd, fuming over their loss of potential power. I only identify two of them in the mass of people, but I know there are more we'll have to fish out when we're done with the Commander.

My father-in-law fights the entire time as they escort him out of the building and back to his house where he will remain under guard until his sentencing is carried out.

"I'm sorry, Roan," my father says, placing a hand on my husband's shoulder. "I really am."

"I know, thank you, sir." He turns to face my father. "I'll be okay."

"I know you will, son. You've got a good head on your shoulders. Just remember that we're all here for you as you testify tomorrow."

Eventually we all slip away to our homes. The trial will begin early.

CHAPTER 25
ROAN

ade wears the hairpin Mr. Eroh left on our counter to the sentencing, clearly a note to my father. Sophie wears the matching necklace. The two sit in the front row, watching my father squirm.

My mother clenches my hand in hers as she waits for the sentencing to be passed. It's been a week of torture for us all.

She sobs when he's taken out of the room. I hold her, trying to calm her tears.

To my father's credit, he never gave up the names of the people involved with his schemes—he probably thinks they'll be able to get him out after his sentencing. That just makes our job a bit harder as we work to uncover those complicit in his crimes.

"I know this is a hard day for all of us," I finally stand when my father's shouting is too distant to hear. "None of us expected this. Until he threatened my wife and I started looking into what my father had done, I had no idea what he was capable of doing. My family extends their deepest apologies to all who have been hurt by my father. If you want me to step down as Commander, I completely understand."

"I don't think that will be necessary, Roan." My father-in-law stands by my side, placing a hand on my shoulder. "If anyone has a right to be angry at the Diamond family, it's me. I lost my wife and nearly lost my daughter and sister-in-law to Robert Diamond's vendetta. But I have complete faith in Roan to run this country. I fully support his leadership.

"He's already shown us he is a man who will be for the people. He wants your input and in the short time that he's been in charge, we've seen drastic improvements toward giving freedom and choice back to the people."

"Here, here," Mr. Artemus says, tapping his cane against the floor.

"We, of course, will take a vote later this month once everything has settled down," Mr. Zuckerman adds. "For now, we will go back to business as usual. We will meet again on Sunday for our open forum where I know we will have several announcements for you as well as plans for moving forward and deciding what direction the country will go in."

"Until then, if you have any questions for us, please don't hesitate to ask," I remind them gently. "Thank you for your time and dedication to this matter."

I wait until the room clears out, leaving my wife and father-in-law, Lucas, Mr. Eroh, Mr. Zuckerman, a few of the other politicians, and my mother, still sniffling in her chair.

"Are you all right?" I sit down next to her.

"I don't know what I'm going to do," she whispers.

"We'll help you, Mom," I assure her. Jade looks like she wants to help but she keeps her distance in case my mother isn't accepting of her attention at the moment.

Maybelle walks up from the back to help my mother up.

"I'll take care of her tonight, Roan. You go home and rest—you must be exhausted." Maybelle gathers my mother, allowing her to lean on the slightly older woman for support. "You all did a good job this week."

This will be Maybelle's first time back to the house since the trial commenced and she officially started her new job in the Command Building. Up to this point, that has meant being at the trial, but she will officially start her new duties this week.

We all agree to meet in the morning and go our separate ways.

I hold Jade's hand in mine as we walk home. She seems lighter now and I imagine if it weren't for my hand grounding her, she would float away.

"You realize," Jade murmurs a few feet from our house, "that if your father had won, I would have died yesterday, don't you?"

I freeze. I hadn't realized that.

"But he didn't, Jade. He didn't win."

I have the sudden urge to pick her up and carry her into the house and protect her from the world. I clutch at her hand, nearly dragging her up the steps like I had done once before—the day I promised not to hurt her.

"Roan," she tries to convince me to stop.

I don't.

Throwing the door open, I pull her inside.

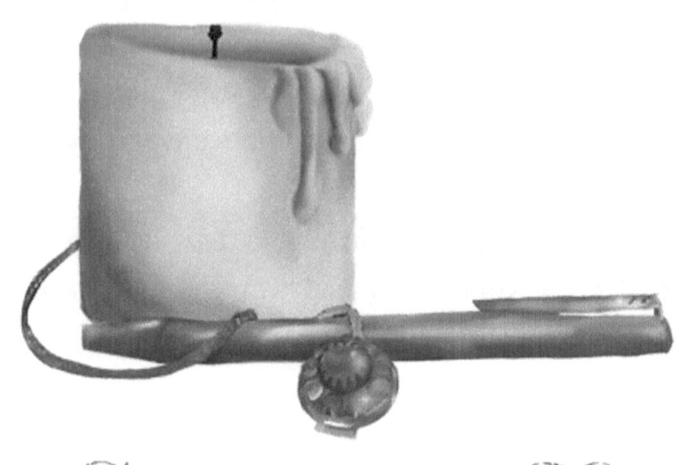

CHAPTER 26
JADE

 stumble inside, following Roan's lead. He's possessed with an idea and it's all he can think about right now.

"What's going on, Roan?" I ask, waiting for him to turn around and face me. I'm terrified this is a reaction to his father's sentencing.

"Jade," he croons instead. I melt. Everything around me is electrified.

He looks at me with such ferocity. His finger lightly grazes the side of my arm.

No, this is about me.

"Jade," Roan whispers as he nuzzles my hair, forcing a shiver down my spine. It feels like every organ in my body has dropped six inches before crashing to a halt and weighing heavily in my skin.

Closing my eyes, I weave my fingers up his arms, tangling them in his blond hair. I'm lost in a moment of overwhelm.

I'm finally free. Free from the Commander. Free from expectations. Free from fear.

Roan lowers me to sit on the arm of the couch, resting his hands next to me on the cushioned seat.

"I love you," he says, bringing me out of my haze.

"I love you too, Roan." I smile back at him.

My husband stares at me, mirroring my careless grin. He reaches up and tucks my hair behind my ear.

When he's near me, all I can smell is his aftershave—sweet and spicy. Miraculously, it's the only scent I'm not allergic to and it's perfect for him. His hand glides over my cheek as he repositions my tresses.

"Marry me," he whispers.

I look at him blankly.

"I *am* married to you," I say with a grin.

"Marry me *for real*, Jade," he says, equal parts elation and pain for all we've been through together. "I want to be your husband—not because we were forced to wed, but because you *chose* me."

I try to stand, attempting to fly to my feet, but he holds me down where I sit perched on the arm of the couch.

"Jade, I love you," he continues. "I want to be yours forever—for better or for worse. I want you—*all of you*—every part of you, every single thing about you.

"You're the most magnificent thing that has ever happened to me and I couldn't be more wrapped up in you if I tried. I *need* you, Jade." He drops his voice to a whisper. "I love you, and I'm yours if you'll have me."

"Roan, I…" he interrupts me by sinking to the ground propping himself on one knee. He takes my hand in his and watches me, eyes pleading for me to accept him. Slight terror hides there, as if, perhaps, I might turn him away.

"Roan," I say again, this time reaching out to brush his hair and face. "I love you. With every breath I breathe, with every thought I think, I know it's you. It's *always* been *you*.

"Even before it *could* be you, it was you. You're all I've ever wanted. You're all my mother ever wanted for me. I can't help but want to be your wife. I want to be with you every moment of every day. I can't imagine life without you, my dear, sweet Roan.

"You've opened my eyes to so much and I know I could never live without you. So, Roan, I'm yours. In every way, I am yours."

He rushes at me, knocking me over onto the couch. He only pushes himself up off of me for a moment, just long enough to realize that neither of us wants him to move. Our lips meet again and again, fast and furious, then fading into a slow simmering burn.

"Then it's settled. We're getting married." He grins above me.

"Again," I add.

"*Again.*"

I giggle as I rest my head against the couch cushion. Roan lowers himself along side of me, wrapping me in his arms.

"It will be perfect Roan…like your painting." I breathe, eyelids heavily drugged with the sensation of Roan's closeness.

"It will be small—just our closest friends and your family," he murmurs in my ear, brushing my skin with his lips.

"That sounds perfect." I run my hands through his hair. "It sounds perfect."

"*You'll* be there, so of course it will be," he whispers, sending a few of my locks trembling around my cheeks. He chuckles before whispering my name, "Jade."

All too soon he walks me to my room and says goodnight. Tomorrow we will plan a simple ceremony and inform our loved ones. In a few days, I will be married—this time *for real.*

I step out of my house, draped in a white dress that I have altered for the third time. It matches the painting Roan created for us.

My father—overwhelmed with joy—waits for me at the bottom of the steps, elbow ready to escort me to where my future husband waits for me.

When we told him yesterday, he couldn't contain his tears. It seems some of them must have managed to stay in order, however, to be of service today. He smiles at me with glassy eyes.

"You look beautiful, my sweet girl. Your mother would be so proud."

Lucas gives me an adoring look as he stands by Roan, *finally* approving of my choice. Erica sits on the bench near Alice and Maybelle.

Mr. Eroh presides over the ceremony as Sophie stands by my side. She's lent me my mother's necklace for the occasion. My aunt nods approvingly as I take my place.

Not even the extra flowers bother me. Alice had them draped over every surface imaginable for the wedding.

She's still tentative about me, but she's accepted me as part of Roan's life.

The ceremony is beautiful.

Afterward, we go inside and enjoy a meal together prepared by Erica and Maybelle, who, coincidentally, get along very well.

"You're all coming to my surprise, limited-admission unveiling on Friday before the big community debut on Saturday, right?" Roan asks as we eat.

I reach up to tuck one of the fake flowers back into my hair. My bouquet sits on the table nearby, cascading with fake floral pieces.

Everyone nods at Roan's request—I don't think any of them know what this surprise is. I'm rather curious myself.

He winks as he takes my hand under the table.

Eventually, it grows late and everyone wanders home.

Carrying me into my room, Roan sets me down just inside the door. I begin to turn to him but find myself frozen. My entire body begins to shake.

"Jade?" he asks, reaching out to stroke my arm. Happiness and terror coarse through my veins.

I will myself to face him, barely catching his eye. Somehow I end up further away from him than I meant to be.

"Jade, we don't have to…" he starts softly, reassurance in his voice.

"But I want to," I whisper. His eyes widen at my words.

I can tell he's scared to spook me, but I have no intention of changing my mind.

I take a fragile step toward him, placing my hands on his arms. Slowly, carefully, he lifts his arms around my back, bringing me into his chest.

"It was a beautiful ceremony," he says softly. I don't know how he can focus on talking.

"It was," I murmur.

"The party was nice too. Our friends looked happy for us."

"Mhmm," I mumble, eyes tracing a line from his lips to his chest.

I swallow.

"Were you happy, my dear?"

His question forces me to look up at him. Meeting his eyes is the biggest mistake I could have made.

"I'm happy," I whisper. My throat is dry and my

breathing is uneasy. Everything about this moment is nerve-wracking.

His fingers trace from my jaw, along my neck, to my shoulder, sending an electric force flooding through me under his touch. I lean forward and kiss him.

"Are you sure this is okay, Jade?" he asks, unsure once again.

"Roan, I am your wife. You are my husband. I've wanted this for a long time." My voice, soft at the start, ends once again in a whisper. "I want *you.*"

I look him in the eye, willing him to want me as much as I want him.

"We're married now—this time of our own accord." I smile at him. "I wouldn't cross that line before, and I know you wouldn't either, but now we're committed to each other…for always."

"For always," he echoes quietly.

I nod slowly, giving him the permission he's been waiting for from me. Roan's kiss starts slowly, flooding over me. He slowly moves us away from the door.

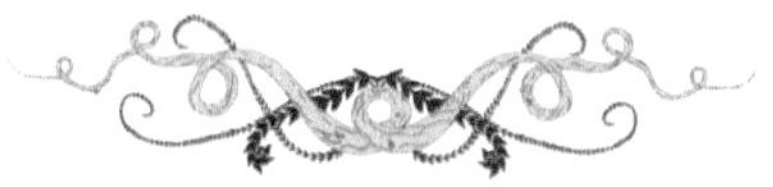

Waking up next to Roan may be the happiest feeling

I've ever felt— he's so beautiful. My hands dance over his skin, gently waking him from his limited sleep.

"Wife," he greets me with a smile.

"Husband." I grin back.

He sighs as he pulls me close.

I wrap myself around him, holding him to me. The way he looks at me makes me want to live in this moment forever. I couldn't be happier. Nothing could be more right. My husband loves me and the world is perfect.

But perfection can only last for so long.

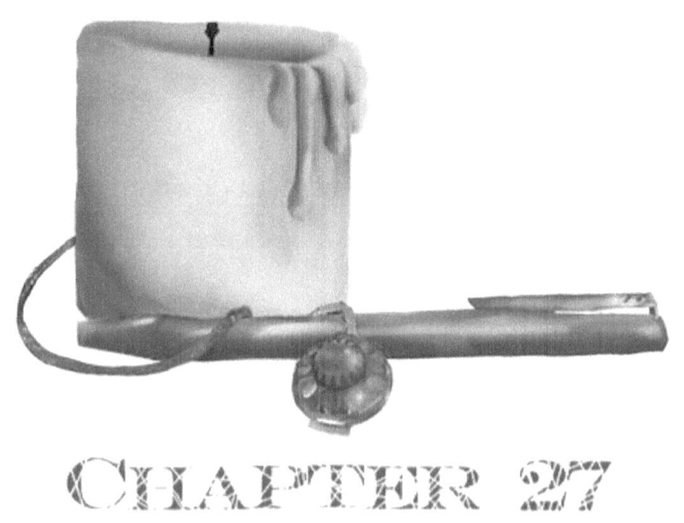

CHAPTER 27
JADE

riday morning finds me carrying a bag with unknown contents toward the far side of town. Roan refuses to give me any clues as to where we are going. We meet our family and friends and continue on with Roan in the lead.

A tall building looms ahead of us, surrounded by dark-colored walls.

"This is it," Roan announces.

I gaze at him quizzically. He chews on his lip adorably as he takes my hand and guides me toward the entrance.

When we round the corner, the world comes alive. Colors are splashed on the walls in giant murals. The sunlight sparkles off of the crystal blue pool water. It bounces off of every surface, dancing and shinning enough to make me feel like I've been transformed into a mermaid.

A multi-tiered waterfall cascades down on one side of the pool, mimicking a tropical oasis that I read about in a book once.

"What is this?" Lucas asks.

"It's a public pool," I laugh. "I can't believe you did this."

Roan beams at me when I turn to him. He nods to the far wall.

A butterfly, beautiful and bold, takes flight on the wall.

"And not a bird in sight," he whispers in my ear. I elbow him making him laugh loudly. "Do you like it?"

"It's perfect," I say, dropping the bag off my shoulder. "I assume this is a swimsuit?"

He nods.

"So that's why you suggested going to the pond after," Lucas mumbles.

I turn to my father to see if he will be joining us.

"I knew this was coming," he holds up his hands. "Amos and I are going to enjoy the tables in the shade over here. Go have fun."

Roan guides us to the changing rooms, which are just as stunning as the pool area. I consider tying my hair up to keep it dry but I'm positive I'll end up dunking Lucas at some point and I know retribution will be swift. Hair ties and wet hair do not mix.

The water is warm and inviting. We splash around for a few minutes before migrating to the deep end of the pool near the waterfall.

"We need a plan for figuring out who was working for the Commander," Lucas jumps right into business.

"Have we located Sean yet?" I ask. "He probably has a good idea of who his competition was. I'm worried one of them might think they can continue to help the Commander."

"Not yet. We're not sure where he is," Roan says as he treads water.

"That's comforting," I reply.

"We'll find him. Mr. Eroh's people are on it. Frankly, I'm surprised Annie hasn't found him—she was furious when I told her he was in on it the other day," Lucas adds, reaching up to push his hair out of his eyes as it drips down his forehead.

"You told Annie?" Erica asks quietly. "You shouldn't have done that. *That woman on a mission* is a scary thing."

She smiles, softening her words. Erica is frighteningly good at holding her voice and face steady when she speaks.

"They'll have to come out at some point," I respond.

"We'll just have to be sure to keep an eye out for them and prevent them from doing any more damage."

"And trust no one until we're sure they're on our side," Lucas adds. "Because we all know how easy it is to fool these two."

He slaps his hand against the surface of the water, sending a cascade of it in our faces—I was right about dunking him.

We spend the next few hours testing out the pool with Erica and Lucas before having a repeat of our first kiss in the driers.

I had anticipated more of a somber atmosphere for the open forum on Sunday, but it appears that the grand opening of the pool yesterday has lightened the mood for everyone.

The fans on the ceiling help move the air around, keeping everyone from over heating inside the hall, though it's noticeably warmer than usual.

Roan finishes thanking everyone who worked on the pool project with him to a round of applause. Several of the elementary-aged girls swoon as he raises his hand to say thank you.

We transition into a discussion on the community gardens, listening to input from people on how they would like it to be run. The crowd seems much more pleased with the new arrangements for the service, and so am I.

Roan beams next to me as I work with the group to cultivate a plan of action most of us could agree to try. He brushes my hand briefly for a moment but then realizes he is in charge and can do whatever he wants. He takes my hand in his as I continue to lead the discussion. Annie and Maybelle giggle louder than they should have.

I can see our entire lives unfolding before us. We'd continue to work with the community and build our country up. Whether the people vote to keep us as leaders of the country or not, Roan and I plan to work to grow this world for our friends and neighbors.

Alice is starting to come around to me, even attempting to have small conversations with me. Sophie is recuperating quickly. Maybelle loves her new job working along side Janine in the Command Building with us. Mr. Eroh is thrilled to be working with his team to uncover people who might still be loyal to Robert Diamond. Lucas and Erica are finally going on public dates. My father is transitioning the group working in his building to give them more responsibilities. Most importantly, Roan and I are growing together and building a life.

I'm happy.

"Now, speaking of growing," I say, slipping away from my husband. "We should talk about what we're going to be planting. I have some samples of different types of seeds over here and I've already started growing a handful to test."

I walk toward the window on the far side of the room where I left the packets of seeds and my test sprouts. Light filters in through the muted windows as specs of dust float in the air. They sparkle as they catch the light, reminding me of the art house.

A small piece of paper is propped up against one of the tiny brown containers where my bean sprouts are growing. I pick it up to read it.

My heart races.

Pay attention.

I turn to find Roan over my shoulder, knowing something bad is about to happen. Worry washes over his face as he sees my rapid movements.

From the angle I'm at, I can see the timer glowing red tucked behind the podium on the stage. I scream for everyone to run.

There's still time left on the counter, but it doesn't matter—the bomb detonates anyway, the perfect ending to the Commander's twisted tale.

CHAPTER 28
ROAN

he explosion was meant to wipe out the top leadership of the Command. Two days after it destroyed most of the stage area in the hall, our people located Sean Flint. He claims he was following orders, though we know my father would never have risked my life—I was an extension of my father in his eyes, and killing me wouldn't look good for him and would take away any hope he had at getting power back one day.

After hours of interrogation Sean finally admits to trying to take out the people who knew his connection to my father. His goal was to work his way up the ladder to fill our positions after taking up the banner to find the person he framed for placing the explosives on the stage, covering up his involvement.

Sean admits to crimes we hadn't realized he had committed during his interrogation. His involvement with the accident during the pond workday, his connection to Sophie's abduction, even his connection to some of the things that happened before my father went after my wife.

I sit on Jade's bed—*our* bed—with her mother's letters in my hands. The music box Mr. Eroh gave her not too long ago sits on her nightstand next to the green jewel he gave me, begging me to open it and play its song just one more time.

Tears stream down my face as I read her mother's words to her husband and child. If I could have strangled my father, I would have.

The shaking begins when I find Jade's first letter. It's addressed to me.

"My dearest Roan," I choke the words out. "You deserve much better in life than what you were given. You deserve happiness and security and overwhelming love."

I lean forward, trying to calm myself.

"If you're reading this, I'm no longer with you to tell you how I truly feel about you, so please hear my heart in these letters," my voice comes out as a whisper. "You are my soul in every way. You give me life and keep me going."

It was cruel of Jade to write such things knowing she was going to die. It's even crueler for me to find them now. My heart pounds in my chest as I continue.

"I love you more than these simple words can say," I choke out the written words, needing to hear them to understand. "Roan, don't give up. I know there is so much you probably don't understand right now—I promise I'll explain in these letters—but I don't want you to get lost in this. I want you to survive, and not only that, but I want you to *thrive*, my incredible husband.

"I know you'll go on to do great things. I want you to find someone to love and start a family. I want you to do incredible things for our country.

"And, Roan, it's okay to move on. I loved every minute I spent with you, but it's okay to find happiness elsewhere."

My entire body shakes in frustration.

"Take care of my father, Roan. Please look after him and Sophie for me. Be sure to watch Mr. Eroh too. He seems strong, but he's going to need people."

This is as hard to read as the note she left in the art house all those months ago, promising me forgiveness.

I quickly hold the paper away from me to avoid tearstains on my wife's words. Trying to focus through the tears isn't easy at this distance.

"You have the ability to change the world, husband, so give everything you have and do what no one else could for this country.

"My heart breaks to be separated from you—" I stop speaking as I set the paper down. I can't finish.

My fingers work their way through her other letters. They explain everything that had happened, detailing what my father had done and how each missing piece should fall into place—much of which I know from the trial, but not everything. I learn things she hadn't even told me once Lucas and I discovered what was going on.

Mixed with her mother's letters, Jade herself is the perfect ending to her mother's story.

One day I'll show these to James, but not today.

Eventually, Lucas knocks on the door of the house. When I don't answer, he lets himself in. He finds me slumped over on the bed, hovering just out of reach of sleep, exhausted from reading the letters.

"It's time to go," he says gently, waiting for me to right myself.

I tuck Jade's mother's letters in my bag, leaving the ones from my wife under her pillow.

He pushes back the sleeve of his dress shirt, coat slung over his arm while he waits for me to lock up.

"Want to talk about it?"

I shake my head.

"Letters from Jade when she thought she was going to die...*again*."

"Broke your heart, huh?" Lucas smiles. "That girl has a way of doing that to people."

I calm myself on the walk. The early moments of my relationship with Jade flash in front of me, all the way until the explosion.

The image of Jade sprawled on the ground, hair everywhere, haunts me. She was so still and lifeless.

I held her in my arms begging for someone to help her as the debris settled around us. I picture Lucas' face as he tries to get people out to safety but still runs back to help us. Even worse, I can see Jade's father and her boss rushing toward her as she lay in my arms.

Fear and overwhelm clutch at my chest.

"We're here," Lucas calls me back from my thoughts.

I step into the Jareau house. James sits on the couch, quietly looking something over.

"Hello, boys," he says somberly.

The house is darker than usual, but then, so is the day, filled with dark clouds.

Lucas pauses to give me a moment.

I walk into Jade's old room, fingers darting to the letters in my open bag. I set them on the bed as I sit.

"How are you feeling, my love?" I ask, leaning in to kiss Jade.

"Better," she responds painfully, holding up her bandaged arm. "I wish I could come home though."

"Soon, my dear," I whisper, burying my face in her hair.

Her kiss is gentle against my neck. A strangled noise escapes her lips. Even a simple kiss is too much strain on her at times.

After the explosion, she was moved to her old house because it was closer than ours. It also had the added benefit of her father being able to take care of her many injuries thanks to her mother's training.

"I found your letters," I whisper, smiling at her. "That was cruel."

She attempts to smirk but winces in pain.

"I meant every last one of them."

"The part about finding someone to start a family with sounded pretty nice."

She snorts trying to hold in a laugh before moaning in discomfort.

"We might have to wait on that a bit." She blinks back her misery.

"I'll wait as long as it takes," I promise. "But no more dying, okay?"

"Relax, Roan, I was only dead for a few minutes before they brought me back," she objects.

"The worst few minutes of my life. It's a good thing your father knows how to keep both of us alive."

"That it is," she smiles. "Mom taught him well."

We watch each other for a moment before she tips her chin toward me.

"I don't care," she says, begging me to kiss her despite the obvious pain she's experiencing.

I oblige.

"I love you, Jade Jareau Diamond."

"I love you too, Roan. More than I ever thought possible."

"So your letters said," I tease.

"Seeing as how only one of us can write now, perhaps you should use all this time waiting around to write *me* a few love letters," she suggests, holding up her badly damaged arm.

"Dear Jade," I say, pretending to write a letter in the air. "You were brave enough to change the world. Now, it's our turn."

"*Our* turn?"

"Everyone *other* than you. I don't need you nearly dying again, so it's time to let somebody else step up and do something good."

"Message received," she giggles. "It's someone else's turn. Someone like...*you.*"

Her smile convinces me to do everything in my power to change the world.

ACKNOWLEDGMENTS

From the very beginning of Jaded, I always knew Jade was meant to die. It had been my plan all along and then about half way through Risen, the story progressed differently than I had anticipated. At the last minute… well, don't hate me—I managed to save her! Really, you should be thanking me.

No? Still a little miffed that I made you think she was dead? Sorry. I still love you though!

Thank you, dearest reader, for seeing Jade and Roan's story through until the end! I have *adored* this girl for so long and I could cry happy tears that she gets to go on and have a beautiful life with all of you!

Please forgive me for wrecking your emotions throughout this series. Fear not, the support group from Jaded is still alive and well, and probably very necessary after the ending of Risen.

Thank you to everyone who has lent their support to this series—I couldn't have done it without you!

Special thanks to Elissa and Jess for everything you've done to help with this project! Your skills are unmatched!

Yentl, thank you for everything! Your encouragement and willingness to go into battle for me are amazing!

To my street team, Elites, and Valkyries, thank you for all you do!

Thank you to the immensely talented Alexis for the gorgeous chapter headers for Jade and Roan!

Most of all, thank you, dear reader, for being here on this journey with me. A year ago, I couldn't have dreamed that we would build this wonderful community together. I thank you for your kindness, participation, support, and love.

Keep reading to find out how to get bonus scenes, play an interactive game to help Mr. Eroh as he tries to SAVE JADE behind the scenes of the story and then see how your actions played into the book—no really, if you read Jaded again, you can see what you did to move the story forward—and more!

Don't forget to check out the Jaded boxset/omnibus for a special exclusive novella from The Jaded Duology that you can't get anywhere else! Trust me when I say you don't want to miss this!

Stay inspired,

-K.M. Robinson

Want to read a bonus scene from Jaded? We're giving out an exclusive bonus scene over on the K.M. Robinson Facebook page where you can read a scene from before Jade's wedding that motivated Jade to dye her wedding dress in rebellion.

Get them by sending the page a direct message at
www.facebook.com/kmrobinsonbooks

We're constantly giving out additional bonus scenes for

preorder swag, giveaways, and more, so watch the social media pages carefully for the next scene giveaway.

K.M. Robinson also has bonus scenes and extras from all of her books on
newsletter.kmrobinsonbooks.com

Sign up now for weekly emails with special bonuses, extras, live broadcasts replays and upcoming dates, events, coloring pages, games, introductions to new authors+live broadcasts with them, and more.

Ready to learn exclusive facts about The Jaded Duology and other K.M. Robinson Series?

World Portals are now available on
www.kmrobinsonbooks.com

Learn behind the scenes facts, watch videos, play games, check out our book filters, find out where to get bonus scenes, view fan art, and get access to other secrets we've hidden away inside the World Portals on the website.

The World Portals are constantly changing and information is being taken away and added all the time, so check back frequently for new content!

SAVE JADE GAME

Join Mr. Eroh on his mission to save Jade from Commander Diamond, his son, Roan, and their revenge mission to murder an innocent woman.

Join the battle for Jade's life and go on a mission for her mentor to help save Jade.

This interactive, choose-your-own-adventure game is played through Facebook messenger so you never miss a mission. Played over the course of two-three days, Mr. Eroh will send several missions which you can then go back into the story to see how your choices affected Jade's journey.

PLAY THE GAME

at

savejadegame.kmrobinsonbooks.com

Mr. Eroh will send a series of missions over the course of a few days, with gaps of time in between so you can "complete the missions" and report back. He will be in touch!

Have fun running missions to help save Jade and then go back in the story to see how your choices directly affect Jade in the story.

Want to get your hands on some incredible Facebook filters for Jaded? Now you have the ability to get filters for the story, characters, etc right inside your phone.

You can use these on your photos, profile pictures, videos, and live broadcasts. All you have to do is like my author page and they will automatically show up in your filters!

I've even taken these clips and put them on Instagram Stories by saving them to my phone and uploading them to Instagram.

Visit www.facebook.com/kmrobinsonbooks to grab these filters for your photos, videos, and broadcasts! Bonus points for tagging me @kmrobinsonbooks so I can see how you're supporting The Jaded Duology.

ABOUT THE AUTHOR

K.M. Robinson is a storyteller who creates new worlds both in her writing and in her fine arts conceptual photography. She is a marketing, branding and social media strategy educator who is recognized at first sight by her very long hair. She is a creative who focuses on photography, videography, couture dress making, and writing to express the stories she needs to tell. She almost always has a camera within reach. Visit her at her website: www.kmrobinsonbooks.com

The Golden Trilogy

Book One: Golden

Forged: A Golden Novella

Book Two: Locked

Book Three: Edge

The Complete Series Boxset/Omnibus with Tempered: an exclusive bonus novella

The Jaded Duology

Book One: Jaded

Book Two: Risen

The Complete Series Boxset/Omnibus with exclusive epilogue

The Siren Wars Saga

Book One: The Siren Wars

Book Two: Darker Depths

Book Three: Beyond The Shores

Origins of the Siren Wars: Prequel Novella

Book Four: Forbidden Waters (coming soon)

The Legends Chronicles

Along Came A Spider: A Prequel Novelette

And They'll Come Home: A Prequel Novelette

The Archives of Jack Frost Series

The Revolution of Jack Frost

The Redemption of Jack Frost (coming soon)

Stealing Steam Series

Book One: Lions and Lamps

Book Two: Pistons and Prisoners

Book Three: Railcars and Rulers

Top Hats and Telegraphs: A Prequel Novella

The Complete Series Boxset/Omnibus with Vambraces and Victories: an exclusive bonus novella

Virtually Sleeping Beauty: A Novella Retelling

The Goose Girl and The Artificial: A Novella Retelling

The Sinking: A Little Mermaid Novella Retelling

Cindrill: A Cinderella Assassin Novella Retelling

Sugarcoated: A Hansel and Gretel's Witch Novella Retelling

Blood Is Silent: A Red Riding Hood Circus Retelling

**Goldilocks wasn't naive. She was sent on a mission
and Dov Baer is her new target.**

When Auluria tricks the Baers into letting her into their
home, they have no idea she's actually been sent by the
enemy to destroy them. Intent on gathering information
for her cousin to hand over to the Society seeking to
destroy all of the rebel factions—including her own—
she's willing to sacrifice Dov Baer to save her people...
until she realizes her cousin lied to her.

Now that she's seen who Dov truly is, she has to decide
between staying loyal to her only remaining family or
protecting the man she's falling for. If her allegiances are

discovered, either side could destroy her—assuming the Society doesn't get her first

Available now!
Learn more about The Golden Trilogy at goldeninfo. kmrobinsonbooks.com

THE SIREN WARS: BOOK ONE OF THE
SIREN WARS SAGA

War has hovered around the kingdom of Scylla for generations ever since the original sirens left the mer collection generations ago after nearly drowning the human prince. Over the years, select mermaids from the royal bloodline have been trained as spies to work for the reigning kings and queens, keeping the collection safe from sirens and humans.

Celena and her partner, Merrick, work covertly for the royals—not even her twin brother knows. When they discover the sirens have broken through the barriers the mer set up to keep the sirens out, Celena and her friends must race to the old kingdom of Metten to stop them from starting a war within their borders.

When she's dragged to the surface, Celena realizes that the war above the waters is as deadly as the one below the waves—and sacrificing herself may be the only way to protect her family.

The Siren Wars have only just begun.

Available now!
Learn more about The Siren Wars Saga at sirenwarsinfo.kmrobinsonbooks.com

All wishes require sacrifice...*are you willing to pay the price?*

Cyra spent the last seven years being trained to steal an airship in a brutal competition that leaves the victor with millions. Last year, she won.

Aladdin spent the past year fighting to get enough money to take his mother away from Horallen after his father was murdered. Now, his evil uncle Kacper wants to force him into the competition and straight to his death inside the Collection Cave.

When Aladdin discovers a genie said to have been banished a century ago, the competition becomes even deadlier, and he knows he can't trust the girl who snuck into the competition this year...but Cyra might not survive his ruthlessness either in a game where only the lion's heart can win.

All wishes require sacrifice, and someone is going to pay the price for the Stourbridge.

Available now!
Learn more about The Stealing Steam Series at
lionsandlampsinfo.kmrobinsonbooks.com

Little Hacker Muffet
sat on her tuffet
destroying her cords and Way.
Along came a hacker named Spider,
who sat down beside her
and frightened his opponent away.

When Fet, one of the most skilled hackers in the Legends, discovers her best friend and leader of her group has been abducted and held for ransom, she must escape unnoticed and find Peep before it's too late.

When Spider, a new recruit training to join her hacker ring, slips out with her and claims to have a plan to save her friend, Fet is forced to bring him along. As she discovers he's not who he claims to be, she faces grave danger and learns just how deadly a spider bite can be.

Now available!
Learn more about The Legends Chronicles at
acasinfo.kmrobinsonbooks.com

VIRTUALLY SLEEPING BEAUTY

To wake her up, he has to enter the game and help her beat it...

Surely the class president wouldn't illegally over-juice to stay in the virtual reality game citizens are allowed to play for four hours a day, but when Royce's aunt calls in a panic because her goddaughter hasn't left the game yet, his only option is to go inside the game and drag the girl out.

The golden knight quickly discovers the princess' absence in the real world isn't of her own doing—*she's trapped inside the game by unknown forces*—and if she can't escape soon, she could die for real outside of the game. He's even more shocked to discover that Rora outranks him inside of the game, which means she'll have to fight to *protect herself* from the evils locking her inside a dangerous world.

Can Rora and Royce work together to outsmart a vicious queen and evil magician, and defeat digital dragons, or will Rora slowly fade away until there's nothing left but an empty shell and the game ranking she will leave behind?

Now available!

Learn more about Virtually Sleeping Beauty at
vsbinfo.kmrobinsonbooks.com

THE REVOLUTION OF JACK FROST

No one inside the snow globe knows that Morozoko Industries is controlling their weather, testing them to form a stronger race that can survive the fall out from the bombs being dropped in the outside world—all they know is that they must survive the harsh Winter that lasts a month and use the few days of Spring, Summer, and Fall to gather enough supplies to survive.

When the seasons start shifting, Genesis and Jack know something is going on. As their team begins to find technology that they don't have access to inside their snow globe of a world, it begins to look more and more like one of their own is working against them.

. . .

Genesis soon discovers Morozoko Industries, but when a foreign enemy tries to destroy their weather program to make sure their destructive life-altering bombs succeed in destroying the outside world, only one person can shut down the machine that is spinning out of control and save the lives of everyone inside the bunker—Jack.

Now available!
Learn more about The Revolution of Jack Frost at
jackfrostinfo.kmrobinsonbooks.com

THE GOOSE GIRL AND THE ARTIFICIAL

What would you do if your artificially intelligent hand-maiden stole your identity?

Threatened by her Artificial, Arta, Princess Goselyn is forced to switch places and pretend she isn't human when she reaches Prince Corinth to negotiate a treaty they both need to be able to take their respective crowns one day. If she doesn't comply, her Artificial, controlled by her evil cousin, will not only kill Goselyn's mother, but Prince Corinth and his father as well.

Can the quiet princess outsmart a machine created to be more intelligent than she is, all while surviving the other

Artificials and robots working against her in the foreign palace, or will Corinth and his father find out and destroy her chance to save them all?

378

Learn more about The Goose Girl and The Artificial at goosegirlinfo.kmrobinsonbooks.com

THE SINKING

**The sea witch wants to silence her, but not for the
reason you think.**

When a quirky older woman pawns a fancy seashell
necklace at her mother's antique shop on the pier, Cara
doesn't think much about the story the woman spins
about the wearer turning into a mermaid.

On her way home, she accidentally drops the necklace
into the ocean and is swept out to sea where she meets—
a merman who volunteers to take her to his mother, the
sea queen, to help her get her legs back.

· · ·

Cara soon learns that it's Quay's eighteen birthday—a day that has been a curse for his family—and is meant to be one for her too. Now she must fight to survive the sea with Quay at her side.

Fans of The Little Mermaid will love this twisted take on the beloved story.

Now available!
Learn more about The Sinking at
thesinkinginfo.kmrobinsonbooks.com

CINDRILL

Cinderella is an assassin out to murder the prince...*but he's hunting her too.*

The nanobots Cindrill's master gives her to use as a mask allow her to slip into the ball wearing a face that isn't hers, but when the assassination attempt goes sideways, Prince Davin doesn't understand why her face changes when he injures her, slicing her foot open around a unique pair of shoes as she runs away.

When Cindrill runs into the prince the next day without her nanobot mask on, he doesn't recognize her, but immediately decides her skills will be useful on his hunt for the would-be-assassin woman who nearly killed his father and his fiancée the night before.

Both are tasked with the job of murdering the other, but things don't quite go as they had planned when Cindrill's master and Davian's fiancée interfere as the two try to decide whether or not to kill the other.

It's hard to recognize a woman when she uses technology to change her appearance, but Cindrill is going to use that to her full advantage as she destroys the prince. ***Will either survive?***

Now available!

Learn more about Cindrill at
cindrillinfo.kmrobinsonbooks.com

Hansel and Gretel's witch was actually on their side...

Annika's job is to create a cake to match the candy-colored rooftops, nightly firework shows, and daily parades ending in unexpected executions for the mad king's ball, but her true mission is to sneak a thirteen-year-old assassin into the palace using her gift of illusions.

Hansel's job is to protect his little sister, Gretel, once she assassinates King Levin and ends the destruction in Candestrachen, using his power over light to rescue the young girl from the chaos her influence over life and death will create.

.   .   .

When the entire forest reconstructs itself under Gretel's command while trying to save herself from a king's guard, Hansel and Annika must put their feelings aside and ensure their plan holds true—even if it means one of them has to sacrifice themselves to protect the mission.

Her illusions were meant to save her....but not everyone will survive the assassination attempt.

Learn more about Sugarcoated at
sugarcoatedinfo.kmrobinsonbooks.com

Red Riding Hood is a circus aerialist and the wolf is ready to cage her.

Sienna has grown up working for the circus, dangling off her signature red silks every night. Her grandmother has been known to wander off to train new acts for their boss, but when Sienna tries to find her to bring her back to the show, she doesn't expect the dashing and dangerous Elijah to join her.

When they finally find Grandma Ida has been transformed deep in the heart of the woods, Sienna will stop at nothing to save her—but the wolf has her right where he wants her, and she won't be able to escape his claws.

She was told not to go into the woods alone.

Now available!

Learn more about Blood Is Silent at
bloodissilentinfo.kmrobinsonbooks.com